Ostrich

A Novel

Matt Greene

 Ballantine Books Trade Paperbacks | New York

A Ballantine Books Trade Paperback Original

Copyright © 2013 by Matt Greene

All rights reserved.

Published in the United States by Ballantine Books, an imprint of The Random House Publishing Group, a division of Random House, Inc., New York.

BALLANTINE and the HOUSE colophon are registered trademarks of Random House, Inc.

Originally published in Great Britain by Weidenfeld & Nicolson, a division of Orion Publishing Group, Ltd., London, in 2013.

ISBN 978-0-345-54521-3
eBook ISBN 978-0-345-54520-6

Printed in the United States of America on acid-free paper

www.ballantinebooks.com

9 8 7 6 5 4 3 2 1

Book design by Mary A. Wirth

To my parents, to whom I owe everything
(at a relatively competitive rate of interest)

Prologue

I can tell my parents are unhappy by the way they smile at waiters. In that small act of ingratiation I can see the custody battle to come. It won't be fought in the courtroom but in HMV and Game. Stocks in Nintendo will soar as my affections are auctioned off to the highest bidder. My teeth will rot.

I can already feel them starting to decay as my mum orders from the Specials Board. It's obvious what she's doing. She's forming an alliance. She even does her French voice, singing along to the chalkboard like the accents are markers on a karaoke screen. (The hat accent on top of the *A* is called a circumflex. It indicates that something is missing. I think a hat always indicates this.) In History we are doing Entente Cordiale. If Mum is the United Kingdom and the waiter is France, then Dad must be Germany.

Dad will order from the Specials only when the waitress is pretty. She is not, so he gets a steak. "Rare."

"How rare?"

"Cooked long enough that his family aren't in denial but not so long that they're at acceptance. Anywhere between bargaining and depression. Just so long as it's seen the inside of a warm room."

Rare meat aggravates my dad's diverticulosis. He just really likes the joke. It's the same impulse that makes him introduce Mum at parties as his first wife. He does it even though he knows it may cause irritation. (He takes "cow's juice" in his coffee even though he's lactose intolerant.)

I order number 28 because it is a perfect number and because I don't like talking any more than is absolutely necessary.

When the food arrives, the only noise is the scrape of cutlery. The silence is familiar. It takes its place at the table like a second son. Then, when it realizes that only three places have been set, it goes on to take the floor. (This is a metaphor. I will probably use some more of them, because you have to in order to get top marks in Composition, which is what I'm practicing for, because it's what you need to get a scholarship. You should also say however instead of but and moreover instead of also, and, whenever possible, make sure that people exclaim and remark things instead of saying them. Moreover, you should talk about past events in the present tense and use at least one semicolon even if you're not completely sure how.)

———

Silence is a game of chicken. Mum always says it's not the winning, it's the taking part. (Dad says you can't win unless you take part. ("Can't win the lottery if you don't buy a ticket.")) So it's not really a surprise when she cracks first.

"What did you learn at school today?"

In Science we are doing magnetic fields. It makes me think of divorce. I will be the iron filings and they will be the poles, taking it in turns to see if they will attract me or disperse me like a water cannon. What they don't realize is that the experiment is flawed because they are both like poles. I can tell this because they repel each other.

"La Paz is the highest capital city in the world."

"Is that right?" asks Mum rhetorically.

"Yes, it is," I say (because I am my mother's son). And then, to further fuel the conversation, "What does *precocity* mean?"

"Why?" Mum. Non-rhetorical.

"Because Miss Farthingdale asked if I knew what it meant, and I said I did."

Dad throws back his head. At first I think he is laughing at me (which he does sometimes), but it's the steak. He's given up chewing, gulping it back in chunks, dolphin-style.

"*Ms.* Farthingdale," corrects Mum.

This time he does laugh. Mum doesn't. She does the opposite of laughing, which is like not laughing but more so.

"You'd prefer he grow up a misogynist like his father?"

She catches herself a second too late. The words slipped out by accident, like a glob of spit hitching a ride on a capital *P*. They drip down Dad's cheek, and for the first time since we've sat down she looks him straight in the eye, pretending not to see it, hoping he hasn't noticed it.

Grow up.

If he has noticed, he doesn't show it.

"Don't you mean *ms*ogynist?"

He gulps back another hunk of beef as a reward for his trick and leans across the table to plant a kiss on Mum's cheek. She recoils at his touch, like the sea from the ugly pebble beach in Brighton where we used to go on holiday. (We don't go on holiday anymore. (Mum says being on holiday is a state of mind.))

"Ah, come on, Lou, he's not so bad!"

Sometimes my parents will talk about me like I'm not here. (This is called the third person. (I think that's why they haven't had any more children, because they're used to me being the third person.)) Dad has been doing it more and more lately.

Is everything all right?

It's the waitress. On closer inspection, she is almost pretty. If you were to describe a pretty girl to one of those police composite artists that they have on American TV shows she is what you might get. All of her features are correct, but somehow they don't link up properly, like they don't belong together. Her hair is fuzzy, as though it's been drawn with a 2B pencil. She is frustrating to look at (like a wonky picture), so I don't.

(I am starting to notice these things, which makes me think that perhaps I am my father's son after all.)

My parents beam at her as though she's the sun and they are solar-powered. I notice that Dad doesn't look directly at her, either.

"Are you needing for anything?"

"Just the recipe!" says my mum, who doesn't cook.

"And how's that number 28?" She flashes me her teeth. They aren't quite white. The French word for white is *blanc,* which is a better one for her teeth. They are blank and she is unfinished.

"Perfect," I remark.

No one knows that I am being clever (and funny). Question: If a tree falls in the woods and no one is there to hear it, does it still make a sound? (Answer: Yes. (Obviously.))

I excuse myself.

The picture on the door of the Men's has got no neck. His head just floats there above his shoulders, totally unconnected to the rest of his body. I decide to use the disabled loo instead, because the only thing strange about this man is that he's sitting down, which I find more relatable than having been decapitated.

I open the door by taking my middle finger and pressing as hard as I can down on the part of the handle closest to the doorknob until the blood pools under my fingernail and my palm starts to ache. Another thing we learned in Science is that a door handle is a First Class Lever and that levers are actually machines (even though we have them in our bodies) because a machine is just something that changes the size or direction of an applied force. (Levers are a way of lifting a heavy load over a small distance by applying a small force over a bigger distance. They work by using a fulcrum, which I like to think of as being a bit like an equals sign. (Imagine you're reading a book out loud and you come across the number 1,000,000,000,000, 000,000,000,000 and you don't know how to pronounce it. This is when you might want to use a fulcrum. So instead of struggling with such a heavy load you could just call it a billion billion, which takes a bit longer to say but is easier than knowing the word quadrillion. This is exactly the same principle behind levers.)) By pressing down here, though, I'm basically doing a manual override. This is how I know that no one else has touched this part of the handle before, which makes it much more hygienic.

I use my elbow to lock the door behind me and turn on the tap, and then I stare at my reflection until it becomes unfamiliar. Usually I can make this happen with less than a minute of actual, concentrated looking (I need to repeat my name only twenty-two times before it sounds like someone else's), but today it isn't working. I try taking off my hat.

David Driscoll says I look like I lost a bet, which he should know about because his dad has a gambling problem and he's had to wear the same trousers since Year 6 even though he's had a growth spurt and he claims he has to shave now. He calls my hat my gay-lid, by which he means it locks the gayness in rather than being gay itself. (It's a white baseball cap, and white is gay only if you refract it through a prism.) I think he thinks homosexuality is like body heat and that you lose 80% of it through your head. (I saw an 18 once where the homophobic bully turns out to be gay, which is called Overcompensation, but David Driscoll isn't gay, because he's always talking about sex with girls. (I mean the sex is with girls, not the talking. (He never talks to girls.)))

It works. A stranger stares back at me from the mirror. I hold his gaze, being careful to keep perfectly still because I am in screensaver mode and the slightest movement could break the spell. We burrow into each other's eyes. (There is no sign of recognition in his, either.) Then I notice something protruding from his head.

Someone has written something behind him in the space between the paper towel dispenser and the help cord:

ɘɿɘʜ ƨɒw I

It makes more sense when I turn around.

I was here

The message slides down the wall, starting at *I* and ending at *e*. (If the help cord is a y-axis and the top of the towel dispenser is x, then it displays a relationship of Inverse Proportionality.) The letters are jagged and sharp. Some of them start off normal and end up in italics, and the *W* looks like an underwater shark. When I take a step toward them I can see that they aren't written at all. Someone has carved them into the wall with a knife, which seems like a lot of effort to go to, especially if you know that *I was here* is a tautology. Whoever left this can't know about tautologies, because if he did he'd have known that he was wasting his time. He might as well just have scratched *I* or *was* or *here* (or even just a full stop) because any one of them would have meant exactly as much. (A tautology is when you say the same thing twice, like *safe haven,* or *tuna fish,* or *I thought to myself* (because it's impossible to think to anyone besides yourself (unless you believe in telepathy (which I don't))). You can lose marks in Composition for tautologies, but people use them all the time in life because they like the sound of their own voices.)

Back at the table it's obvious Mum and Dad are arguing, because that's the only time they're polite to each other. The way they fight is to see which of them can keep the calmest, because the calmer you are, the more rational you're being. Even from a distance I can see that Dad is winning on points. He's doing this thing where he measures out his words between his palms like he's boasting about a fish he caught, which he thinks makes them sound precise and authoritative (but which I think makes it look like they're in brackets). I edge closer until I can hear them.

"I appreciate that, I hear what you're saying, Lou, I recognize its validity, and for the record here, no one's actively disagreeing with you."

"I wouldn't suggest you were. I apologize if you got that impression. That said, if you'd let me finish—"

"You're right, I will, I'm sorry. However, before you do, let *me* first just say this . . ." He takes off his glasses and pinches the bridge of his nose between his thumb and forefinger, like I do when I get a nosebleed. "It does him no good to see you like this. It doesn't do any of us—" He spots me over Mum's shoulder. He stops mid-sentence so I know *him* is me. A smile cracks open his face. "Bloody hell, if it isn't Titus Oates! D'you get lost? We were about to send a search party. Don't forget to change your watch back."

I sit down, adding Titus Oates to my mental To Google list. (I don't ask Dad about these things anymore, not since I embarrassed myself in English by telling everyone that a Palindrome is where they race Michael Palins.) The plates have been cleared. I hadn't finished. Mum has something in her eye, which is a little red. Dad tops up my Pepsi and throws an arm round my shoulders.

"Well, now you're here, Alex, you can settle a debate."

Mum lowers the napkin that she's been using on her eye and shoots him a look.

"Who's tighter, your uncle Phil or your uncle Tony? Because Phil serves soup on plates, but your uncle Tony buys time secondhand."

And then the lights go out.

The room inhales. The walls contract.

I see the flash before I hear the clap because light travels faster than sound.

If you count the seconds between seeing and hearing and divide it by five then you can calculate how far away the storm is. But there's no time for that, because it's already upon us.

"I don't know what I've been told, no I don't know what I've been told, but someone here is getting old, oh someone here is getting old."

The waiters march out from the kitchen in procession. Ours is in the middle, holding aloft an ice-cream sundae, sprouting sparklers (the sundae, not her). By the way she's carrying it you'd think it were the Olympic torch. She leads the chorus, singing the song against its will.

"I don't know but it's been said, no I don't know but it's been said, someone's face is turning red, yeah someone's face is turning red."

Dad starts clapping along and Mum spills a laugh down her shoulder as she cranes round to see what's going on. I appear to do nothing, but actually I'm busy empathizing (which is like sympathizing but better, because you actually put yourself in the other person's shoes). I want whoever the storm is headed for to know I feel their pain. I try to implant this thought in their mind, but I don't believe in telepathy, so it proves difficult. I want them to know I won't laugh at their discomfort. I'll do the opposite. Maybe if they're really embarrassed I'll even act. I'll stand up.

"It's *my* birthday!"

Maybe it will catch on. Maybe everyone will want a free dessert. It will be like the end of that film.

"It's *my* birthday!"

"It's *my* berfday!"

"It's *moy* boithday!"

The sundae lands in front of me.

"The good news is we sing for free, the bad news is we sing off-key."

Blood races up toward my head so quickly for a second I think I might black out. My face turns red and my eyes turn green with envy for everyone else in the whole world in this exact moment right now. (I'm an effing traffic light.) The waiters form a semicircle round our table. Everyone is watching. It's nothing like the end of that film. I look to Mum for help, but she's laughing tears. I look at Dad.

"Don't look at me."

"Happy birthday, happy birthday to you!"

It is not my birthday.

Finally, Mum steps in.

"I think you may have the wrong table."

Our waitress beckons Mum toward her and whispers conspiratorially.

"It's the only way they'll let us comp desserts." She nods toward me. "We didn't want to draw any, you know, *attention.*"

Then she says this to me: "But we want you to know how brave we all think you are."

We don't tip.

Part One

It's Raining, It's Pouring

Chapter One

In Assembly last year we learned about Rosa Parks, who was the black woman who sparked the Civil Rights Movement in America because she refused to move to the back of a bus. I think it's great that black people are equal now and we don't have racism anymore, but I honestly don't get why she was complaining in the first place. On our bus, sitting at the back is a privilege that is afforded to only the most senior pupils. It has taken me nearly four years to earn this position (during which time I have matured from the bright-eyed nine-year-old who arrived at Grove End with a song in his heart and raisins in his lunchbox to the worldly and cynical almost-thirteen-year-old I am today). Middle school was meant to be only a stopgap. The bus thing is pretty much the only advantage of still being here after all this time. So when I see a Year 5 stumbling hesitantly down the aisle toward me, I know exactly what's going on. A mix of Fear and Excitement struggles to articulate itself on his face. He chews the inside of a cheek with a set of primary teeth and looks up at me, his eyes round with hope. (He knows who I am, but I don't know who he is. That's the way it works. School years are Semi-Permeable Membranes. (Moreover, everyone at school knows who I am.)) I decide to help him along.

"Yes?"

He rehearses one last time in his head and then asks what he's meant to ask. "How are your mum's piano lessons going?"

For a second I feel sorry for him. He's so small. (It's hard to believe I was once that young, even if it was three whole years ago.) He has no idea that he's about to learn a lesson he'll never forget, a lesson that will strip him of a faith in humanity he's so far never had to question. However, it's a lesson we've all learned in our time. I know my lines. I tear up a little, which I can do on demand. "My mum hasn't got any arms."

A breath dies in his throat. It's my second cue.

"Why would you ask me something like that?"

Now his face has no trouble with ambiguity. Terror sweeps across it, freezing his features in place and pricking his tear ducts. At the front of the bus, David Driscoll pops up like a Whac-A-Mole and blasts him with a "Waaaaah!" I knew he'd have had something to do with this.

Your Mum's Piano Lessons is a simple game that requires three players, Older Boy 1 (the instigator), Older Boy 2 (the

accomplice), and New Boy (the mark). It works like this.
Older Boy 1 sidles up to New Boy on a bus trip or on the
playground and asks him if he wants to be part of a really bril-
liant joke. New Boy, eager to please and slightly star-struck by
Older Boy 1, who he instantly recognizes and reveres on account of his seniority, discerning a valuable opportunity to associate with a social superior (and perhaps recalling from a
nature documentary he's seen the levels of protection afforded
to those tiny birds that clean crocodiles' teeth), gratefully ac-
cepts. Older Boy 1 then points out Older Boy 2 (who may or
may not have been previously briefed, depending on his familiarity with the game) and tells New Boy that if he goes over
and asks him how his mum's piano lessons are going, Older
Boy 2 will break into hysterical laughter and everyone will live
happily ever after. Then what just happened happens (the
crocodile snaps his jaws) and New Boy scurries back to his seat
or his corner of the playground, and when anyone asks why
he's crying blubbers something about the high pollen count.

Except this one doesn't. He couldn't move if he tried. He's
staring at my head, transfixed.

"What happened to your hair?"

I'm the only one in school who's allowed to wear nonreligious
headgear (there are four turbans in our year, and Simon Nagel
wears a skullcap in the colors of Watford Football Club) because some of the younger kids don't understand why I'm bald
and sometimes it's easier to hide things than explain them. I get
a lot of looks, but it's okay. Once in Year 6 I forgot to wear my

own clothes on Own Clothes Day and for the whole day I was the only kid at school in uniform, so I already know what it's like to feel ostrichized, which is a better word for excluded (because ostriches can't fly, so they often feel left out). I took my sweater off and undid my top button, but that still didn't stop people from staring at me. It's weird how you can wake up one day exactly the same person as you were the day before except the world has changed around you and now you're the odd one out.

Being ill is a bit like forgetting Own Clothes Day.

(Analogies are also important in Composition because they help people relate things they don't understand to their own experiences (and to tell a good story, you need to write about things that not many people have experienced). Metaphors are just one type of analogy, but there are loads more you can use. Sometimes people don't even realize they're using a metaphor because they've heard it so often that they've forgotten that they're trying to relate to something they don't understand. These are called dead metaphors, and there are some examples below:

1) *Running* water
2) *Head* Master
3) Flower *bed*

Dead metaphors prove that we can understand the world around us only by pretending that it's human and it behaves

like us (which it isn't and it doesn't). That's why we pretend
that chairs have arms and woods have necks and we're so used
to doing it that we've forgotten that that's even a slightly weird
thing to say (which is why you don't get extra marks for using
dead metaphors in Composition).

When my doctor, Mr. Fitzpatrick, explained about my
treatment he used an analogy. He told me to imagine that a
suicide bomber had taken a group of innocent people hostage
in Gamestation and that if we didn't stop him he was going to
blow up the whole of the Harlequin Centre, which is the biggest shopping center in all of Hertfordshire. And then he told
me that if we sent in a Specially Trained Armed Response
Unit they would be able to "neutralize" the terrorist threat,
however, they couldn't necessarily guarantee the safety of the
hostages (who might accidentally get shot), but if we did nothing the terrorist would kill them all anyway, as well as everyone
else in a 10-kilometer radius.

"And that's why we're sending in the SWAT team," he said.
"That's why we're telling them Shoot to Kill."

And when I asked him why we didn't try negotiating with
the suicide bomber first, he shook his head slowly like a cricket
umpire and said, "It is our country's policy never to negotiate
with terrorists."

(So I asked him what were the bomber's demands and he
told me he didn't have any, which I told him was bullspit because the whole point of taking people hostage is getting your
demands met, and if you didn't have any demands there would
be no reason to take hostages in the first place. So then he told
me that the terrorists hated our freedom and that actually the

suicide bomber did have some demands after all, and did I want to hear what they were, because all they were was the systematic destruction of Western culture and the entire American way of life (because Mr. Fitzpatrick is American).

"And besides, even if we could negotiate with him—*which we will not do*—it wouldn't do us any good anyway, because let me tell you something about the terrorist mentality, let me school you here a second, son. The terrorist believes he has God on his side. The terrorist *actually believes* that when he gets up to heaven-knows-where there's seventy-two virgins waiting for him, and every last one of them, they're big-time murder fans—and do you know whose side they're on, cos it sure as bacon ain't Team Infidel."

(And then I asked what a virgin was, because this was two years ago and I was young and naïve (and Mr. Fitzpatrick told me that a virgin was a really good friend with a PlayStation 2). (Being a virgin is like growing up Caucasian in Hertfordshire. You are one long before you know there's a word for it.))

So then I asked Mr. Fitzpatrick why they had to shoot to kill and why they couldn't use rubber bullets and shoot to disarm, which would ensure the safety of the hostages, and he told me that the terrorist has a thick hide like a rhinoceros and that the rubber bullets would just bounce off him. (Which I took to be an insult to my intelligence, so I asked him where exactly he thought the terrorist was from, because if he was threatening everyone in a 10-kilometer radius that would suggest he had nuclear capabilities, which was extremely unlikely, unless maybe he came from North Korea, in which case he'd most likely be a Buddhist and not believe in heaven. And Mr. Fitzpatrick just said, "Exactly.")

But even then I didn't understand why we couldn't just try talking to him, because, after all, even if the suicide bomber did believe some weird stuff and even if he did have Weapons of Mass Destruction (which I sincerely doubted), at the end of the day he was still a person. And that's when the analogy stopped working, because my tumor is not a person.)

The Year 5 is still there. I tell him to get to fuck, which is not in the script.

Normally I try not to swear. I learned to swear when I was seven in Wales when we went to stay with Uncle Tony and he dropped a frozen leg of lamb on his foot. A few weeks later I was watching football with Dad and his team conceded, so to empathize I said "Shit!" Dad washed my mouth out with soap (because it was "dirty" (which suggests he doesn't understand metaphors)). But that wasn't half as bad as the time Mum heard me call Pete Sloss a cocksucker on the way to the cinema. She didn't get angry with me, but that night when she was tucking me in she asked if I knew what one was. And when I said no, she said she didn't have a problem with me using rude words if I felt they were necessary to express myself, but she'd prefer I didn't use words I didn't understand. So she explained it to me. She told me about oral sex and foreplay and lubrication and even flavored condoms (I had previously thought vaginas had taste buds), and finally when she was finished she made me repeat it back to her. After that she kissed me good night, which made me feel queasy.

I can swear in sixty-seven different languages. But I can apologize in only three, which means I could get beaten up in sixty-four countries.

One of the languages I can do both in is French, which is my first lesson on a Monday. In French class we're not allowed to speak English. Instead, we have to do everything *en Français*. There are a lot of things I do *en Français* that I'd never do in English. For one thing, I help out around the house a lot more. Every weekend I spend a minimum of one hour passing the Hoover in my bedroom, and each night I set and clear the table before and after dinner (respectively (obviously)). I have a younger sister who calls herself Marie-Clare (who has nine years (whenever anyone tells you their age in French it sounds like they have a terminal disease) and enjoys horse-riding), and what is more, an older brother (Serge) who likes to play football. Moreover, I have a diet that consists exclusively of the potato in its various incarnations (plates of chips, bags of crisps, and baked), a father who is a doctor (because I don't know the word for a driving instructor), and a mother who works at home (because I don't know the word for sexism (or legal secretary)). Every summer the five of us go on holiday without fail, and always to the same place, La Rochelle, where we practice windsurfing and pass a fantastic week with one another and our dog, who calls himself Sausage. I even have a different name in French. (Madame Berger made us each choose one at the start of the year and explained that in her class that is what we would be known as. At first it felt a bit like we were losing our identities, like we were going into prison and being given a number, but actually now I quite like my French name.) It's Marcel.

"Marcel?"

"*Oui, madame?*"

"*Qu'est-ce que tu as fait le weekend dernier?*"

At first the question confuses me because I don't know if last weekend means the weekend that's just passed or the weekend before that. Both are in the past. I can tell that because I'm in French class.

"*Le weekend?*"

"*Oui. Le weekend* dernier. *En* passé composé."

In truth, it doesn't matter which weekend. Madame Berger was only trying to be helpful. But in French I do the same thing every weekend: "*Samedi j'ai joué au foot avec mon frère et dimanche j'ai lu un roman.*" (I am a much more active person in French, and I read novels only, because I don't know if the Internet is masculine or feminine.)

"*Ah, oui. C'est vrai?*"

This is *une question rhétorique.* However, I decide to answer anyway, because Marcel is a keen conversationalist. "*Oui. C'est vrai.*"

"*Et pour aider tes parents, tu as fait quelque chose?*"

"*J'ai passé l'aspirateur dans ma chambre pour deux heures.*"

"*Comme un bon fils, n'est-ce pas?*"

(Marcel is a good son. I take some vicarious pride from this, which is when you experience something as a result of something someone else has done.) Madame Berger is beaming.

"Et est-ce que tu as fait quelque chose hors de l'ordinaire *peut-être?"*

I pretend to scan my brain for an irregular past participle, but really I knew the question was coming. *"Oui, j'ai ri à un film."*

(In many ways, my life is so much simpler in French. I don't get headaches or déjà vu in French, because I don't know the words for them. Moreover, I don't worry about my parents' marriage or my own mortality or why I haven't had a wet dream, because these are emotions I am not able to express. Sometimes I'm jealous of Marcel. I think that if I moved to France I'd be a completely different person. (For one thing, I'd agree with people a lot more, and for another, I'd spend much more time in libraries and swimming pools.) Do you know what the French call a Lost Property Office? They call it a Found Property Office. (But then again, they call a Potato an Apple of the Ground.))

"Et qu'est-ce que tu feras *le weekend prochain? Dans* l'avenir."

I don't know the French for brain surgery. So I cheat.

"La même."

Our next lesson is the one I've been waiting for. English. Miss Farthingdale hands back our Compositions in reverse order, starting with the worst and ending with . . . Simon Nagel's. *Effing eff-word!*

I come third, with 16 out of 20, behind Simon and Chloe Gower. As punishment, I decide I have to coat my forearm in the fluid from the white end of my ink eraser pen and rest my nose on it for the whole lesson. (It's made from pig urine.)

Simon Nagel is an Alkaline Jew, and his grandfather was in a concentration camp (I forget which one. It's definitely not Auschwitz, but it would be one of the other top answers in *Family Fortunes* if they ever did that round). He always finds a way to write about the Holocaust, whatever title we get set, which is why he always wins. Chloe Gower is an albino and comes from a Broken Home. Her skin is the same color as the correction fluid she uses to write *Manic Street Preachers* on her rucksack, and her parents split up a year and a half ago (which is about the time she dyed her hair black (which is not a good look for an albino (because it makes her face look like apartheid))). Every few months when her dad picks her up from school in his convertible there'll be a new woman in the passenger seat. They always look roughly the same, like younger, prettier versions of her mum. It's a bit like her dad's casting for an American Remake of his life. I tried to talk to her once about the Manic Street Preachers because I quite like that song they do about being tolerant, but when I told her this she sneered and told me she liked only the early stuff. Then she gave me one earpiece from her minidisc and played me a song called "She Is Suffering" and asked me what I thought. I think that being a Manic Street Preachers fan who prefers "She Is Suffering" to the Tolerance Song is like being a Christian who prefers the carpentry to the miracles. But I told her it sounded cool, and now when we cross each other in the corridor we nod.

Chapter Two

(The Composition was A Life in the Day, which is absolutely not the same as A Day in the Life. A Day in the Life is a snapshot of a particular day from the time you woke up to the time you went to bed and all the things that happened in between. We don't do A Day in the Life anymore, because it's too easy.

A Life in the Day is much harder. In A Life in the Day you have to give an account of an average day in your life to show what it's like to be you. To do this, you have to focus on all of the thoughts and feelings you have about the places, people, and routines that make up an average day in your life.

On an average day in my life I have milk on toast for breakfast (or maybe Honey Nut Cornflakes with Peanut Butter). There is such a thing as an average day in my life, but I don't think it tells you anything about who I am and what it's like to be me. In fact, I'm not sure that life really has all that much to do with days in the first place.)

Chapter Three

When the anesthetic practitioner came to visit, he weighed me like I was a fish he'd just caught and asked me if I had a phobia of needles, which I told him I didn't because a phobia is an irrational fear of something and my fear of needles is 100% justified. (I don't understand why people insist that they have phobias of things like heights and snakes and small spaces and open spaces and other people when all of those things can kill you. I hate how people think that not walking under ladders makes you superstitious, when actually it's just common sense. You wouldn't call someone superstitious if they didn't want to live under a flight path. (I am not superstitious.))

Then he asked if I had any questions. I could think of only

one, but it didn't seem relevant (If Stephen Hawking got his CapsLock key stuck, after a while would he start to lose his voice?), so instead I shook my head.

"It's a real game of chess," remarks Dad.

I have always wanted a TV in my room. There's a bed (which I'm in), a bedside cabinet with a call button, an armchair (which Dad's in), and an unusually high number of three-pin plug sockets (six). I thought about asking the nurse what they were for, but then I figured it out myself. (Three are for personal use, three for medical use. (Three to charge my minidisc and three to charge me.)) In the corner of the room, Chelsea are playing Liverpool.

I look up from my crossword (*24 across: uncooperative (9)*, which is either difficult or *difficult,* in which case it's easy (and 19 down is *basic*)), because I prefer chess to football. At first I can't see any similarity, and I'm just about to dismiss Dad's claim as a bad metaphor when one of the Chelsea defenders reaches the opposition's goal line and is replaced by a better player who can move forward, backward, and diagonally. Dad seems pleased by this and lets me go back to my crossword. A few minutes later, Liverpool mount an attack that ends in an acrobatic save by the Chelsea goalkeeper. Dad tells me to look at the screen: "Because that's what a pedigree goalkeeper looks like, son."

This means that both of his parents were goalkeepers and you can trace his ancestry back through an unbroken line of them.

During the halftime analysis I get déjà vu while they are replaying the save, which is like having déjà vu squared.

When Mum returns with a cup of coffee, Dad turns off the game guiltily without her having to say anything. She asks if I mind her drinking in front of me (because I am NBM, which means I can't eat or drink anything), which I don't, and then she asks if I'm okay.

"Ah, he's all right," says Dad. "It's not like it's rocket science!"

I wonder when Dad last made Mum laugh.

Once when I was very young, Mum and Dad left me with Aunt Julie and Uncle Tony because they were going to the Alps for a weekend for their anniversary. I remember after dinner on the night before they went watching Dad count out some strange-looking notes at the table. "Are those Francs?" I asked, because I didn't recognize the markings, but I knew from the care that Dad was taking that it must be money.

"No," said Dad. "They're mine."

It was the best joke I'd ever heard. And Mum agreed. It took the legs from under her. I remember she was standing behind him and she skied her hands down his front in a snow-plow until they crossed and she was draped over his shoulders like a knotted jumper. She laughed so hard nothing came out, and finally, when she had enough air in her lungs, she kissed the spot that's now his bald patch. It made me feel queasy to look at them because it was the only time I can remember that they didn't look like parents.

For ages afterward, whenever I watched Dad counting out money he'd get a glint in his eye, which would be my cue. "Are those Francs?" I would call, melting into laughter before he even made the joke. Which didn't stop him.

"No, they're mine!"

Then he'd cheer and throw his hands up above his head like he was trying to start The Wave. When I'd join in, he'd swoop down to tickle my armpits or hoist me up onto his shoulders and parade me around the house until we found Mum. And then we'd restage the whole thing for her benefit. This time, though, he'd play around with the wording. Sometimes he wouldn't give us exactly what we thought we wanted. Instead, he'd just nudge us in the direction of the punch line and sit back as we raced to the end.

"Are those Francs?"

"Well, it's funny you should ask that . . ."

"NO, THEY'RE MINE!"

This was my favorite version of the joke. It was like we were running a relay and Dad was handing me the baton for the final straight. He'd already blown away the competition, and all I had to do was hold on tight and break the tape at the finish line.

Then it was Mum's turn to run with it. The joke became how much she liked the sound of this Frank fellow, and did we happen to know if he was single? After all, Frank was a billionaire. While Dad could claim ownership over only whatever amount he had to hand (and would happily do so whenever I asked him to), Frank didn't need to boast. Whatever modest sum Dad wasn't joking about belonged to Frank. And then the joke became how much more eligible Frank was than Dad in other departments. By Dad's own admission, not only was Frank richer, he was better-looking, too, and a better listener and (as Dad got older) a better dresser and (as I got older) better in bed, until eventually Frank was Dad's superior in every respect and Mum would openly fantasize about the day he'd rescue her from her life with us and whisk her away to his private island (France).

However, none of this stopped me from pitying Frank. Because for every point he scored over Dad there was still one thing that he couldn't do. He couldn't make Mum laugh. (For everything that Frank had, my parents had each other.)

Around the time of my first seizure, Mum and Dad had another trip booked to France, to the same resort they'd gone to half my life before. In the end, they canceled it to be with me at the hospital, but not before Dad had changed some money over. The night they were supposed to leave, we ate together in the hospital canteen, and when it came time for Dad to pay I noticed in his wallet an unfamiliar note sandwiched between fifteen pounds.

"Are those Frank's?" I asked, expectantly.

"No, they're Euros," he replied.

———

I don't think my dad has made my mum laugh since the introduction of the Single European Currency. (I sometimes think all it would take for them to find what they've lost is if we all took a trip to Switzerland. (However, there's only one reason sick people go to Switzerland.))

"Why don't you get yourself a paper?" suggests Mum.

"From where?" asks Dad.

"From Smiths."

"Where's that?"

"You know where it is."

"So humor me."

"It's where you went last time to buy a pack of gum."

"Great. I'll just ask for the blue plaque."

When Dad's gone, Mum sits down on the edge of my bed and tells me I have nothing to be afraid of. Sometimes I think she's in denial. (It's the way she ruffles my scalp.)

For a long while we say nothing, which is the same as not saying anything only when you look at it from the outside in. Finally, Mum asks what I want to eat when I get home. I pretend to think about the question so as not to hurt her feelings.

Spaghetti Bolognese is my favorite meal, which is lucky, because it's the only meal Mum cooks. She doesn't follow a recipe, I think because she doesn't like being told what to do and recipe books are always full of imperatives. If you want Mum to finely chop two onions, then the worst thing you could do is tell her to *Finely chop two onions*. (Instead, you should follow these instructions:

Spaghetti Bolognese

1 Kitchen
1 Chopping Board
2 Onions
1 Cutlery Drawer
1 Saucepan Lid

Preparation time: 5 minutes, Cooking time: 1 hour

Serves 3

1. Enter the kitchen, loudly. If anyone is in earshot, announce your intentions to make a Bolognese sauce. If no one is in earshot, loudly announce your intentions to make a Bolognese sauce.
2. Take out the chopping board and place the onions on it, loudly.
3. Clatter around the kitchen, being sure to make as much noise as possible. Pretend the cutlery drawer is a percussion instrument and play it, badly, in 5/4 time.
4. Await arrival of Mum.
5. Answer the question "What on earth are you doing?" with "I am looking for a knife."
6. Send subliminal message by playing F Sharp on the saucepan lid.
7. Leave for 1 hour and season to taste.

(If Jamie Oliver ever wrote a storybook about a kid who nicks an artery making a red-wine reduction, then Mum would be a Michelin-starred chef inside a year.))

Because Mum has never read a recipe in her life, her Spaghetti Bolognese isn't like any other Spaghetti Bolognese. She calls it her signature dish, which I suppose is appropriate, because it looks nothing like the thing it's supposed to represent and it's never the same twice in a row. (I think what she means, though, is that it's unique to her, which is definitely true.) Dad says Mum's Bolognese is the culinary equivalent of a black hole because everything gets sucked into it, which is true. Sometimes it's made of beef, other times lamb, sometimes it's got bits of broccoli in, or sometimes peppers, and once even frozen peas. He says we shouldn't even call it Bolognese, and that if we do we might as well throw a pillow out the window and call it a bird of prey.

I don't know what the rules are for what is and isn't a Bolognese (or for where one thing ends and another thing begins in general), but I don't think we ever could call what Mum makes something else, because for something to be a word at least two people have to have tried it separately. Otherwise, there'd be no point in naming it in the first place, because you wouldn't have anyone to discuss it with. (I try and remember this whenever David Driscoll tells me about rusty trombones or space-docking or munging. I know it's bullspit, because there's no way two people would ever have tried those things independently. So even if you were sick enough to give it a go, you wouldn't bother giving it a name, because you wouldn't assume it was a thing. (Which means someone's just made up the word without doing the thing (which is like having a door without a room behind it).))

I suppose Dad does have a point, though. If you think about it (which I have), it is a bit weird we call Mum's sauce Bolognese, because if you asked anyone else in the world to make a Bolognese, theirs wouldn't even be close. However (thinking about it), that's probably why it's my favorite. It's like a really bad private joke that's funny only because no one else gets it. It makes me feel like we've got our own secret language, because only our family has that picture in our head when we hear the word *Bolognese.* (So even if it does always taste better in restaurants, my mum's Spaghetti Bolognese is my favorite meal because it makes me feel safe.)

I realize I haven't answered the question out loud.

"Spaghetti Bolognese," I intone.

Mum smiles. "You mean my signature dish."

"Why do you call it that?" I ask.

Mum considers the question.

"Because by now I'm stuck with it."

And then we finish the crossword.

Chapter Four

"I bet you know your five times table, don't you?" asks the anesthetic nurse, apparently without irony, after I've been wheeled out of my room and down a long white corridor past at least a dozen hand-washing checkpoints and into and then subsequently out of a lift that requires a PIN number to operate, which is a tautology (because PIN stands for Personal Identification *Number*), and which Mum and Dad weren't allowed into, and then down another three much quieter corridors and into the room I'm in now, which is called the Anesthesia *Station,* which implies I'm going on a trip somewhere, which is the opposite of reassuring.

Having people talk down to you is the absolute worst part

about being a kid. I hate when someone tries to talk to me *on my level* (especially when it's someone whose job a drug addict would probably be overqualified for). Instead of answering, I concentrate on remembering my calming techniques.

"How about counting? You can count to ten, can't you?"

"I'm doing it right now," I say.

(Another tree falls in the woods.)

"Okay, well, when I say so, here's what I want you to do. I want you to try and count all the way up to ten. Will you give that a go for me?"

"In what language?"

"Say what now," says the nurse, so it sounds like she's reading stage directions off an autocue. She is Specials Board pretty (which probably means no one's ever told her how annoying she is). My surgical gown is membrane thin. Suddenly I'm worried about erections, but, luckily, when I remember that my bum's on show all the blood in my body gets diverted to my face.

"In what language would you like me to *try* and count to ten?"

"Well, how about just in numbers for now."

(I didn't know it was possible to feel superior and a breeze between your bum cheeks at the same time. (I thought they were mutually exclusive sensations. (If I'd had to draw a Venn diagram it would have been two separate circles. (Like a pair of breasts.)))) The blood reroutes back toward my penis. I manage to suck some of it back up to my cheeks by remembering the time I called Miss Farthingdale Mum. (It's like one of those Test Your Strength games you get at fairs. (The hammer is my history of embarrassment.)) At this rate, she'll never be able to find a vein.

(Sex is one of the things I know least about, and every day it gets worse. You know how they say the universe is expanding? That's how it is with sex at our school. Every day there's something new that I didn't even know I didn't know about. It all started last year in Biology, when they split up the girls and boys to show us videos about puberty and the presenter told us (like he was reading the news) how perfectly natural it was for us to be worrying about the size of our penises.

From that moment on, even if we'd never thought about it before (which I hadn't), penis size was all we had on our minds. Whispers spread round the school (like head lice used to) about averages and anomalies and acceptable methods for measuring. Everyone had a figure (me included). The first weird thing I noticed was how everyone else somehow knew without being told to use inches. Everything else in our lives up to this point had been measured in meters and centimeters (graph axes, sports day events), but now all of a sudden our genitals were mini–metric martyrs. The only other time I'd heard inches as a unit of measurement was when Dad was showing off his new wide-screen TV, and I couldn't escape the feeling that there was a connection between the two things. It was almost like Sony wanted to encourage us to make the association, as if they realized it was mainly men who bought wide-screen TVs and they knew what impressed us most. But whether it was a coincidence or not, I knew from the moment I started calculating the size of electrical appliances as a factor of my own penis that something fundamental had changed.

For an entire week after they showed us the video, debate raged in the playground about what made for admissible data. We all recognized the need for standardization, but we weren't all agreed about what it was we were actually measuring. Some of us argued that the penis was just what you could see with your own eyes (and hold in your own hands (which some of us had started to do, apparently)), while others maintained that the shaft actually began before the balls. (One or two even measured from their bum holes forward, which reminded me for some reason of an argument my mum had once had with Aunt Julie about abortion. (Aunt Julie thought it was okay, but Mum just kept saying that *Life began at the moment of conception*.)) Eventually, we reached an agreement that the penis was the protuberance alone, and for a week or so this looked set to be our Magna Carta, until someone with an older brother raised the subject of *girth*. Then it was back to the measuring tapes. In seven days we'd gone from blissful ignorance to this. There wasn't a man among us who (with a little application and a Casio FX-83) couldn't have calculated his volume to twelve decimal points.

For a few days we were as happy with our new knowledge as Mr. Carson was with our sudden interest in π. However, slowly it began to dawn on us that a penis in isolation, whatever size (large, medium, or travel), didn't actually mean all that much in real terms. It was only when correlated against the depth of our classmates' vaginas that the data became useful. And that's when the boys started talking to the girls.

———

That was the term that Susie Beckman spoke to me. Susie Beckman was the first girl in our year to get breasts, which means she's even more of a celebrity than I am now (which means I don't know anything about her). She didn't need to say hello, because I had tracked her approach all the way across the playground (which she must have either seen or assumed). Instead, when she arrived, she announced that she had made a bet about me.

"It's about the clitoris," she explained, unwrapping a stick of bubble gum and sliding it between her lips until it squashed against her teeth and folded up like a sound wave.

I had no idea what the clitoris was. (I'm still not sure I do entirely.) My guess was it was something sexual, because we were living through the second great Age of Discovery. The clitoris must be some new Newfoundland, I figured. Maybe Susie Beckman had discovered it accidentally while looking for India.

"The clitoris?" I asked, casually tossing off the word with false familiarity.

"Yeah, it's whether or not you know what it is."

Eff-word. I examined my options and realized quickly I didn't have any. (One thing I could have done was just own up to my ignorance (*own my ignorance*), but technically if you've got only one option, then it isn't an option at all.) I could feel the sweat starting to gather in the small of my back. (In that moment, my Hydroelectric energy potential was vast enough to power a small Peruvian village.) To buy myself time, I asked how much was riding on my answer.

"Pound tuck," retorted Susie Beckman, in a double-berry-flavored speech bubble.

"And what did you bet?"

"I said you didn't know, but Chloe Gower reckoned you would and I should leave you alone."

Here I looked up and spotted Chloe fifty meters away in the tuckshop queue, oblivious to its flow, like a pebble in a stream, a stethoscopic Y of headphone cord disappearing at her throat into a dark swathe of anti-uniform. Her eyes were pointed our way, and when she saw me notice she pivoted gracelessly, flicking up the hood of her non-regulation sweatshirt and dislodging an earpiece as she did so. Suddenly, I saw a chink of light. Maybe there was a way Chloe Gower could be the loser here and not me. After all, it would serve her right for believing in me.

"So if I don't know, you get a pound?"

"Oh my God, you know how a bet works!"

(Judging by how early Susie Beckman discovered it, Sarcasm is an island just off the coast of Portugal. (But I didn't mind, because now I had a plan.))

"Well, in that case"—I tapped my nose—"how about I don't know and you owe me fifty-p tuck."

Susie Beckman's face scrunched into a frown. She looked down her nose at my stomach, because we were roughly the same height.

"You what?"

"Let's just say what *I don't know* can't hurt you."

I held her gaze. (I was all in on a pair of Dinosaur Top Trumps. I was playing a man's game with kids' cards.)

"So you're saying you *do* know?"

"I'm saying for a can of Lilt, I can forget."

Susie Beckman never did give me my fifty pence (in fact, that was the last contact we've had), but if she did suspect I was bluffing, she never called me on it. And if she wanted to now, I'd be ready for her, because that night clitoris fast-tracked itself right to the top of my To Google list.)

I start thinking about all the items on my current To Google list. All of the names I've heard for things I've never got round to looking up. All of the doors I've never opened: Walter Cronkite, Cassius Clay, Capsicum, Sir Vantess, Tess of The D'Urbervilles, John Cougar Mellencamp, The Dow Jones Index, The Duckworth-Lewis Method, The Rhythm Method, The Footsie 500, The Daytona 500, The Birmingham 6, The Aurora Borealis, The Cuban Missile Crisis, Christian Guru Murphy, The Bay of Pigs, Pig Latin, Jerry Mander, Mandy Patinkin, Monica Seles, Mnemonics, New Radicals, Free Radicals, Flea Markets, Fixed-Rate Mortgages, Double Penetration, The Corridor of Uncertainty, Squeaky Bum Time, Tennis Elbow, The Ottoman Empire, The Six-Day War, The Hundred Years' War, Hamid Karzai, Prince Naseem Hamed, Prince Albert, Albert Pierrepoint, Pierre van Hooijdonk, Donkey Oaty, Titus Oates. (It's like browsing the index to a book I haven't read.) And that's when it hits me.

What if something goes wrong?
What if this is the last conversation I ever have?

For the first time, I feel myself starting to panic.

"Where's the other one?"

"What other one?"

"The other one. The anesthetic practitioner. What happened to the other one?"

"Oh, honey, he's not a doctor. Don't worry, there's nothing to be afraid about."

"Why does everyone keep saying that?"

"Because it's true."

"If it's true, they wouldn't keep saying it," I hear myself say.

I try to breathe normally, but my heart is beating in my throat. I feel like I could cough it up right into her lap. The nurse flicks a dewdrop off the end of a syringe. "Look, this really doesn't hurt, I promise, just so long as you can keep calm. Will you do that for me?"

I think of things to reassure myself:

1) It takes sixteen years to qualify as a neurosurgeon, which means that Mr. Fitzpatrick has been studying how to do this sort of operation since before my parents met. (Before we left for the hospital, I googled the 100 biggest hits of 1988, and I'd only heard of seven of the artists in

the list.) Mr. Fitzpatrick is so well qualified that people don't even call him doctor anymore. You get to be called Mister only after you've qualified on top of qualifying to be a doctor. (It's a bit like sports day. If you run the 100 meters, then you end up 100 meters away from where you started, but if you run the 400 meters you end up in exactly the same place.)

2) *Trepanning* is a word, which I know about from another 18 I saw. It's when you drill a hole in someone's skull to cure them of headaches or madness (or, in the film, demonic possession), and apparently it's the oldest surgical procedure that they've ever found evidence for, dating back at least as far as the prehistoric era. Even though no one knows how widespread it was, the fact that it has a name means they must have done it at least twice. Which means it must have worked.

3) *Pour trouver le bureau des objets trouvés continuez tout droit.*

The nurse is rubbing cream into the back of my left hand and talking about nerve endings. The veins run blue like motorways on a roadmap. They are the quickest possible way to my heart. (We are not interested in taking the scenic route.) I look away and think of all the must-see films I've never seen.

She taps on the skin to bring up the vein. My blood is hiding from the syringe, running scared. It's in the last place she would think to look.

"All you'll feel is a tinsy prick, like a wasp sting."

People use analogies when they're trying to explain something you don't understand.

"I'm allergic to wasps."

"Then a small electric shock."

I've never been electrocuted. We have plastic socket covers. I am totally unprepared for this. I have a Personal Best stiffy.

"Now, remember what I said about counting to ten . . ."

I refuse to give her the satisfaction. If this is to be my last act, let it be one of defiance.

I decide to do a Fibonacci sequence.

Ice shoots up my arm.

"1 . . . 1 . . . 2 . . . 3 . . . 5 . . ."

And then I die.

Chapter Five

(Question: Bungee Jump is to Suicide as General Anesthetic is to _____?

Answer: <u>Lethal injection</u>.

(You know the difference only on the way back up.

(Which is why right now I think I'm dead.)))

Death is a bit like being in screensaver mode, except the mouse is unplugged.

That your life flashes in front of your eyes before you die is such a cliché (and Miss Farthingdale says that in Composition you should avoid clichés like the plague. (Dad says clichés are clichés because they're true, but this is also a cliché.)). I never thought my death would be so mosaic, which is a better word for dull.

I always imagined a blooper reel.

I am walking hand in hand with my father along unfamiliar streets. There are no signs or numbers on the doors, and the houses and the driveways feel unimagined somehow, unrealized, like the outskirts of a computer game level (as though no one ever expected us to venture this far). We stop outside one such house. The gravel under our feet makes no sound. The door is without detail. I don't believe there is a thing behind it, but Dad presses the buzzer anyway. It makes the noise of a circular saw. After a moment or quadrillion a gigantic man answers. Beneath a tangerine beard, his face is slate. Hair licks his forehead like fire. A lock darts down his face and bursts into flame in his fierce blue eyes. (They are the hottest part. (As he looks down at me, I think I might melt.)) Dad talks to him in an adult language I don't understand. It's a series of clicks and fellas and laughs and curses, and before long they are old friends and we're expected. Dad squats down weightlifter-style, and for a minute I think (hope (pray)) he's going to hoist me up, carry me away from here. But instead he tells me he'll be back to collect me after his lessons and I'm to behave for Mr. Driscoll.

Mr. Driscoll shuts the door with me on the other side of it, and the room starts to load around me. For the first time in my life I realize that we are well off. Sunlight from a broken shade bushwhacks through the murk and slices a cross section of the living area. The air is heavy with dust. Breathing is like the last half-bowl from a packet of Rice Krispies. (The world record for holding your breath is nineteen minutes and two seconds. (Dad's lessons are an hour each, and Saturday is his busy day. (He spends all day Saturday "on road" or "in car." (His weekends are so busy he doesn't have time for determiners.))))

David is on the sofa in front of a small-screen TV, an N64 controller at his feet. A mushroom cloud of dead cells rises around him, so I know he has sat down recently, but he is pretending to be asleep. His snoring is stagy. I sit down next to him on a newspaper front page (Illegal immigrants have been lashing themselves to the underside of freight trains. (Something must be done.)). Even in the near dark I can see that his skin is angry, his face pockmarked and raw.

Which is when I remember why I'm here.

David is the second-to-last one in our year to get chickenpox.

I am the last one.

I am here to contract his.

(Life is flashing very slowly. It's all happening at half-speed but also kind of at once. Looking around the room smears. Time has lost its shape, like a rubber band stretched beyond its elastic limit, and now that they're no longer tethered by tense, every action is a present participle. Moreover, even the nouns are starting to behave as verbs. It's hard to explain, but it's kind of like Antarctica, which most people think of as a continent but is really just sea. (*Everything* is an -ing word.))

Outside, through the missing slat, a neighbor is washing a

Ford Escort with a garden hose. The spray off the bonnet makes a bastard rainbow.

And then I remember why I'm back here.

Today is the day that it rained.

I know what Mr. Driscoll is going to say before he says it. I hear it in my head before it's out of his mouth, so it's like he's being badly dubbed.

"Money's on the fridge like. Acting the maggot I'll hear about."

The door opens. Light yawns in, like air into a lung, and just as quickly it's gone. I watch Mr. Driscoll climb into a van. There's time enough to read the slogan on its side before it shivers awake and pulls out of view: *An office without plants is like the Amazon without a rainforest. Love plants. We do.* (The sickle of the question mark has peeled away. (Now it is an imperative. (*Love plants!*)))

On the TV, Mario starts snoring.

David stops.

"There's only one control," he says, riding the sofa cushion down onto the floor without looking at me. Mario backflips up a wall and eats a coin. "If you want, you can watch," he adds, after what could be a minute or a decade. And then: "If you tell anyone you were here, I'll kill your pets."

(I never did tell anyone. I have taken it to my grave, David Driscoll. When you returned to school, your black eye a septic yellow, and told whoever asked that you fell down the stairs (which you must have learned from a thousand bad TV shows in which someone convinces no one that they haven't been punched), I did not tell them that you live in a bungalow.)

For lunch we order pizza and eat on the floor from paper plates, which reminds me of birthdays. David eats first. When the grease has stained his lips orange and the light from the ceiling has seeped through his plate and into the carpet, he turns the box round to me. As I open the box its jaws split like a snake's, and for a second I forget who's eating who. A cheese-and-tomato tongue beckons me closer, and as I reach shakily through fangs of corrugated cardboard the smell is science experiments and swimming lessons. I'm overwhelmed by the feeling that at any moment this box could swallow me whole (that I would disappear completely), but before it has the chance, David swivels it back round and takes the last slice. I want to tell him that he's saved my life, but he's on his feet before I can shape the words.

The room gulps another breath as the front door opens and I remember the stray dog tied to the lamppost. David frisbees the empty pizza box into the Ford Escort owner's front garden and sets the slice down where the flea market can catch its scent. He galumphs greedily toward it, his eyes wide with thanks, but when the meal is a half-foot from his mouth (when he can taste it in his nose), the tether snaps back his neck, and David laughs. As he wheezes and strains against his leash I can see the first tears of rain making Venn diagrams of the hose-pipe puddle. (The first drop is *Butterflies* (hairless, diurnal, chrysalis), the second is *Moths* (furry, nocturnal, cocoon). They hit the surface in a photo finish and burst and sprawl and inter-

sect (antennae, six legs, Pterygota (which is a subclass for insects who are winged hexapods)). The third drop is *Bees* (hairy
legs, feeds on pollen), the fourth is *Wasps* (smooth legs, feeds
on parasites). They meet in the middle (stings, yellow, Hyme-
noptera (which is the biggest order of insects)) and then become indistinct. In seconds there is an ecosystem falling from
the sky (set by set), and by now it's impossible to spot the differences. (Everything intersects. (One thing becomes another.)))

Wet gel lacquers David's brow.

His hair will dry in stalactites, which are the ones that point
down.

He pushes past me and slams shut the door.

"Help me get the washing in!"

I don't move. I know what's coming, but right now I'm
mesmerized by the dog. He's trying furiously to catch the rain,
which I don't remember noticing on my first time round.

("Oi! Gaybot! Washing!")

He is good at it, but success brings him no satisfaction.
Whenever he plucks a drop from midair it turns to water on
his tongue, which is not what he wanted at all. He wanted to
take them alive.

"What the . . ."

Now it's David's turn to be spellbound. When I turn round
he's stiller than a bowl of fruit (or a violin). The rest of the
sentence has frozen on his lips. He's standing in front of the
open slide door, staring out at a washing line that sags across
the back patio like a maths problem.

The sun is shining.

There's not a cloud in the sky.

David speaks with double question marks. Wonder slackens his jaw.

"What the *fuck* . . . "

Above our heads, the downpour plays arpeggios on the bungalow's roof, and in front of our eyes the drought falls in sheets from an open sky. It takes a moment for us to realize what should not even need realizing (what is too obvious to even say). It is raining in the front garden and not in the back garden.

The carpet feels like sand between my toes. When I look down I am in only my Y-fronts. But this isn't an anxiety dream, because no one else is in school uniform. David is stripped to the waist. The sores on his back spell out a constellation. He is singing.

It's raining, it's pouring.
The old man is snoring!

(This carpet will bear witness to what happens here today. With bare feet we will trample in mud from the front garden and dirt from the back like we're signing a treaty between two separate planets. (For one day only, David Driscoll's house is a portal between worlds, and as we run shuttles from slide door to porch we are in both simultaneously. (This is Greenwich to the power of infinity. (We are at the center of the Universe. (Today we can win any argument because the Earth *does* revolve around us.)))))

He went to bed and bumped his head
And he couldn't get up in the morning!

A duckbilled platypus lays eggs and has a beak, but it is a mammal and not a bird. I do not know where Bolognese stops and Ragú begins. Once I was riding up an escalator when it stopped working, and then I was walking up a staircase. (Mood swings are one of the symptoms of my illness. Last year when Mum refused to write me an Off Games note I told her that I wished she was dead and I didn't get into trouble. "It's not you saying it," she told me. Which scared me, because I don't always know what is me and what is the illness. (I really do think I wanted her dead.))

There are so many things I don't understand.

But me and David Driscoll know where the rain starts. And for now, at least, that means we understand everything.

For the first time in my life I know I will remember something until the day I die.

(Which I have.)

Part Two

Taking an Interest

Chapter Six

It's funny how time works in hospital. When you come in the front door they put you in the waiting room, where time goes backward, but the farther in you get, the more of a rush everyone seems to be in. I'm as far in as you can go and still come back. They call it the ICU. In here I'm hooked up to an ICP (through a hole in my skull), an EKG, and two IVs (which makes eight in Roman Numerals). Everything in the ICU has an abbreviation, which proves how much of a hurry everyone's in (except me). (If the ICU were a person, it would be the sort who walks up escalators, which would make it a walking tautology.)

In the other wards I've been in, the nurses do things ASAP, but here in the ICU they do them asap. The fact that asap is two syllables shorter than ASAP means that it conveys a deeper shade of urgency. (The extra two syllables it would take the nurses to say ASAP would eat unacceptably into time that could be better spent starting to do whatever it is that needs doing.) While the nurses and doctors buzz around like flies I have a lot of time to think (which hurts less than I thought it would). One of the things I've been wondering about a lot is the first time someone used the abbreviation ASAP.

Although we probably won't ever know the exact circumstances that this happened in, I have decided that it's reasonable to assume two things:

1) That the person who first coined the term was in a rush. It is reasonable to assume this because the one thing we do know about him for certain is that he needed something done as soon as possible.
2) That the person who first heard the term didn't understand what it meant. It is reasonable to assume this because no one had ever said it before.

Therefore, it is also reasonable to assume that the conversation probably went something like this:

MAN 1: I need you to do something ASAP.
MAN 2: What does that mean?
MAN 1: It means that I need you to do something as soon as possible.

MAN 2: Well, why didn't you say that, then?

MAN 1: I did say that.

MAN 2: No, you didn't. You said you needed me to do something ASAP.

MAN 1: ASAP is short for As Soon As Possible.

MAN 2: Since when?

MAN 1: Since now.

MAN 2: Says who?

MAN 1: Says me. Think about it. People only ever say "As Soon As Possible" when there isn't a second to spare, right?

MAN 2: So?

MAN 1: So if there isn't a second to spare, then surely it makes sense to have an alternative phrase that takes a third less time to say. Which is where ASAP comes in.

MAN 2: Well, that's all well and good. But how the eff did you expect me to understand that "I need you to do something ASAP" meant that you needed me to do something as soon as possible?

MAN 1: I didn't. But sometimes you have to speculate to accumulate. Moreover, I hope now you can see that, if anything, my decision to risk confusing you by using an unfamiliar abbreviation was, in itself, testament to the exigency of the circumstances that we currently find ourselves in.

If you think about it (which I have (a lot)), this represents a net loss of 264 syllables, when all Man 1 was trying to do was save himself two in the first place. In conclusion, this means that in this situation saying ASAP was exactly <u>44</u> times less efficient than it would have been to say As Soon As Possible.

(All this is really unlucky for Man 1 and Man 2 (because by the time Man 1 was through explaining, their house would most probably have burned down), but for me, it's great news. I don't know how many hours it took me to figure this out because I fell asleep and had to start again quite a few times, but the fact that I can still do mental arithmetic means I don't have major brain damage.)

This time when I wake up, Mum and Dad are Siamese at the foot of my bed. Mum faces away from me, her hair lank and shapeless and her head bowed into Dad's clavicle, which is another word for collarbone. Dad is looking right at me. Stubble hangs like fog over his mouth, and his eyes are set back in his head like two marbles in a pocket. I see him before he sees me.

Dad?

He continues to stare as though he hasn't heard me. (I wonder if this is what an absence seizure looks like, but it can't be, because they're not genetic.) I count eleven Mississippis before he notices me.

"He's awake. Lou, Lou, he's awake. Son, can you hear me?"

Yes.

"Son? Can he hear us? *Excuse me, nurse!* Can he hear us?"

I can hear you.

"Nurse!"

Am I okay?

Mum and Dad detach. A string of snot links them still, from Mum's nostril to Dad's shoulder. (It's like he's her ventilator.)

Mum?

"He can hear you: Talk to him. He might not have the strength to talk back."

Mum turns to face me, and the mucus tube snaps free from her nose. She looks blurry, like someone has turned down the contrast on her face. I can't tell the difference between her skin and her lips.

Am I okay?

"Okay, son, do you want the good news or the bad news?"

Am I okay?

"Good news is girls love scars."

Am I okay?

"Bad news, me and your mum have been talking and we've decided you've been getting a little too clever for your own good, so while they were at it we got them to go ahead and take a little bit off the top. Nothing too drastic, just a trim, just enough to give me a chance at Boggle."

He trails off.

"Dot dot dot," says the heart rate monitor.

"But you might want to familiarize yourself with that noise right there, cos chances are you'll be hearing it a lot in a few years when Tesco's put you on the tills."

The nurse laughs, which only encourages him. (Mum hasn't moved a muscle since he started talking. (She is starting to scare me.))

"What is that, anyway?"

"It's monitoring his heartbeat, which is perfectly normal. It's called a cardiogram."

"I thought that was a type of stripper. You know, the type that comes dressed in knitwear."

"You're okay," says Mum.

And then I fall asleep again. I don't know how much later I wake up, but when I do, it's like a Spot the Difference puzzle. (I can spot only the following differences:

1) Two silver trails (like a snail's) run in parallel lines down the shoulder of Dad's jumper.
2) Mum's nostrils are crusty.
3) The nurse is black.

Otherwise everything is identical. (Neither Mum nor Dad have moved.))

I don't know why exactly, but I shut my eyes again before Mum or Dad notice I'm awake. After a while I hear a sound like a fart being squeezed between clenched cheeks. However, no one laughs (and I can't smell anything), and I realize it's a chair scraping against the lino floor. Then Dad's voice:

"Well, I don't know about you, but I need a coffee like he needs a hole in the head. Nurse?"

"Mi kyan help yuh wid someting?"

"The cafeteria?"

"Goo a dar an galang de kyarridar."

"Do you want anything, Mum?"

No response.

I listen for Dad's footsteps to drown in the ventilator tides and imagine he's striding out to sea King Canute style. For a while it's silent (relatively, at least), and then it's Mum's turn to talk. However, when she tries to, her voice stalls like Dad's car after he hasn't used it for a while. She coughs and tries again, and this time it takes.

"I was born in this hospital," she says. And then, after quite a bit more time, "You don't remember your grandmother, do you?"

The question doesn't sound rhetorical, but it must be, because I'm doing an excellent impression of sleeping. Either way, though, I decide to think about the answer to check for memory loss. (Another analogy a doctor used once to help me understand my brain was that a seizure was like blowing a fuse. (He told me to imagine I'd had a power cut and I was sitting in the dark, and after fumbling around for a bit I manage to reset the fuse. The lights and the TV come back on, and my computer (which I was using) starts to reboot. However, the homework I was doing in Word has to be rescued from the last saved version, which means some of the data might be missing. (Since he told me this, I always do my homework by hand.)))

"You came to her funeral. Do you remember?"

I open my last saved version and Ctrl F *funeral*.

(I do remember Grandma's funeral. Actually, I don't know if that's true. Maybe it would be best to call it a half-truth (or maybe just a lie (because being truthful is like being naked (because if you're halfway there, you're still pretty much the opposite))). What I mean is I know I was at my grandma's funeral because people have told me all my life about what I said when I saw her there in the open casket in her summer dress ("Won't she be cold?"). The fact is I've been told this story so many times (mainly by Dad, because he's still proud of his response ("Not where she's going")) that I've started thinking of it as my own memory. But actually, when I look back on it, I can see myself in it, which means it's not from my point of view, so it must be someone else's. (I think everyone has some memories like this that don't belong to them. They're the ones made from other people's memories of you, which means you're taken far enough out of the moment to look back at yourself in the middle of it. (I think maybe this is what people mean by having a Photographic Memory, which would also explain why in my memory of Grandma's funeral my mum's eyes are red.) The weird thing though is that even if it isn't exclusively mine, this is still one of my most vivid recollections.))

The floor farts again, and a second later I feel Mum's breath on my cheek. At first it's annoying (it smells really stale), but after a while, once I've managed to align our exhalations, I forget she's even there. Until, that is, she starts telling a not particularly interesting story about the time she told Grandma she was pregnant, which goes like this:

She (Grandma) was baking her signature dish, which was her famous Victoria Sponge (it wasn't really famous, Mum ex-

plains, that's just what Grandma always called it (i.e., My Famous Victoria Sponge (which is an oxymoron, because if you
have to tell everyone that something's famous, then by definition it isn't))). The cake was meant to be a celebration, because
Mum had just passed some exams and when Mum told
Grandma she had something to discuss, she (Mum) remembers
that she (Grandma) had just started beating the eggs . . . Here
Mum fades out. Her voice is uneven, and the way she's talking
reminds me somehow of the stairs up to the assembly hall.
They're the sort that are too far apart to be taken in one stride
and too close together to be taken naturally in two, so instead
you have to choose between a series of dainty ballet steps or
these ridiculous trouser-splitting lunges like you're a football
referee pacing out a free kick. (Neither of which I'm very
comfortable with. (Hence, I think, the sudden association.))

When Mum starts up again, she's skipped a few steps:

"She didn't say a word. The whole time I was talking, she
just kept whisking, faster and faster. And when I was through
talking, when I couldn't think of any more words that I
knew . . . I don't remember what I'd said. I think I told her you
were the same size as a lychee."

(I think about the only other thing I know of that is measured in fruit, which is the reason I'm lying here in the first
place. (However, I don't have to worry about that anymore.))

"But I remember exactly what she said," Mum continues.
"You will always be my daughter, and whatever you decide to
do, you will have my support." Here Mum breaks off again and
pauses too long for it to be dramatic, especially considering I
can easily deduce the end of the story (the fact I'm here listen-

ing to it is pretty much the ultimate spoiler). "So that night I told her I was moving out. Because there wasn't a decision to make. Because I already loved you more than I knew I'd ever love anything again."

Her lips are scratchy against my forehead. They linger there for a second after the air's gone out of the kiss and the suction's worn off. (I am so glad she thinks I'm asleep. This would've been a gadzillion times worse than the time she explained blowjobs. (And a gadzillion isn't even a real number, because it's too huge for anyone to actually imagine.))

When I feel Mum's body start to shake, I assume she's crying about Grandma, which I've never seen her do. However, after a bit she lets out a stab of laughter.

"And that," she says, "was the fluffiest sponge she ever baked."

Chapter Seven

I'm pretty much the best person I know at Spot the Difference, because I've trained myself to use it to recognize absences. Absences usually last for only about thirty seconds max, so you have to be very observant beforehand and afterward to know that you've had one. For example, two weeks ago in Maths class Mr. Carson turned round to write a problem up on the board and the next thing I knew Simon Nagel was bleeding. He had all these red blotches on the back of his white shirt, and at first I thought someone had stabbed him with a compass (because we were doing Geometry) but then I noticed that David Driscoll, who was sitting next to me, was writing down the problem with a red fountain pen. So I knew I'd had an absence and David Driscoll had been ink-flicking again (so I told Mr. Carson, and now he has to use a Bic biro).

(Before we knew about the absences, a lot of the teachers used to think I was daydreaming or just being lazy (which is why Miss Farthingdale wrote in my end-of-year report that I was like the English Language because we both had two moods and no future). I'm doing much better at school now (especially in Maths and Science), and in a weird way I think my absences have helped me out because they've taught me to be more vigilant, which can be really useful for English Comprehension.)

One of the things recently that I've been spotting differences in is the behavior of Jaws 2, my Russian Dwarf hamster, who is named after the film. (He isn't named after the film *Jaws 2*, which I've never seen, but he is my second hamster and the first one was Jaws 1. (Although at the time I only called him Jaws, because I didn't know he was going to die and be replaced (in History one time they gave us a newspaper cutting that was meant to be from 1916 and we had to figure out whether it was genuine or fake, and I knew it was fake straight away because they called it the First World War, which didn't make sense because they wouldn't have known that there'd be a Second World War (which is why at the time they called it The Great War)).)) Jaws 1 (as he's now known) died on Christmas Eve 1999 when Dad batted him out the window with a slipper. Dad claims he thought Jaws was a rat and that he leapt at his throat, which I've never believed, because I called him

Jaws to be ironic since he was actually the most docile hamster in the shop. On Christmas morning when Dad found The Great Jaws clinging to the drainpipe outside his bedroom window, frozen stiff, he realized his mistake. He wrapped him in cling film, like he was a present, but instead of putting him under the tree he put him in the freezer, where he remained until April, when we gave him a proper burial in the back garden. By the time the ground had thawed and we were able to dig him a grave I already thought of him as Jaws 1 because I'd had Jaws 2 for a month and was well on my way to forgetting what had happened. But that Christmas I was distraught. I refused to have dinner or open my presents, and it wasn't until well into the next Millennium that I spoke a word to Dad again.

In the February when I finally felt ready to move on, Mum took me to the pet shop. Having witnessed my response to the passing of Jaws 1, she tried to talk me out of getting a Russian Dwarf because of their average lifespan, which is only eighteen months (although no one can tell me whether that's mean, median, or mode). The whole time we were at the pet shop she spent cooing over this dopey-looking Long-Haired Syrian, but the second I saw my Russian Dwarf I knew he was going to be Jaws 2. (I know what I said earlier about dead metaphors and realizing that not everything is human, but when we first saw each other I could have sworn we shared a moment. (This is going to sound stupid, but when he nibbled my little finger through the mesh it felt like we were shaking hands.)) Jaws 2 is like *The Empire Strikes Back* of pets because he's a sequel that's even better than the original.

Even though Jaws 2 is coming up to his fifth birthday, which must be some kind of record for a Russian Dwarf hamster, until recently he was very energetic. Hamsters can run up to 4.8 miles a day on their exercise wheels, and sometimes Jaws 2 reminds me of a falsely imprisoned inmate in a prison film doing press-ups all day in his cell while plotting some terrible revenge against whoever it was that framed him. Which is why I like to make sure he gets an hour's yard time, which means letting him explore the house in a see-through plastic sphere. On the day I got back from hospital, I decided he should have an extra-long session in his sphere to make up for all the ones he'd missed while I was gone, but when I took him out to the garden he just sat there in the middle of the patio, looking around like he didn't know where he was.

(According to Google, there is a thing called jamais vu when you don't recognize something even though it's really familiar to you, a bit like when I say my name twenty-two times until it doesn't mean anything. Apparently, jamais vu is the opposite of déjà vu (which I know lots about), but really they don't sound so different from each other, which is the weird thing about being opposites. If you think about it (which I have), for two things to be opposites they have to have quite a few things in common in the first place. So even though cold is the opposite of hot, it doesn't mean they're all that far apart, because they're both to do with temperature and they can both be

about days or food or how close you are to something in a
game of Hide and Seek. I always used to think that being the
opposite of something was being as far away as you could from
that thing, but just off the top of my head I could name a
dozen things that are further away from cold than hot:

1) A Table
2) The Internet
3) Racism
4) Family
5) Nostrils
6) Synesthesia (which is when you can smell colors)
7) Medicine
8) Banana-Flavored Condoms
9) Horse Power
10) An Oxbow Lake
11) France
12) The Clitoris

Which means that being the opposite of something is actually just like being the same as it is, only with one thing different. So even though I've never had it, I think I must know how
Jaws 2 feels, because both jamais vu and déjà vu are about
memory and the past and confusion and feeling powerless.)

When I mention this to Dad at tea he tells me that the excitement of having me back home has probably just worn Jaws 2
out a bit, and he'll no doubt be back to usual in a day or two.

And then he changes the subject by telling me that while I was napping I had a visitor.

"Who?" I inquire.

"A girl," he says and smirks. "She didn't leave a calling card. Said she had some homework for you. She's coming back to-morrow."

"What did she look like?"

Dad thinks for a minute. Then he says, "A Zebra Crossing."

The next day, when Chloe Gower rings the bell I'm expecting her. From my bedroom I can hear Dad answer the door and greet her as "M'lady." Chloe asks if she should take anything off (which obviously means her shoes) and Dad says, "Steady on! Why don't you wait till you're alone first." While he's laughing at his own joke I have time to find my white baseball cap and wonder whether albinos can blush, and when he knocks on the door there's just long enough to realize I've never had a girl in my room until now before I say "Come in." The door swings open, and Dad announces Chloe's arrival with a wink.

"I'm downstairs if you need anything. But don't worry," he says, "it's a thick ceiling. I wouldn't hear a thing." And then, like a hit-and-run driver, he's gone.

Chloe rolls her ankle in the doorway and surveys the scene. She's wearing her favorite thick black hoody, the sleeves pulled tight over fingerless gloves, even though, like usual, she smells of sun cream. (The dye from her hair has started to grow out. Where it parts across her scalp there's a double yellow line, which means no parking at any time.) I realize she's waiting for me to invite her in. I indicate a beanbag.

"Do you want to sit down?" I ask.

"S'cool," she replies.

"School?" I inquire.

"It's cool," she responds.

"School is?" I query.

"What?" she retorts.

"Is school cool?" I catechize.

"S'okay," she rejoins. And then I realize the nature of our misunderstanding.

(Mum said once that girls are like spiders because they're more scared of me than I am of them. (I'm sure I read somewhere that female spiders eat the male ones.)) I decide that under the circumstances the polite thing to do would be to stand up, too. I notice Chloe notice my bed, or rather the mattress on the floor that I sleep on. Her brow starts to curl up in a question mark and her mouth rounds out like the dot.

"It's so I can't fall out of bed. You know, in case of fits," I explain.

Chloe nods. "But you're better now?"

"Yeah," I say. And then, because sometimes I talk way too much when I'm nervous: "They took it out. The tumor, I mean. It's pretty much the riskiest surgery you can have. There was this one woman who had it and they thought it had gone okay, but when she woke up she had a Chinese accent, which was really weird because she wasn't Chinese. So now she can't eat Chinese food because every time she goes to a Chinese restaurant all the waiters think she's doing an impression of them so they probably spit in it or something, which was one of the main things I was scared about because I really like duck pancakes, but in the end it went fine, so I guess I'm not epileptic anymore.

"But I still might get them for a bit, they think. The fits, I mean. They call them Wind-Down Seizures."

"So when are you coming back to school?"

"Don't know. They said I'd probably be too tired for a couple of weeks. Probably after they take my stitches out. Why? Am I missing much?"

"Dunno. Not really. Rock formations. A bit."

"Rock formations?"

"Yeah, you know. Batholiths and that."

"What's a batholith?"

"Dunno . . . But whenever Mr. Rose says it I get drenched," says Chloe. And then she does a really good impersonation of Mr. Rose's lisp, which officially breaks the ice.

(Breaking the ice is a weird metaphor, because figuratively it's a good thing, but to do it literally is really dangerous. (In the cold snap of 1999 that claimed the life of Jaws 1, Letchmore Pond froze over and a boy in the year below drowned when he went to retrieve a football because he didn't know that you're supposed to spread your body weight over the largest possible surface area, because in Science you don't do Pressure until Year 6.))

——

"What's your hamster called?" asks Chloe, once we've sat down on the mattress.

"Jaws 2."

"After the film?"

"No," I tell her. "After the shark. I haven't seen *Jaws 2*."

"Me either. Have you seen *Dawn of the Dead*?"

"No. Can you watch 18s?"

"Pretty much, since my parents got divorced. Dad lets me do whatever I want, and Mum lets me do whatever I tell her Dad lets me do. He's going to buy my sister a sports car when she passes her test."

"I know. My dad's teaching her."

"I know. Can I touch him?"

"What?"

"Jaws 2."

"Oh. Yeah, okay."

I get the cage and explain the correct way to pick up a hamster. You've got to pretend you're scooping up water. Then I open the door on top of the cage and Chloe reaches in.

"Cocksucker!" she exclaims. "He bit me!"

(I wonder if she knows what she's saying, especially the cocksucker part.)

"Are you sure?"

She shows me her thumb. Sure enough, there's a bead of red.

"You probably just caught it on something. His name's

ironic. He's a pacifist, which is like being a coward but idea-
logical."

I reach in to show her, and a beam of pain breaks through
my medicine fug. I pull my arm free and bolt shut the cage
door. My contents finger is bleeding and my feelings are hurt.

Chloe sucks the sauce from her own wound and says "cocksucker" again.

"That's so weird," I say. "He never . . . Are you wearing
perfume?"

"*Shut up!*" Chloe ripostes. "Why would I be wearing perfume? I only came to give you your homework."

"It's just . . . Ever since I got back he's been acting really . . ." I try and think of another word for weird, because in
Composition you should avoid repeating yourself. "Queer."

"*Queer?* Like effeminate?"

"No, like . . ."

I have an idea. I go to the cupboard and collect the LEGO
maze that I made by splicing DNA from the Death Star and
Cloud City. Then I set it down beside the cage and take out a
box of tissues from my bedside cabinet. I can feel Chloe watching me as I open it from the side. In cross section you can see
that the box is hollow. A dozen or so tissues lie on top of four
variety-size cereal packets (two of which you can see from this
side), the top tissue sprouting out through the box's slit like a
weed through concrete. As I slide out the Frosties pack and
remove a block of Parmesan I can sense from behind Chloe's
surprise.

"It's his favorite," I offer by way of explanation, snagging off
a piece and placing it down under Lord Vader's supervision at

the heart of the Death Star. Then I reach back into the cage, pinch Jaws 2 at the scruff of his neck, and lift him free like an arcade crane.

At the gates to the gas refinery Jaws 2 strikes. Instead of embarking fearlessly on the heroic trench run that hundreds of times before has seen him lead the Rebels to victory in the Battle of Yavin and free the galaxy from the evil clasp of the Empire, he sits down hard and tries to eat Lando Calrissian.

"Weird," I say.

"Very," Chloe agrees.

"He never does that," I say, rescuing Lando and drying him on the carpet. "He hasn't been himself lately."

Then it's Chloe's turn to have an idea. "Jaws 2," she calls in a singsong. "Jaws 2." He doesn't react, but this only seems to encourage her. "I think I know what's happened," she says carefully, giving each word space to stretch out like they're in First Class. "He's in a fugue state."

And then, for half an hour, Chloe tells me all about fugue states, which apparently is what happened to Richey from the Manics (which is what she calls the Manic Street Preachers). What happened was this: On the first of February 1995, Richey Edwards (who is also Richey James (who is also probably one of if not the greatest lyricist that ever lived)) was supposed to be flying to America with James Dean Bradfield (who is the lead singer of the Manics) to promote the Manics' new album *The Holy Bible,* but instead he checked out of room 516 of the Embassy Hotel in London at 7 a.m. and drove to Cardiff. (When James Dean Bradfield got the porter to open up room 516 (which he could do because he was the front man (but not the one with the actual talent)), all he found was a packed suitcase full of Richey's clothes and a note that said *I Love You,* which probably wasn't intended for him, because Richey definitely isn't gay.) He was reported missing the next day. On Valentine's Day 1995 his car, which was a Vauxhall Cavalier, got a parking ticket at the Severn View petrol station, which is right next to the Severn Bridge, and because the Severn Bridge is a notorious suicide hotspot (which means lots of people have jumped off it (which proves that even in death everyone just wants to conform)) and because Richey was twenty-seven years old (which is the age that all good musicians die), everyone just assumed that he'd committed suicide. But that's not what happened, because Richey would never do a thing like that, because he was too strong a person. (It's like he said in "Motorcycle Emptiness": *survival's natural as sorrow (sorrow (sorrow))*.) Which is why they've never found his body.

What actually happened is the fugue state. You know how if you put a magnet on top of a floppy disk you can wipe it? Well, apparently, that can happen to people, too, only the magnet is a kind of psychiatric or physical trauma (which in Richey's case was success), and the floppy disk is our entire identity, which is pretty terrifying. But that's not even the weirdest thing about fugue states, because not only do they make you forget who you are (which would be queer enough), but also when you're in one you invent a whole new life for yourself. (I guess if you forget your name you need to invent a new one (because you know that if you don't have one you can't be a real thing) and then, once you've got a name, you must know that you need a history to go with it, otherwise your name wouldn't mean anything (like another door without a room behind it).) Fugue states usually last for only a few days, but technically there's no reason they couldn't go on indefinitely, which is what happened to Richey, which explains why he's been spotted all over the world since he disappeared but he's never answered to the name Richey Edwards (or Richey James). Even though some people who didn't really understand him reckon that he faked his own death to escape his burgeoning fame (which he would never do to the fans who he loved and got), the only explanation that makes any real sense (if you actually think about it (which Chloe has)) is that he's been stuck in a fugue state since 1995. One day hopefully he'll snap out of it and start writing songs again, but until then he's trapped in somebody else's life, which must be like being stuck in Madame Berger's French class for a decade.

And that, Chloe concludes, must be what's happened to Jaws 2.

"So what's the magnet?" I ask.

"Dunno," says Chloe (whose French name is Agnes) with a Gallic shrug. "Could be anything. Maybe a near-death experience. Who was looking after him when you were in the hospital?"

"My mum."

With a smile that I can tell she fondly imagines is enigmatic, Chloe rests her case. Then, to make sure I know what she's insinuating, she says, "Well, there you go."

―――――

By the time I sneak Chloe downstairs to show her out, the extractor fan is roaring in the kitchen, which means that Mum's home from work, and Dad is getting ready for a lesson. He is by door, putting on jacket in preparation for going out in car. (You might think from this that he's the kind of man that would walk up an escalator, but actually, if it's an option, he prefers to take the adjacent staircase and race against the gliders. I think he thinks he's proving a point somehow, taking a stand instead of just standing still, but personally I think walking parallel to an escalator is like using an abacus in the IT Lab (i.e., Stupid).)

"M'lud," he says when he sees me, doffing an imaginary hat with one hand and twiddling an air mustache with the other. "Does the lady require a carriage?"

I hate that he's showing off for Chloe, so I decide to play chicken and not say anything until he talks properly. Chloe seems to know the rules of the game herself. She averts her eyes and picks at a scab of varnish on the banister, and sure enough, after a quick dose of silence, Dad dusts down his pretend cap, returns it to his real bald patch, and tries again:

"Seriously, you're Ella's sister, right? She so happens to be a patient of mine. I'm passing your place now." He turns his back on us and starts shaking the hat stand like he's scrumping for apples. "Did you have a coat?"

Chloe doesn't rush her answer. First she finishes liberating the flap of laminate, which gives me just long enough to do a quick calculation in my head: (MUM + CHLOE) ÷ ME >

DAD + CHLOE. Only once she's peeled the strip all the way down to the banister's knuckle (revealing a runway of raw, pink skin underneath) does she let out a sound. But before her lips can shape it into words, I cut her off.

"Do you think it would be okay if Chloe stayed for dinner?"

Chapter Eight

(Another thing you need to do to get top marks in Composition is paint a picture with words. There are no guidelines for how much space you should dedicate in your Composition to description, but the rule of thumb I subscribe to is that a thousand words is equal to one picture. (Once we had to write five hundred words about the street we grew up in, and David Driscoll handed in a doodle he'd drawn of Miss Farthingdale performing inflatio on a wall of dicks (it looked a bit like a climbing wall). When Miss Farthingdale handed back our exercise books she told David that she couldn't mark his because he had massively exceeded the word count. (And then he had to see the school counselor.)))

Mum's face is characterful, which means it has lots of lines on it, especially by her eyes and across her forehead. If Mum were an algebraic equation, then you could make the following deductions from the symbols on her face:

1) Mum's right ear is much greater than (>>) her right eye.
2) Mum's left eye is much lesser than (<<) her left ear.
3) Mum's left temple is roughly equivalent to ($\approx$) her right temple.

The good thing is, though, you can see these sums only in a very particular light and at a very particular angle, because the trenches on Mum's face are so shallow. (They remind me of when you take a message at the kitchen table and the pen imprint shows up in the wood grain when you've taken the pad away, which is why you're not supposed to take messages at the kitchen table.) In fact, it's almost like she's a hologram sticker, because in the same light and at the same angle as you can read the messages on Mum's face you can also see the red tint in her hair (which is called Toasted Auburn (and which Dad never notices)).

Another place that Mum has character is around her mouth. These are called nasolabial folds, but most people call them laughter lines, but since Mum hasn't laughed since Monetary Unification, I prefer to think of them as nasolabial. The funny thing about Mum's nasolabial folds is they have the effect of making her mouth seem less important than the rest of her face by putting it in parentheses (which is a better word for brackets). This is ironic, because Mum doesn't like to waste words like Dad does. When Mum was my age she had a really bad stutter, which she told me about once when I was nervous about a presentation I had to give on the Vikings. Sometimes, she said, she'd get stranded all the way out in the middle of a sentence, too far into it to retreat to the beginning (because by now people were listening) and not far enough through that she could pretend to be done. Every second that passed before she could get out what she wanted to say would ratchet up the suspense, and as she would stall and splutter and trip on consonants (like the alphabet was the 110-meter hurdles (my analogy, not hers)) she could actually see her audience's expectations rising. She told me it was like their hopes had grown feathers, and as she watched them float off impossibly toward the horizon she would begin to realize that whatever form her conclusion took, it would inevitably be a disappointment. This realization would only make matters worse because now Mum wouldn't just be worrying about the sounds of the sentence but the whole point of it in the first place. Her mind would start racing, frantically searching for other exits (clever puns, surprise twists, anything to justify the wait), and eventually she'd get so caught up thinking about the ending that she'd forget where it was the sentence had even begun. Finally, when she got the next word out it would be in the wrong tense, or the wrong number (or just the wrong part of speech altogether), and the whole thing would come crashing down around her in a cloud of gibberish. Which is what taught Mum to think carefully about what it is she wants to say before she opens her mouth. And about whether it needs saying in the first place. (I sometimes think this must be the thing that Mum resents most about Dad, that he can make her talk pointlessly just by being more comfortable in silence than she is.)

Pete Sloss was the first person at school to say that my mum was fit, which is partly why I called him a cocksucker. I hadn't really ever thought about whether or not Mum was attractive before he told me about making a deposit in his wank bank on the way to the cinema, but in fairness to Pete I suppose Mum does possess many of the qualities that men have traditionally found sexually alluring. For example, people of various cultures have always been attracted to symmetrical faces, and Mum's is perfectly symmetrical (except for the mole above her lip on the right-hand side as I'm looking at it (which only makes the Roughly Equals sign on her brow more appropriate)). According to the Internet, a symmetrical face is a good way of telling that someone is genetically healthy (because your face gets shaped while you're an embryo), and this is why we find it attractive. Because subconsciously when people choose a mate what they're looking for is someone they can make healthy babies with.

Mum's best feature (besides her general symmetry (and her slender fingers (which are like a piano player's (ironically)))) is her eyes, which is why she sometimes allows herself to wear eyeliner to work (because it lets you put your eyes in bold). As a rule, though, she won't wear makeup. This is because makeup is deceitful, and Mum believes in candor, which is a better word for honesty. Mum has always been really honest with me, even when I was young and naïve and used to ask her things like why the sky was blue (which it isn't (it just reflects blue light)). The one time she did lie to me was because she didn't want me experimenting with alcohol (which I never would've done anyway), so she told me my grandpa drank himself to death. I found out a few weeks later from Dad that actually he'd had an aneurysm in the fast lane of the Finchley Lido and had drowned before the lifeguard could fish him out. When I confronted Mum with this, she apologized and explained that she had only been trying to keep me from harm and that she wouldn't lie to me ever again. (In this instance I forgave her because eventually I recognized that she had been trying to protect me, and also because technically she hadn't actually lied, because drowning is the same as drinking yourself to death, only quicker.) Today is obviously one of the days she's applied eyeliner. I can tell this because onion tears have dribbled three streaks of black ink down each of her cheeks, so she looks like she's sponsored by Adidas.

"My mum says that if you put the onions in the freezer for a bit before you chop them they won't make you cry," says Chloe, pushing Bolognese around her bowl like she's trying to prove the second law of thermodynamics (which is that Entropy always increases (which is just a clever way of saying that nothing lasts forever)).

At first Mum doesn't seem to have heard her. Then, as if to confirm this impression, she says, "Pardon." However, before Chloe can repeat herself, Mum runs back the tape and catches up on what she's missed. "Oh," she continues, wiping at the eyeliner tracks with the back of a hand (and, like a disloyal athlete, turning the Adidas logo into a Nike tick). "Thank you. I'll have to remember that."

Meanwhile, I arrange my pills at the corner of the kitchen table and pretend they are points on a graph. There are six of them in total (three sorts of painkiller, two anticonvulsants (which I need to keep taking in case I get Withdrawal Symptoms (which is what Dad calls babies)) and a laxative (because one of the painkillers is also a cure for diarrhea (and because I'm not supposed to strain on the toilet because I could reopen my surgery scar))).

"And what does your mother do, Chloe?" asks Mum.

"Dunno," says Chloe. And then, after considering the question some more, "Sleeps mostly. She's got depression."

I look back down at the table and trace a line of best fit between the pills. The graph displays a relationship of Direct Proportionality, but the anticonvulsants are both anomalies. I extrapolate the line out beyond the laxative and toward the salad bowl. In between them, something is scratched into the grain:

Aunt Julie called

It's a message I took years ago, before I'd learned to write joined-up (certainly before I'd passed my fountain-pen test). In this light it's invisible, but if you know where it is (which I do) you can read it like Braille. As my finger rides the *U* in *Julie* I have a really morbid thought. If I had died in the hospital, these letters would be my fossilized remains. In centuries to come, this is how I would have been remembered. An interesting fact I know is that Julius Caesar has two months of the year named after him: July and August (which is why *Oct*ober, which comes from the Latin meaning eighth, is the tenth month and *Nov*ember and *Dec*ember are the eleventh and twelfth, respectively). I don't really understand how they found space for the extra two months (although I suspect it's got something to do with the universe expanding), but that's not the point. The point is *Aunt Julie called* isn't much of a legacy, especially when you consider that Julius Caesar has a sixth of all time named after him (not to mention my aunt Julie).

Chloe kicks my shin under the table, which I take as my cue to begin the interrogation.

"How was Jaws 2 while I was away?" I ask Mum, looking down at my food so as to appear uninterested, because the key to a good interrogation is that the person being interrogated shouldn't know that they're under suspicion, which in this case should be easy enough because I don't suspect Mum of any wrongdoing.

"Well, I think he missed you," she answers, spearing a brussels sprout and then thinking better of it.

I'm not quite sure how to proceed, but it's not something I need worry about, because by now Chloe has picked up the scent. She clamps it between her teeth to free her hands, and with them takes the reins. "How would you know that?" she snaps (with the manner of someone who's obviously watched enough films to know about the Good Cop Bad Cop dynamic). "Unless you mean he was acting differently?"

Even though it's Chloe who's addressed her, Mum directs

her answer to me. But before she does so, she takes a moment. She looks at me like I'm a Magic Eye puzzle and someone's told her if she stares hard enough and relaxes her eyes there's a dolphin on a motorbike. It's a weird sensation, like she's looking straight through me and out the other side. (It's almost as if I'm not here. Like she's looking at me in the third person.) "We all did, sweetheart," she says eventually. "We all missed you."

At the front door when I'm showing her out, Chloe tries her enigmatic smile again. However, this time I decide if she has anything to say on the matter she should say it out loud.

"What are you smiling about?" I ask, Bad Cop–ly.

"You heard."

"Heard what?"

"How she avoided the question."

I lower my voice to a whisper, which means sacrificing some of my natural authority. "Mum would never do anything to harm Jaws 2."

"What?"

"You heard," I say (cleverly) in quotation marks.

"No, I didn't," says Chloe. "You were whispering. Try speaking up."

"She wouldn't. She'd never hurt him. And if anything happened to him, she'd tell me. We have an open relationship."

"That doesn't mean what you think it means."

"Yes, it does. It means neither of my parents would let my hamster come to harm. That's just a fact," I say in conclusion, pretending my finger's a sparkler and dotting the air with a full stop.

"So what happened to Jaws 1?" asks Chloe rhetorically, ignoring my finger punctuation and adding three air full stops of her own (which doesn't even work, because it actually makes things less final (it's not like a triple exclamation mark)).

"And by the way," she adds. "You know you owe me a pound."

"How come?"

"Cos you didn't know what a clitoris was."

"But I really didn't know," I protest. "I was only pretending to. I was bluffing."

Chloe sighs, like I've been missing the point all afternoon.

"I know you didn't know," she says. "That's why you owe me."

Chapter Nine

On the way to the hospital to have my stitches taken out we pass the lamppost that Dad calls Morrissey. It always has a bunch of flowers tied to it, which means that someone's died and someone else is trying to remember them. Flowers symbolize this, because smell is the most important sense for memories.

Whenever someone tells Dad about a car crash that they've been in, they always use phrases like *all of a sudden* and verbs like *appear*. For example:

1) The car in front braked <u>suddenly</u>.
2) A badger <u>materialized</u> in the road.
3) We came to the junction <u>forthwith</u>.

This is Dad's Number One Pet Hate. He says that nothing on road happens suddenly. The problem is, he says, people don't look ahead. And if you don't look ahead, then you end up reacting to hazards instead of anticipating them.

Commentary Driving is a lesson Dad gives his students when he thinks they think they know how to drive. What they have to do is imagine there's a blind man sitting in the back of the car (although not literally, because his weight would affect the stopping distances) and describe to him exactly what they're doing at every step. The point of Commentary Driving is to focus the mind on the act of driving a car, to ensure that no part of the process becomes automatic, and at the same time, to allow the driver to reach a higher plane of awareness and perception. Dad calls this last part Lifting Your Vision.

What Dad finds with Commentary Driving is that when they first try it his students see it as two separate activities: 1) The Driving, and 2) The Commentary. They begin by driving the car just as they normally would, except maybe a little slower, to give them extra time to fit the words in, and then they start talking Dad through what they've just done like they're trying to justify their actions. For example:

1) I just changed down to second gear because I saw the traffic lights change.
2) I checked the mirror before indicating.
3) I reversed back over the badger because he was suffering.

This is what Dad calls Two Different Strudels, which means that they have given him two separate things when what he asked for was both of these things combined. It is only when Dad bans his students from using the past tense that they start to get it right. Eventually, the words catch up to the action, i.e., the lag disappears (or where once there was Apple Strudel and Wild Berry Strudel, there is now Fruits of the Forest). This is a big improvement, because now, instead of having applied the brakes because they saw a light go red, the students are applying the brakes because the lights are changing, which means they are living in the moment.

However, seizing the moment is not the same as anticipating the next one. The magical thing about Commentary Driving is when the words overtake the actions and you start talking about what you're planning to do, stuff that hasn't even happened yet. The second Dad hears a student talking about what's going to happen at the end of the street he knows they're going to pass their test. This is because now they are commentating on The Future, which is exactly what Dad means by Lifting Your Vision.

When I first used to get déjà vu I thought it meant I had lifted my vision. I don't think I'll ever forget how powerful that made me feel. (It made me think I could live forever.)

The Christmas after Miss Farthingdale wrote in my report that I had No Future like the English Language I spent a lot of time trying to figure out what she'd meant, which is why on our first Friday back at school in the new year I missed my bus home. When the bell rang at the end of her lesson and the rest of the class bottlenecked at the classroom door, I remained seated.

"Why did you say I had no future like the English language?" I asked, once my classmates had decanted themselves, giggling, into the weekend. Miss Farthingdale was at her desk, packing a briefcase full of Days in the Lives. When she looked up, she didn't seem at all surprised to see me.

"Because," she replied, "you're an extremely capable young man, but if you can't get your daydreaming under control you'll never come close to realizing your potential. I'm sorry if you felt I was being unfair, but if I didn't hold you to a higher standard than some of your classmates, then I'd be doing you a grave disservice. Do you understand?"

I did, but that wasn't what I'd meant. I meant why did the English Language have no future. "Is it to do with China?" I asked.

This made Miss Farthingdale laugh and call me a curious boy (which is a double entendre).

Then she took out some chalk and wrote the words *I'M THERE* on the blackboard.

"Does that make sense to you?" she asked.

"Yes," I replied.

"Why?"

"Because I've heard people say it."

"Because you've heard people say it," said Miss Farthingdale, swilling my answer around her mouth like she was taking the Pepsi Challenge. "In other words, it makes sense because it's familiar?"

"Right."

"But it shouldn't make sense, though, should it? Not if you think about it. Are you thinking about it?"

"Yes," I said. And then I started to think about it.

"What tense is the verb?" asked Miss Farthingdale.

"Present."

"And what does the present tense mean?"

"Now."

"Exactly." She smiled. "And how could I be *there* now?"

I thought about the question for a minute. When I spoke, it was because I knew I hadn't for too long. "Is that a rhetorical question?"

"Are all unanswerable questions rhetorical?" asked Miss Farthingdale.

"Yes."

"Then yes, it was," she said. "Where was I?"

"There."

"Exactly right," said Miss Farthingdale. "But that was then and this is now. And there's only one place I could possibly be now, isn't there? And, I'll give you a clue, it isn't *there*."

"Could you say that again?" I asked, because I needed some time to catch up.

"Did anyone ever tell you the world doesn't revolve around you?" said Miss Farthingdale.

"Sorry," I mumbled. "I've got waxy ears."

"Don't be sorry. Answer the question. Did anyone ever tell you that?"

"Yes. My mum."

"Well, guess what. She was wrong. It's precisely *because* the world revolves around you that I can promise, without fear of contradiction, that at no point in your life will you ever actually *be there*. Because no matter how far away *there* is to begin with, the second you arrive it won't be *there* anymore."

"It won't be there?"

"Well, that's really more of a Geopolitical question. But whether it is or isn't isn't important. The important thing is it won't be *there*. Because by the time you get there—by virtue of your presence—it'll be *here* instead. Do you see what I'm saying?"

I thought so. "That I am here?"

"Exactly right! In fact, I'd go one further. I *is* here. And always remember, wherever that happens to be is neither here nor there. Now"—she grinned, rapping the board with the chalk stub—"does that still make sense to you?"

I looked at the board again. As if on cue, the letters scrambled before my eyes and the words they spelled (if indeed they ever were words in the first place) stopped making sense.

"So how come people say it?" I asked.

"Well," said Miss Farthingdale, hushing her voice and beckoning me closer, "that one's easy. It's because they're not talking about now. They don't mean I am there in the present. They mean I am there *in the future*. Tell me, what are you doing this weekend?"

"I'm playing football with my brother," I answered automatically.

"You are playing football with your brother?" asked Miss Farthingdale.

"Why wouldn't I be? He's called Serge."

"I see. And when you *are* playing football with Serge, what tense is the verb?"

The question swung open like a trapdoor.

"Present?" I ventured carefully (a bit like Indiana Jones in *The Last Crusade,* when he has to spell *Jehovah* to get across the tiles in the Temple of the Sun without falling through to his death and old James Bond reminds him with telepathy that in Latin it starts with an *I*).

"Exactly right!" said Miss Farthingdale. The teeth of her briefcase snapped into place. "Because in English we don't have a Future. So if we want to talk about it we have to use the Present. Because so far that's the best idea anyone's come up with."

"But that doesn't make any sense," I protested, when Miss Farthingdale was already half out the door, which made her stop with one foot in the weekend.

"Oh, I don't know," she mused. "I think it makes a whole lot of sense, imagining The Future's something you can hold in your hands. It's quite reassuring, don't you think? Gives you a lovely false sense of control. And it certainly beats believing in Fate, if you ask me. Which is precisely what you did. And now that I've answered, if you'll excuse me . . ."

But I had one more question before I could excuse her, and I promised to keep it quick.

If the whole point of having a language was so we could

describe the world that we lived in, then how was it that we didn't have a Future tense?

Miss Farthingdale looked from me to the classroom clock (which was five minutes fast, because David Driscoll had wound it on during form period) and then back again.

"I would have thought that was fairly obvious." She shrugged. "I think a capable boy like you can figure that one out for himself."

I sometimes wonder if it was a coincidence that that was the weekend I had my first seizure, or whether Fate, which at that time I didn't believe in, had something to do with it. Like all of the seizures since, I don't remember anything about it except for two things:

1) Waking up exhausted in a me-shaped sweat puddle on the floor of Paperchase (because one of my fits can take up more energy than running a marathon ("And it's twice as hard to collect sponsorship for," as Dad said when the pretty MacMillan nurse told us that fact last year)).

2) The déjà vu that came first.

I was riding my bike into the Harlequin Centre because it was almost my parents' anniversary and I needed some final materials to make them the card that I'd been planning. (I had decided to make my own card, having browsed the selection

available in WHSmith the week before and found it to be un-
satisfactory. Five of their cards featured birds touching wings,
which I found particularly offensive. Of these five avian cou-
ples, two were penguins, two swans, and one mallards, all of
whom are famous for mating for life, which is supposed to be
romantic somehow, except it isn't because it's not difficult for
birds to be mahoganous because they don't have the capability
to imagine being happier with another partner. (This is what
Miss Farthingdale had meant when she said English had two
moods. We have the Indicative Mood, which is for things as
they are, and the Subjunctive Mood, which is for things as they
aren't, which is what lets us do Conditional Thinking, which
is what separates us from animals.) Moreover, mallards are rap-
ists. (I did, however, see one thing in WHSmith I'd liked,
which was a quote from someone I'd never heard of called
Anon that I decided to weave into the theme of my own card.))
I had done most of the work already, and all I needed now was
some good quality white paper so I could print out the pictures of the dung beetle and the dung heap, and a new Pritt
stick so I could mount them on the card under the quote I'd
stenciled: "Love isn't about being perfect. It's about being perfect for each other."

The way I know I'm about to have déjà vu is the taste I get in
the back of my mouth. I spent most of that weekend thinking
about what Miss Farthingdale had said, especially what she'd
meant by the last bit, and the stuff about being able to hold the
future in your hands, which I think I'd understood most out of

everything because whenever I get that taste at the back of my mouth it feels like I'm Tasting The Future. It tastes metallic, and I got it that day while I was pedaling up Granville Road.

As I turned right into King Street with pennies in my saliva, I noticed the wind had painted a crisp packet against the fork of my bike, right at the axis of the front wheel. It was red (which means danger (and Ready Salted)), and as my wheel raced around it, it plucked furiously at the spokes, letting out a motorized howl that for a second made me imagine I was a Hell's Angel blazing down an open highway. The sun glinted off its foil innards and danced on my retinae (which is the correct plural of retina), and as I leaned forward to free the bag from its accidental roulette my vision lifted and I saw exactly what was about to happen.

I remember foreseeing it (in what was a sun-bleached, almost nostalgic haze). But I don't remember it happening.

As I lay on the pavement I could still taste copper on my tongue, but as I dribbled a rope of pink saliva into the gutter and felt the tear in my cheek I realized it wasn't the future. It was blood. At first I didn't understand. I had used my super power. I had foreseen all of this (that my finger would get caught in the spokes, that I would catapult myself over the handlebars, that I would land hard and bruise my mouth). I had looked into the future and perceived the hazard, which should have made me invincible, but instead I was somehow powerless to avoid it. (It was like I'd lifted my vision and seen the cliff, only someone had cut my brake cords.) I looked down at my grazed palms, at the raw runways of pink skin, and

considered the other times I'd had déjà vu. Now that I thought
about it, it always seemed to come halfway through something
(like a sentence or a fish-finger sandwich) and never at the
start, and moreover, I always seemed to finish what I was doing
before stopping to remark that I'd just had déjà vu. Even
though I knew while it was happening that I was in the middle
of a prophecy and (by knowing) I surely had the power to
prove it wrong, I never did. Instead, I always played it out exactly how it was in the script, even though the words in the
sentence no longer felt like my own and the fish-finger sandwich tasted of air.

It was as though the future I had glimpsed into had already
happened.

And that's when I understood what Miss Farthingdale had
meant. (She was right: It was obvious.) We don't have a future
in English because there's no such thing. It was just like she'd
said. We liked to imagine we could reach out and touch it,
hold it in our hands (and taste it in our spit), because that's
what let us believe we were in control, but we never could be,
because that could never happen. Because the future dies at
our touch. Which would explain why I couldn't not fall off my
bike that day. Because when I lifted my vision and saw myself
flying improbably through the air, it wasn't the future I was
looking at.

"I am noticing the Asian woman at the wheel of the Vauxhall
Cortina," says Dad, flicking on the indicator (back in car (on

road on the way to hospital (in the present tense))). "And I am preparing for the worst."

But he can't commentate on the future any more than a dog can catch raindrops.

He is predicting the present.

Chapter Ten

The indicator ticks like a metronome, which makes me think of David Driscoll and Mum's fictional piano lessons as Dad slides across the broken line and slots in behind the Cortina. The time is 4:21:48, which means two things:

1) In 1.091 seconds the hands of my watch will be perfectly aligned (except my watch is digital, so it doesn't have any hands).
2) We're going to be late for my appointment with Mr. Fitzpatrick.

———

"We're going to be late for my appointment with Mr. Fitzpatrick," I tell Dad, extending my arm to show him my Casio SGW100 (which is the exact one the deep-sea divers use).

The two lanes of traffic merge into one like a deck of cards being shuffled.

"Coast," replies Dad, without looking at me.

I answer (correctly) without thinking (because I don't have to), "Concentration Observation Anticipation Space Time." Then I repeat myself, making sure to change the wording because if you repeat something furbatim (which means the exact same way), it means you're lying. "We are running behind schedule for my consultation with Señor Fitzpatrick."

"Don't you worry about Mr. Fitzpatrick," says Dad, straightening up the wheel. "Ever asked an American when World War Two started? They're not so hot on timekeeping." The indicator clicks off. "Poor Old Walter," he adds, thoughtfully. "Dies Every Ruddy Year."

I turn to look out the window and mindlessly list all the things you should check before a long drive: "Petrol Oil Water Damage Electrics Rubber You."

(It turns out I knew exactly what Mnemonics were all along, even before I googled them. I just didn't know they had a name. (To help me remember it, I have invented one of my own: Memory Never Escapes Me Officer Now I Construct Sentences.))

"Correct," says Dad. "But *you* should come first."

———

From our new position, my view of the roadside is unob-
structed. Frost-glazed sports fields stretch out to our left, the
markings vague and sort of implied, trampled underfoot by
another ruddy year of touchline dribbles and parents' pride.
The goals are naked. Stripped of their nets, they have no backs
or fronts, which robs them of their purpose. We pass sixteen of
these sad arches (which makes a total of eight pitches (which is
roughly the surface area of four small intestines)) and each one
of them seems somehow more listless (which is when you have
nothing left To Do). All the while Dad concentrates on the
road ahead, being careful to leave a gap of exactly two chevrons
between us and the Asian woman in front, which makes me
think of Mum again (because now we are much greater than
the Cortina (just like Mum's ears are much greater than her
eyes)).

I asked Dad once why they didn't make the distance between two chevrons twice as long, because that way you'd have
to keep only one chevron apart.

"They were like that when we found them," he said, and
laughed.

(I sometimes wonder if civilization had to start again from
scratch how much stuff we'd reinvent. I realize that the odds of
life existing in the first place are about 1 in a googolplex
squared (which is a number so big you couldn't write it in your
entire lifetime), but I just can't imagine that wax fruit could
happen twice.)

The blanket of frost on the fields reminds me I'm cold, so I
tug my sleeves down over my knuckles, clamp my hands be-

tween my thighs, and watch my breath cloud in front of my mouth like a wandering thought bubble. To my surprise, there's a question in it: *Can my soul be given away?*

I don't know who's asking, but my best guess is the goalposts. I watch them slide away in the vanity mirror and say the question over to myself. *Can my soul be given away?* I'm sure I've heard it somewhere before. The words are familiar yet strange. (I both recognize them and don't at the same time, like the taste of toothpaste in the afternoon.) The harder I look and the farther away the goalposts fall the more sense it makes. Maybe a soul is like a net. It's the thing that stops other things from passing straight through you without you noticing them.

The Asian brake lights blush two chevrons toward tomorrow, which brings me out of my daydream. Dad shifts down through the gears and repeats himself: "Can My Soul Be Given Away?"

Forthwith I know where I've heard it before. I respond automatically. "Course Mirror Signal Brake Gear Accelerate."

"Okay, then," says Dad, flicking the indicator back on with a smile. "I think you're ready."

And the next thing I know we're in car off-road.

"What about my appointment?" I protest, as we rumble down the footpath at a perfect right angle to where we're supposed to be going.

"There are more important things in life than perfect attendance," says Dad (and then immediately lists none) as the foliage forms a Guard of Honor above our heads. At first the wind rustling through the leaves reminds me of applause, as though we're a visiting sports team being clapped on to the pitch, but with the end of the tunnel just a pinprick in the leaves, the lane tapers and the roof starts to collapse. Dad grinds down on the accelerator, and I breathe in deep as though me and the car are one. "Hold on tight!" he exclaims, as branches drum on the windscreen and the hedgerow pins back the wing mirrors like a plastic surgeon performing an Otterplasty (which is the proper name for cosmetic ear surgery (which is what Beckie Frogley had after David Driscoll invented the term Blowjob Handles)). We speed ahead through the raking thorns and the canopy falls like dusk, dressing the entire car in black (except for my watch, which is glow-in-the-dark). Dad karate chops on the headlights. They peer forward into the dark, peeling back the night until they trip on something ahead in the path. It's a fallen log. Half sunk into the mulch of mud and fallen leaves, it lies in wait like a Sleeping Policeman.

"In for a penny, in for a pound!!" double-exclaims Dad. "Hold on to your ____"

But I don't hear what I'm supposed to hold on to because I'm holding on to my head. My fingers lock behind the occipital bone, my elbows point to my toes, and my wrists plug my ears.

(My pulse sounds like the sea.)

("There are lots of people in an operating theater," explains Mr. Fitzpatrick before the operation. "But I am The Captain of the Ship." (*So what does that make me?* I wonder.))

———

We hit the ramp at what must be at least 150 kilometers an hour, causing Dad to say a four-letter word, into which he manages to squeeze about twenty vowels. We are suspended in midair for five and a quarter seconds by my count (five Mississippis and a Yangtze (which, ironically, is longer)) during which time I can feel my sphincter tighten and the tunnel walls contract around us like a womb so that it sort of makes perfect sense that when the *T* explodes from Dad's lips, the fart thumps into my seat, and the ground slaps open my eyes I find we've been birthed into a field.

"What the *eff* are you thinking?" I ask Dad in italics, once we've skidded to a halt (and I've checked my head like you're supposed to check cartons of eggs in the supermarket before you buy them).

"Now," he says, jerking up the handbrake, turning off the engine, and handing me the key, "I'm thinking that if you're old enough to drive a car you're old enough to swear like a fucking grown-up." And then he makes us switch positions.

(If I were to describe what happens next in my French Oral exam the outcome would be one of the following:

1) I would fail for incorrect vocab, which would mean I definitely wouldn't get the scholarship for my new school.

2) I would have to see the school counselor, who would ask me if everything was "cool beans" at home and make me

point to a color on a Dulux color chart that he calls his
Happiness Graph.
3) I would be taken into care.)

"Well?" says Dad, gesturing out across the land from the passenger seat as though he owns everything our headlights can
see and one day it will all be mine. The field is bordered on
one side by a guard of assiduous black trees, silhouetted against
the sinking sun, and on the other by the hum of distant traffic.
Even in the rising dark I can see that winter, like old age, has
flecked the grass white, which makes my dad look like a young
man in comparison, which is appropriate, because he's grinning childishly. (I wonder if this is his idea of a joke. (After all,
a car crossing a field is almost the opposite of the chicken crossing the road which means they have nearly everything in
common.))

"Charlie Blithely Accepted Handouts," Dad continues,
pointing out the clutch, brake, accelerator, and handbrake respectively, all of which I know already, but not from this angle.
"Right. What are we waiting for?"

I select an answer from a brimming quiver. "My seven-
teenth birthday."

"Why?" He sighs. "You know how to drive, don't you?"

"Maybe in theory," I concede. "But there's a difference between theory and practice."

"See," says Dad, tapping his nose, "I have a theory that there
isn't."

———

Turning the key in the ignition is (doubly) illegal because people with epilepsy aren't allowed to drive cars unless they can
prove that they've been seizure-free for a year (and children
aren't allowed to drive cars unless they can prove that they're
adults). The engine catching makes me a criminal, so I make a
mental note of it in case I ever embark on a life of crime and I
need to pinpoint the moment it all went wrong (for example,
when I'm tattooing my autobiography on to the face of my
screaming cell mate in maximum-security prison or if I ever
have to give a careers talk as a criminal cum reformed criminal
slash bestselling author).

My first three attempts at pulling away I fall short of the
biting point, rushing up on the clutch and causing the car to
stall violently, which means actually I have to turn the key in
the ignition four times in total. (To make sure I don't confuse
any of these later turns with the decisive one that set me off on
my path to delinquency, I do them with my eyes shut.) The
fourth, fifth, sixth, and eighth time I overcompensate like the
secretly gay homophobic bully in the 18, plunging too deep
on the accelerator so the car squeals with impotent fury, and
the seventh time I brake instead (which is a tautology, because
we're already stationary (which is already as slow as you can
go)).

The ninth time is the charm. When he thinks I'm not looking, Dad sinks his foot into the passenger-side pedals and the
clutch ghosts out from under me. In response I pump the accelerator and the car wheezes and strains against its leash. And

then when Dad takes my hand in his and presses my thumb to
the handbrake (just like the policeman will when he takes my
prints), we lurch forward, tearing free from an umbilical vine.

"Fuck," I remark.

"Fuck," he concurs.

"What if I have an accident?" I inquire.

"Then propose and get a job," he opines. "But for now just
remember to keep your hands on the outside of the steering
wheel, because it's significantly harder to hitchhike with two
broken thumbs. Now, put your left foot down and your left
hand on the gear stick."

I put my left foot down and my left hand on the gear stick.

"Paper covers rock," says Dad, putting his hand on top of
mine and jiggling the stick back into second gear.

In second gear the car feels a lot less skittish, and after a few
minutes learning how to steer (you must *never* cross your hands,
which Dad explains by asking whether I've seen *Ghostbusters*
(yes (sleepover)) and whether I know what happens if you cross
the streams (yes (every molecule in your body explodes at the
speed of light))) I'm almost starting to enjoy myself. Driving
isn't really so different from riding the bumper cars on Brighton Pier, which I used to do with Mum when I was a kid.

When I feel like I've got the hang of it, I ask where we're
going.

"Where do you want to go?" Dad answers, unhelpfully.

"Where do you want me to go?" I answer, less helpfully.

"Where do you want me to want you to go?" I expect him
to say, taking the joke too far, like he always does. But instead
he puts on his serious voice, which is his normal voice but

slower. "Seriously," he starts (unnecessarily), "if you could go anywhere in the world, where would it be?"

However, before I can answer he tells me not to now but to think about it (which I really don't have to, because it's an easy question). So instead I ask him why he never took me on the bumper cars. At first he doesn't answer, so I start to repeat myself in case he hasn't heard, but before I'm through he interrupts me.

"I heard you," he says. "I was thinking about it. I guess if I'm honest I probably thought it was a bit of a busman's holiday. I'm sorry. That's not a very good reason. Did you want me to go with you?"

I tell him I would probably have liked that, yes, because Mum never wanted to hit anything (which I knew would be the case before we even started, because she insisted I call them *dodgems*), and then, so he doesn't think there's any hard feelings, I ask where he wants me to want him to want me to go.

Again, though, Dad doesn't answer for a really long time. Not until we bounce over a hump, the headlights lift, and the full beam strikes the base of a rusty protuberance sprouting through the frozen earth.

"I want you to score a goal," he says slowly, pointing into the distance at the ghostly scaffold.

By my estimate we're twenty meters from goal when all of a sudden Dad appears to lose his mind.

("I don't think we should tell your mother about this," he says at forty meters.

"About what?" I ask at thirty.

"This," he says, pinning me back against my seat with his right arm and with his left spinning the wheel toward him.)

The passenger-side door takes the brunt of the impact, so Dad has to climb across the gear stick to join me in the penalty box, where we survey the damage in silence. The boot has popped open and won't close properly, but it's definitely the goal that's come off worse in the collision. At the point where the car thudded into its post, the soulless skeleton is painfully misshapen.

"Well," says Dad proudly, tying the boot shut with his shoe-lace. "Now we've done bumper cars together."

And then he gives me a stick of chewing gum, which I'm not allowed.

Chapter Eleven

I open the door into a blinding flash of white.

"Smile!" says the voice behind the camera.

Both of them (the voice and the camera) belong to Mum, whose new hobby is photography. Ever since I got discharged from the hospital after the operation she takes my picture at least a dozen times a day. She's even turned the utility room into a darkroom, in which she spends about two hours every night and from which I'm barred in case I accidentally overexpose any of her pictures (even though most of them are of me anyway).

I used to hate having my photo taken, which is why there

are no pictures of us all as a family from when I was a kid. Every time Mum tried to take my picture I would start crying, or, when I got a bit older, do something deliberate to sabotage the composition, like making my eyes racist. Which is why if you looked through the photo albums that Mum gave up keeping around the time I turned seven you wouldn't even know I existed. (You'd just think that my parents were two grown-ups who enjoyed spending a disproportionately large amount of their free time at petting zoos.) The one good picture Mum and Dad do have of me from when I was young is a portrait taken against our front door on my first day of school, which now sits on top of the TV. The idea, apparently, was to document this milestone with a picture of me dressed from head to toe in my smart new uniform. At the time Mum's ambitions apparently stretched to a whole series, one picture to be taken each year on the first day of Winter term, each one charting in stages my growing into (and eventually growing out of) this uniform, with the glass panels of our front door behind my head acting as a measuring stick. The pictures would then be lined up on the mantelpiece like a sort of human staircase, providing a convenient visual aid for any distant relatives who wanted to remark how much I'd grown since I'd last seen them (i.e., "Last time I saw you, you were only four panels tall!"). The reason, so the story goes, that the only remaining evidence of this project is the single mischievous mug shot on top of the TV is that I was so against the idea of having my photo taken every year on the first day of term that I poked my penis through the flies of my new school trousers.

Now that I'm grown up, though, I don't mind Mum taking my picture so much. In fact, I have devised a game to amuse myself while she does so. As soon as she tells me to "Smile!" I pretend I've just heard a really hilarious joke or seen someone I don't like getting hurt. This way, when she takes the picture, she catches me in what looks like a moment of wild hysteria. The point of the game is to trick my older self into thinking I was a deliriously happy twelve-year-old and remembering my childhood more fondly. This time, though, I don't smile because I don't want her to see the wad of gum pouched in my cheek.

"You didn't smile," says Mum, looking over my shoulder at Dad. "Is everything all right? Did everything go okay with Mr. Fitzpatrick?"

"Yes, thank you, Mother," I say, which certainly isn't the whole story, but isn't a lie, either, because Mr. Fitzpatrick did see us in the end even though we were an hour late. (He removed my stitches without saying a word, but when he was finished he asked to see Dad alone for a moment. I waited in the corridor, and when Dad came out nearly fifteen minutes later he was grinning like a pupil who's just been told off really badly and doesn't know what else to do with his face. I asked him what Mr. Fitzpatrick wanted to talk about and he just told me to keep the dressing dry.) And then, to explain why I don't want my picture taken, I tell Mum about the Aborigines in Australia who believe that having your picture taken is tantamount to having your soul stolen.

"Oh," she says when I'm through explaining. "And do you believe that, too?"

(I think about the goalposts and really can't see the connection. But Dad's already been told off enough for one night, so I decide to protect him.)

"Yes," I lie. "And accordingly, I would appreciate it if you didn't take any more pictures of me."

However, I can't stop her from seeing the car.

From my bedroom, if I'm completely still, I can hear the politeness rising through the floorboards. It's obviously a big argument, because no one's raising their voice by so much as a decibel. I put Jaws 2 in his roaming sphere and push my mattress into the middle of the floor so I can sit on the carpet in the corner, directly above the kitchen, but even then I have to really strain to hear the utility-room door being gently closed and the crack of Dad's beer can as he slumps down on the sofa to watch TV.

After a half-arsed exploration of a faded Airfix paint stain (a patch of carpet that he's long since claimed in the name of Russian Dwarfs the world over), Jaws 2 reverts to sitting and staring at me from the middle of his plastic quarantine. He looks thin. When I lift him out of the sphere and cradle him, muzzling his teeth between a Vulcan salute, I can feel his ribs pressing against my palms like matchsticks. There's no denying he's lost weight. Moreover, when I turn him over to inspect his belly I notice a thin strip of white fur that definitely wasn't there before.

Google confirms that both rapid weight loss and white hair are symptoms of emotional trauma, which supports Chloe's fugue state theory. I decide to run some tests.

The best way to test for brain function abnormality is to measure the fluctuations in voltage from the various ionic currents between the billions of neurons in the brain during a variety of mental states, which sounds complicated but isn't really, especially if you consider that neurons are a bit like dogs (but not really) and ions are a bit like water (but also not really). The neurons (dogs) spend most of their time swimming through the ions, which as well as (not really) being like water are also (not really) like magnets, because they have either a positive or a negative charge. The ionic currents start when the neurons (dogs) have a message they need to deliver. They climb out of the ions (water) and "fire off," which is (not really) like shaking off the excess water (ions). But because the ions aren't really like water, because they're all (kind of) magnetically charged, they repel any other nearby magnets (water) with a like charge. This starts something (not really) like a domino effect, because when those secondary ions (magnets) are pushed out, they in turn push out a whole other set of like-charged ions, which in turn push out another set, and so on and so forth. What this creates is a current of ions (water), which crash out toward the edges of the brain. These are what we call brain waves, which are *exactly* (not really) like waves. And it's these brain waves that carry the electrical charges of the ionic currents all the way up to the scalp, where they can be detected and measured if you glue loads of electrodes to someone's head and link them up to a special computer.

I don't have any glue, so I decide to use a free sample of Shock-waves Power Hold Gel, which I took from a magazine I once found in a doctor's waiting room (because I was too embarrassed at the time to ask Mum to buy me any). The reason I never ended up using the free sample was that the waiting room I found it in belonged to the doctor who gave me my own EEG test, which lasted twelve hours because he wanted to study the ionic currents of my brain during one of my seizures (which he would only call "events" until after the results came back). The glue that he used to stick the electrodes to my head reminded me so much of the gel I'd seen lacquered across David Driscoll's forehead that I decided at some point in that twelve hours that I didn't want Mum to buy me any after all. (I also can't eat Polo mints now, either, because they remind me of CT scans.) When Mum found the hair gel sample a few weeks later in the back of the washing machine I'd already had to shave my head, which is why she suggested I keep it as a reminder that one day my hair would grow back. I told her I had no idea what she was talking about, and when she showed me the sample denied all knowledge. However, later I fished it out of the kitchen bin and hid it in one of the compartments in my tissue box. I was saving it for a ceremonial quiff to mark the return of my plumage, but through the ages men have made bigger sacrifices for science.

———

Using my ingenuity and teeth, I am able to construct a near-exact replica of an EEG scanner from my Smithsonian Elements of Science Mini-Lab (Ages 14+), which I got (by request) for my ninth birthday. In layman's terms, this involves connecting a mini-LED bulb to some wires, and fusing them to Jaws 2's scalp with a dewdrop of gel. In thirty seconds it sets, "redefining" his "look," and completing the circuit. Now all I need to do is give the dogs (neurons) some messages to deliver.

The experiment is simple. If Jaws 2 is able to receive the messages, then it will mean that the neurons in a particular part of his brain will have fired off, which will then have set the ionic currents rolling, which will then have gathered into brain waves, which in turn will have delivered the electrical charges to his scalp. If this happens, then the LED bulb will light up. Different messages require different dogs (neurons) to shake off (fire off), so the more messages I can give them, the more accurate a picture I can get of Jaws 2's brain activity.

The first message is Exhaustion. I lower Jaws 2 back through the hatch into his cage, carefully feeding the wires behind him, and once he lands nudge him toward his exercise wheel. He stumbles on lethargically and immediately falls asleep. Annoyed, I try rocking the wheel back and forth, but like a stubborn sunbather determined not to re-hang a wonky hammock, Jaws 2 screws his eyes shut even tighter and dreams more furiously, so I prod him with a 5H pencil, which is the hardest one I have. The wheel fizzes around its axis like a firework as he bolts. I set my stopwatch for seven minutes and hold my pencil in readiness, should his pace slacken. Which it doesn't.

When the alarm sounds, the bulb is unlit. Which is weird. I don't know exactly what I was expecting, but I do know that my brain waves powered a whole computer for the entire twelve hours of my test (which is partly why I was so surprised to find out I'd failed). Next I try exposing him to strobe lighting (which you can get online), then hunger (skewering a Parmesan crumb on a smoothed-out paper clip and suspending it from the roof of the cage just beyond his reach), then sleep deprivation (the 5H pencil again), then sleep (darkness plus patience). At no point does the bulb even flicker.

I don't hear Mum come in. I only realize she's in my bedroom when my computer drifts off into screensaver mode and I see her reflection in the black. Backlit by the pollution from the landing and moonstruck (by the moon (obviously)), there is a ghostliness to her appearance that makes me swallow my gum. When I turn round I can clearly see the chevrons by her eyes.

"I didn't mean to startle you," she says through parenthetical lips.

"You didn't," I lie. "How long have you been there?"

The question seems to stump her. Eventually, she says, "I don't know. What were you doing?"

"Tests," I reply, warily.

"Did he pass?" asks Mum, optimistically.

"I haven't collated the results yet." I cock my head to the side like a TV detective. "It may take up to five working days,"

I add humorously, so she doesn't suspect she's now under suspicion.

"Why have you moved your bed?" she asks.

"I'll ask the question round here!" I want to say.

"Because variety is a slice of life," I say.

"It's the spice of life," she says.

"That's what I said," I say.

"Do you want some help moving it back?" she asks.

"Yes," I admit.

When we've moved the mattress back to the corner of the room I ask Mum to help me turn it 90 degrees so it faces the door instead of the window, which I've been meaning to do anyway, because it would allow easier access to the plug socket and hide the Airfix paint stain on the carpet. But Mum says I can't sleep with my feet facing the door. I don't understand why not, because it wouldn't change the position of my head relative to the wall cushioning.

"Why not?" I ask. "It wouldn't change the position of my head relative to the wall cushioning. And even if it did, which it definitely wouldn't, I could wear my boxing helmet like on sleepovers."

"Because that's how they carry you out," says Mum.

"What does that mean?" I say, trying not to get frustrated. "How who carry you out? What are you talking about?"

Then Mum asks if she can sit down for just a little minute. She slumps down into the beanbag before I can grant permission, and then for exactly seven normal-sized minutes does nothing at all. (Her eyes remind me of David Driscoll's front

door in my anesthesia dream. I don't believe there's a thing
behind them. (I doubt that her brain waves could light the
LED.)) The beeping of my stopwatch wakes her like the click
of a hypnotist's fingers.

"I'm sorry, sweetheart. I was miles away," she says through a
smile that crinkles her chevrons. "Have you got everything
ready for tomorrow?"

I tell her I have.

"You know you don't have to go back yet, if you're not
feeling ready. I've spoken to the school and they say you can
take off as long as you like."

But I tell her that I can't afford to miss any more school, not
if I'm going to realize my potential, at which point the bones
in her knees crack as she hauls herself out of the beanbag and
envelopes me in a self-sealing hug. Over her shoulder I can see
the memory she's left in the beans. For some reason it makes
me think of the green plastic chairs in the hospital waiting
rooms and the overfirm mattresses on the ward beds, which are
all far too hard to remember anyone. I think about what Mum
told me in the ICU when she thought I was asleep and as suddenly and violently as a car crash my mistrust evaporates and I
feel sorry for her.

I stop her when she gets to the door because TV has taught
me that this is the most opportune moment to ask an important question.

"You know how I was an accident," I start.

"You weren't an accident," interrupts Mum. "You were a
happenstance. Like penicillin. Or Coca-Cola."

"Okay," I concede (even though I don't really know the difference). "But you know how you and Dad didn't plan on having me?"

"Yes," says Mum.

I pause for dramatic effect. (This would come directly before an ad break.)

"Do you ever regret it?"

A change breaks over Mum's face, like dawn or an egg. She looks almost angry. "You're not allowed to ask me that," she says. And then she leaves.

Chapter Twelve

According to Google, chewing gum can stay in your digestive tracts for as long as seven years, which is exactly as long as the Seven Years' War and a whole year longer than World War Two. This means that if you ingested a piece of gum in Europe in 1939 in peacetime you wouldn't outgest it until peacetime again on the other side of the war. Which is like if Hazel had hibernated at the start of *Watership Down* and only woken up at the end of the book without ever realizing that the warren had been destroyed.

———

I know there's no such thing as the future, but when you know you've got something inside you that won't be gone until seven years' time, it's hard not to think a bit about what the present will be like then. I don't have any specific prophecies or anything (because History is written by the winners which means that predictions must be written by losers), but it's weird to think that I swallowed this gum as a child and I'll discharge it as an adult.

Chapter Thirteen

Year 5s all look the same to me, except for the black one whose name is Michael. I know for sure that the one standing in the aisle before me isn't Michael, but I couldn't say absolutely whether or not it's the same one from last time. Not until he opens his mouth and starts lisping.

"House . . ." he begins.

But I hold up a hand to stop him. One look at his spit-glazed tongue, crashing against his braced teeth like an exhausted sea lion flopping onto land to escape a killer-whale attack, and I know he has no use for the lesson I'm supposed to teach him. It's obvious from the way the saliva froths like sherbet in the corners of his mouth that he learned long ago that life and the people in it can be cruel. Perhaps I'm softening in my old age, or perhaps I know how traumatized he must already be from meeting David Driscoll, but for whatever reason I decide to take pity on him.

"Listen," I whisper, beckoning him close (but not so close that I'm in range if the spit bubbles detonate). "The joke's on you."

"W-hat choke?" he splutters before I can hold up my hand again.

"Don't talk, just listen." I sigh. "You're a pawn. And I know you've been told if you make it all the way to the back of the bus you'll become a queen."

(This time my hand is quick enough to silence him pre-emptively.)

"But let me school you here for a second, son," I continue, allowing myself to start imagining what a hero this will make me to this poor boy, probably for the rest of his life. "It's an ambush."

(I wonder how he'll thank me. I guess it all depends on what he does when he grows up. I suppose with his speech impediment he's unlikely to become a theologian or a therapist or a scientist or a sage, so maybe one day he'll be an artist or an architect or an alchemist, in which case he might want to erect a statue of me. (I'd insist on something simple. Maybe a *Gulliver's Travels* motif, like a forty-foot me bowed down (to symbolize my humility) with a child (to-scale) standing in my palm, gazing up at me through eyes full of wonder and renewed hope in humanity. Or maybe I'm releasing him into the air like a dove, so he can fly away on wings made of my infinite compassion. But either way, nothing too ostentatious, maybe marble or bronze (unless he does become an alchemist, in which case I suppose gold would have to do).))

"David Driscoll," I say, nodding conspiratorially to the front of the bus. "Looks like a spotty Irish Tintin. He's the one who sent you, isn't he?"

The Year 5 nods (normally).

"And he told you to ask how my mum's piano lessons were going, didn't he?"

This time he shakes his head.

"He jus thaid *it*."

"Said what?"

"He jus thaid to arse you house it gong."

"No, he didn't," I say, wiping dry my cheek (subtly, pretending to readjust my cap, so as not to cause offense). "He said to ask how my mum's piano lessons were going. Because if you'd just said how's *it* going, it wouldn't have made any sense when I told you my mum had no arms."

"Your mumps got no amps?" he asks, suddenly frightened.

"No," I explain patiently, congratulating myself for not impersonating the boy and renewing my resolve not to start. "My mum has plenty of arms. That's how this works. You ask about my mum's piano lessons and I act all upset because my mum doesn't have any arms, and then you start crying, when actually all along there was nothing wrong with my mum, which David Driscoll knew perfectly well or he wouldn't have sent you here in the first place. Because if she really didn't have any arms, then the joke would have been on me instead of on you." I pause, considerately, to let him catch up. Then I smile benevolently down at him for long enough to really sear the image on his retinae, just in case he should want to re-create it at a later date in materials of his choosing. "But don't worry," I continue eventually, "because I'm not gonna do that to you, on account of my infinite compassion. So instead we're just going to pretend that all of what I just said was meant to happen *has* happened, and that way the joke's not on either of us."

For some reason the Year 5 still seems confused.

"But he jus thaid to arse ith you whir okay," he says, the spit webbing his lips like ducks' feet and starting to annoy me.

(I count to ten before replying.)

"That's not a joke," I explain, calmly.

"Tho what?" asks the Year 5, insubordinately.

"Tho, he didn't thay vat," I say.

I can see his eyes start to bubble.

"I'm sorry," I thay, internalizing my growing impatience. "I didn't mean to upset you. I'm trying to help you out here, kid. Try and understand. This is all a joke."

"Ven who sit on?" he foams.

"It's on David," I snap, "because his mum's dead!"

The second before the Year 5 bursts spectacularly into tears David Driscoll pops up at the front of the bus and looks over. Very slightly, more with his eyebrows than with his head, but at the same time absolutely unmistakably, he nods at me.

Even though it was practically undetectable to the naked eye, David Driscoll's nod leads me to pursue some fairly massive trains of thought. To help me manage them, I open my

Maths exercise book to a new page (while Mr. Carson drones on about quadratic equations, which I mastered in Year 5) and divide it into two equal columns. The first one I label "For" and the second one "Against."

In the *Star Trek* episode "Mirror, Mirror," the crew of the *Enterprise* ends up in a parallel universe called Mirror Universe, where they meet their evil twins, who are identical to them in every way imaginable except that their moral compasses are completely inverted so they don't prick themselves when they do something wrong (and Spock has a goatee). This makes the inhabitants of the Mirror Universe the exact opposites of the *Enterprise* crew, because they have only one thing different.

Scientifically, this pretty much all checks out.

My favorite thing about Science is how it's not always that different from Religion, which is probably why they make such good opposites. For example, a lot of scientists still believe that there is a cat in a box in Copenhagen that is both alive and dead simultaneously. The reason they believe this is that in Copenhagen subatomic particles exist in two quantum states at the same time (which means they're in two places at once) until, that is, someone observes them. When someone does observe one of these subatomic particles it stops being in two places at once and starts being in one place at once. This is an example of the Uncertainty Principle, because if you can't ever catch a subatomic particle out (which you can't, because literally the second you see them they stop being so schizo), then you can't really ever know for certain too much about them.

The scientists who believe in the Uncertainty Principle remind me of Mr. Carson when he's writing problems on the board and he's convinced that David Driscoll is misbehaving behind his back. However quickly he spins round he never catches David doing anything wrong. However, this only makes him more annoyed, because rather than taking the sight of David doing nothing wrong as evidence of his innocence, Mr. Carson uses it to reinforce his belief that the act of observation has altered David's behavior. What this means is that the more Mr. Carson turns round and the less he sees David impersonating him having his stroke, the more convinced he becomes that it's happening.

There is, though, one main difference between the scientists in Copenhagen and Mr. Carson.

Mr. Carson is usually right.

However, today he isn't. Today, when he breaks off mid-equation to pivot round toward us with a speed and accuracy you would associate sooner with a professional ballerina than a forty-year-old Maths teacher with a face like the Countdown Clock (because ever since the stroke only one side of it works), he finds David in his usual quantum state of good behavior.

"Driscoll!" he booms, through the good side of his face.

"Sir?" asks David, as though melted butter would resolidify in his mouth.

"Now what are you up to?"

"Nothing, sir."

"Yes, I can see that," says Mr. Carson, frustration ripping wavelike through the good side of his brow. "Don't be cute."

But David wasn't being cute (by which Mr. Carson means clever, which is something he'd never accuse David Driscoll of being). The entire time Mr. Carson had his back turned David was diligently transcribing the equation into his exercise book. And when I looked over at him to confirm the lack of ill discipline in my periphery, *he smiled at me.*

Which brings me on to the cat.

The reason someone decided to put a cat in a box in Copenhagen is because he didn't believe that something could be in two places at once and then suddenly stop being the second someone saw it. His name was Erwin Schrödinger (which is easy to remember (<u>S</u>cientists <u>C</u>rave <u>H</u>ealthy <u>R</u>eason <u>O</u>ver <u>D</u>arkness <u>I</u>n <u>G</u>eneral <u>E</u>xcept <u>R</u>eality)), and the point of his experiment was to prove that it didn't make sense to have one rule for subatomic particles and another rule for pet-sized ones. In his experiment, a cat was put in a box with a tiny bit of radioactive material and a Geiger Counter (<u>G</u>amma <u>E</u>asily <u>I</u>s <u>G</u>ettable <u>E</u>specially <u>R</u>adiation), which was hooked up to a Diabolical Mechanism. This is really bad news for the cat, because if a single atom of the radioactive material decays, then the Geiger Counter will twitch, which will trigger the boot, which will kick the bucket, which will release the marble, which will topple the tower, which will dislodge the ball, which will fall on the diving board, which will propel the diver, which will unleash the hammer, which will smash the vial, which will release the gas, which will kill the cat.

The reason that Schrödinger's Cat is such an important experiment in Science is that it demonstrates a huge flaw in the way quantum mechanics works in Copenhagen. Which is this: If you believe that a subatomic particle is in two places at once until it is observed, then you believe that the radioactive material both decays *and* doesn't decay simultaneously, which means you believe that until you take the lid off the box to have a look, the cat is both *alive and dead*. This is a bit like saying that until Mr. Carson turns round to check, David is simultaneously impersonating him *and* not impersonating him. In other words, it makes absolutely as much sense as Dad refusing to watch penalty shoot-outs in case he affects the outcome. Which is why most intelligent people now believe in Many Worlds.

(*"Freeze!"* screams Mr. Carson, swiveling round again like a sheriff in a Western. But the problem in the class is sitting quietly, so reluctantly he turns back to the one on the board.)

In the *Star Trek* episode, Captain Kirk finds himself aboard the *ISS Enterprise,* which is the exact equivalent of the *USS Enterprise* in a parallel dimension. This is completely realistic because of Many Worlds Theory. Many Worlds Theory agrees with the Not So Great Danes in one major respect: that a subatomic particle *can* be in two places at once. However, it has a much better explanation for what happens inside the cat trap. According to MWT, the cat really is alive and dead simultaneously inside the box. However, the cute part is when you open it up. Because when you do that in MWT instead of making one of the cats (i.e., the living one or the dead one) magically stop existing, what you actually do is lift the lid on one reality *while at the same time another you opens the lid on the other one*. (This is all actually kind of obvious if you think about it (which I am now doing), because if subatomic particles are allowed to be in two places at once in Copenhagen, then why shouldn't they be allowed to be in two places at once everywhere else in the world? And, more important, if subatomic particles are allowed to be in two places at once everywhere in the world, then why aren't we? (I think the only reason people have such a hard time accepting that there's an infinite number of thems in an infinite number of parallel realities is because it makes them feel less special, especially when the alternative is to believe that they're so special they can bring a dead cat back to life just by looking at it.))

This time when Mr. Carson turns round he notices that the two columns I have divided my exercise book into have approximately nothing to do with quadratic equations. After sidling up to me and reading the page over my shoulder he does nothing about this, a fact which I subsequently record in the "For" column. So far it reads:

1) David's behavior
2) Jaws 2's behavior
3) Dad's behavior
4) ~~Mum's behavior~~

4) In theory there is no difference between theory and practice
5) Mr. Carson's behavior

When Mr. Carson returns to the board (pausing en route to check on his unlicensed tribute act, who immediately continues to not misbehave), I think about the look Mum got in her eyes last night when I asked her about moving the bed and decide to whisper her back in at 6) using an HB pencil. Meanwhile, at the board Mr. Carson wipes out the first line of workings to make room for the solution. Noticing I haven't taken any of the workings down, David nudges me.

"Do you need to copy?" he mouths, showing me his transcript.

I shake my head and turn back to my list. But he nudges me again.

"What you doing May twenty-second?"

I shake my head again.

"My birthday," he whispers. "I'm thirteen. Gonna be a party at my house. You're invited."

Here's the thing that doesn't make sense: If I had to characterize the way in which everyone's behavior has been schizo lately, I'd say it's that (with the exception of Jaws 2) they're all being nice to me. However, in *Star Trek*, when Captain Kirk encounters people from his parallel reality, they're the Evil Twin versions of everyone he knows. This is almost always the case on TV and in films, which suggests that if I have somehow passed through a portal into another world, I must have been living in the Evil Twin version to begin with. I add this observation to the "Against" column, where it slots in at 3), after 1) Goatees and 2) <u>HOW THE F★★★?</u>

On the blackboard Mr. Carson marks the spot (x) and then slowly adds two parallel lines (=). He is about to write the answer (which is 7), when instead he whirls round with such force that he almost takes off like a helicopter (or maybe in this world, screws himself into the ground like a helicopter). This time the sight of David Driscoll behaving impeccably is too much for him to bear. His (good) eyebrow trembles, his (good) nostril flares, and his (whole) head jogs on his shoulders like a dashboard dog's. I wonder if it would be of any consolation to him to know that in a parallel world he's just caught David red-handed, his spotty Irish face lolling lopsidedly in its cruelest Conundrum Carson routine.

In the end though consolation takes a different form. His voice cracks like thunder:

"CHLOE GOWER!"

Everyone turns to look.

(In this reality, it turns out albinos can blush.)

Mr. Carson strides toward her, his confidence returning with every step. "Why, is that *for me*?" he asks, holding one hand to his heart in a mean parody of emotion and with the other plucking the note from her stiff fingers. "But you know I've got no secrets, Chloe. If you've got something to say to me, then you can say it to the whole class."

The look that Chloe gives him is withering enough to make fruit think twice about ripening, but Mr. Carson stands his ground. After what seems like forever, she kicks back her chair, gets to her feet, and snatches back the note on her way to the blackboard. With her eyes still fixed on Mr. Carson, who shifts uncomfortably from foot to foot, she unfolds the note, takes a breath, and then recalibrates her gaze to the floor.

"We're all atwitter," says Mr. Carson.

"Meet—" starts Chloe.

"E-nun-c-iate," interrupts Mr. Carson.

"Meet me—"

"Try to project," interrupts Mr. Carson (which is ironic, because he's the one Projecting. You can almost see him coloring Chloe's hair orange and dotting her face with greasy Irish spots).

"Meet me after—"

"Breath from your stomach, not your throat. Try again."

"Meet me after school—"

("Oooooh," says everyone.)

"Stand up straight," says Mr. Carson. "Try and imagine there's a string—"

"Fuck off," interrupts Chloe Gower, and then storms out of the class.

"Well," says Mr. Carson eventually, once the laughter and applause have died down sufficiently for him to be heard. "I'm sure I don't need to tell whoever that message was intended for that if they wish to meet Miss Gower after school they'll be doing so after detention."

When the clock is about to strike half past, I make the *Countdown* alarm sound under my breath, but loud enough to get a detention of my own.

Chapter Fourteen

Alternate Miss Farthingdale calls me the prodigal son outside detention, which I find embarrassing because it reminds me of the time I called her Mum. We are at the entrance to the sports hall, which is all set up for exams and which is where detention is taking place. She asks how I'm feeling, and I tell her fine thanks, and when I make to walk past her into the sports hall she looks confused.

"Are you on the list?" she asks, like she's a bouncer in a film with a velvet rope in one hand and a clipboard in the other (as opposed to an English teacher in a school with what looks like a Pez dispenser in one hand and a clipboard in the other).

I tell her I am, and she asks what I'm in for, but before I can tell her she says, "Actually, don't tell me. That's the first thing you learn in detention. Everyone's innocent." Then she smiles and beckons me close and asks if I'd like a Polo.

"No, thanks," I say (shuddering almost imperceptibly). "They're bad for your teeth."

"What isn't these days?" says Miss Farthingdale, and tells me to hold out my hand, which I do automatically. Then she double-clicks her Pez dispenser and two small round white pills appear in my palm. Their dimensions are identical to the gap in the middle of a Polo, like we're living in a negative. I must look as confused as I feel, because Miss Farthingdale laughs and explains that they're "Polo Holes." And then (as though she knows I'm a visitor from a faraway place) she tells me not to worry because they taste exactly the same.

Inside the hall, Chloe and I sit one in front of the other in the shadow of the godivarous basketball hoops. Because we are far enough out of Miss Farthingdale's earshot and because I'm the one sat behind in alphabetical order, we are able to converse effectively, me whispering and her holding up notes on an A4 pad. The first note she holds up is in pencil and too faint for me to read.

"E-nun-c-iate," I whisper into the darkness of her hair.

"LOL," she writes in biro, even though we both know she hasn't. Then she traces over her original message with the pen.

"what did u find out?" it says.

"Bout what?"

"hampster."

"I think you were right," I mumble (partly to be quiet and partly because I don't like admitting I'm wrong).

"project," she scrawls.

"You're right," I say louder, disguised as a cough. "He's not the same. And everyone's acting really weird."

"weird?" she scribbles, although I don't know if she intends the italics or if she's just holding the pad at an angle.

So I tell her about my driving lesson and about how David smiled at me and how Mum keeps looking at me in the third person and a little bit about Quantum Mechanics. And then, as it occurs to me, I tell her about how my life flashed before my eyes in the hospital and, specifically, how it felt like Time had come loose from its moorings, and how (now that I think about it) this might have been a Relativity-type thing, which would suggest that I was traveling close to the speed of light, and maybe I had died under the knife after all or rather one of me had because maybe death is just another word for reaching The Limit of Infinity, which is the only place in the universe where parallel lines can meet, which maybe, just maybe, might explain how it was I was able to hop across to an alternate reality (!!!) and carry on my life like nothing had happened. (Maybe that's why when someone dies you don't say they've died, you say they've *passed*.) Finally, to illustrate the point, I tear the For and Against page out of my Maths exercise book and pass it off to Chloe as she rocks back on her chair. She studies it for no more than three and three-quarter seconds (three Mississippis and an Amazon) before scrunching it into a ball and starting to compose her reply. It's only four words long (or five if you count the apostrophe (which I don't)), but the way Chloe writes it, turning the pad on its side and slotting the letters between the lines like she's doing nothing more important than playing a game of Connect 4, it takes up a whole side of paper:

| h | e | ' | s | | h | a | v | i | n | g | | a | n | | a | f | f | a | i | r |

At the bus stop Chloe expounds her theory, which is another word for explain.

"He's doing it so you choose him."

"Choose him for what?" I ask. "Doing what?"

"Being 'fun,'" she says, making the inverted commas in the air with only one hand so it looks more like Scout's Honor. "So you choose him to live with."

"What do you mean?" I ask, stupidly.

Chloe sighs. "He's trying to be West Germany. He wants to make sure that when the wall goes up you want to be on his side of it."

And then she tells me the story.

It all started one Saturday morning when Chloe's dad suggested they went on one of their drives together, just the two of them. Already Chloe knew something was up, because they'd never before been on a drive together, neither as a pair or as part of a larger unit. (They had driven to places and then subsequently back from them, but that wasn't the same thing at all.) When she got into the car Chloe had to adjust the seat, which recently she noticed had been set much farther back than she was used to. She could tell this for certain that Saturday morning because when she first sat down she couldn't reach the radio dial, which had been retuned to Heart 106.2. On the motorway her dad asked her lots of questions about her life (what sort of music she was listening to (good), whether or not she had a boyfriend (not), how everything was going at school (s'okay)), and then a few more about her mum (did she like her cooking (s'okay), whether or not she wanted to be like her when she was older (not), how would she rate their relationship on a scale of one to ten (good)). By the time he was done quizzing her, a sign had welcomed them to Surrey.

"Where are we going?" Chloe asked.

"There's something I want to show you," said her dad.

The something turned out to be a house. They were greeted at the entrance gate by a six-foot-tall blond estate agent with a button missing from her blouse, who kissed her dad on both cheeks and told her she must be Chloe. Then she gave them a tour, which took forever because the house had seven bedrooms and a tennis court.

"What do you think?" asked her dad halfway through, when the estate agent had slipped away to take a phone call.

"We don't play tennis," said Chloe.

"I know that," said her dad. "It would be an investment. Charlotte's nice, isn't she?"

"Who?" said Chloe.

"Charlotte," said her dad again, as though Chloe hadn't heard him the first time, which she had. "The estate agent," he added eventually.

"How do you know her?" asked Chloe.

"I make a lot of investments," said her dad.

At the end of the tour, once she'd kissed Chloe's dad on both cheeks again and told him that they should talk on Monday, Charlotte told Chloe what a pleasure it was to *finally* meet her. On the way home Chloe had a lot of questions she wanted to ask, but her dad put the roof down even though it was October, which meant they couldn't talk. As he explained, "You only live once."

In the three weeks that followed, Chloe twice found her dad sleeping on the sofa in the living room. (He must have fallen asleep reading, he said the first time, and he must have fallen asleep reading again, he said the second, although both times Chloe observed that the only reading material in arm's reach was an old copy of *AutoTrader* magazine, which she doubted possessed the requisite rereadability to trigger two separate instances of falling asleep on the sofa.) In these three weeks Chloe's dad took her CD shopping on five separate occasions, each time returning with a bounty of no fewer than four albums, each of which he insisted she copy for him. After she had done so, he would wait a day or two to tell her how much he'd enjoyed it, usually saying how much it reminded him of someone he used to listen to himself (most often someone called Colin Bluntstone, who Chloe and I agree sounds more like a Cluedo guess than a musician). The last dozen CDs she "burned" for him were blank.

It was at the end of this three weeks that Chloe's mum found she couldn't get out of bed one morning so her dad had to drive her to school. He was waiting in the driveway with the engine running when she opened the passenger-side door into a blast of saxophone. "Careless Whisper" by George Michael was playing on the retuned radio, and the car seat had been pushed back as far as it would go. It was when she reached underneath it to pull the slide lever that she found the button. She got the bus home from school that day (from the exact spot we're at now (well, actually, from about two hundred meters down the road, because this one's a temporary stop)), and when she got home and opened the front door she saw the luggage on the porch.

Charlotte moved in with Chloe's dad for a while after the separation, but soon she gave way for Nadine, who was replaced by Anya, who abdicated (after Chloe's sister pissed in her bubble bath) and was succeeded by Nicola. It wasn't until a long time afterward that Chloe realized that her dad's first four post-divorce girlfriends had all been named after potatoes.

"And mark my words," she concludes (in the nick of time) as her bus exhales and its doors flap open, "that's what's happening to you. He's waited till you're better, and now he's going to start Taking an Interest."

That night it's just me and Mum for dinner because Dad's got a lesson with Chloe's sister. Later in bed I have my first Wind-Down Seizure. It's so intense that the sweat soaks all the way through the mattress and the carpet and drips through the boards onto the kitchen floor.

Part Three

Small Things Grow

Chapter Fifteen

At Tallow Chandlers' School for Boys, which is the institution I have decided to attend, all of the football goals have nets. There are three pitches in total, one each for the First XI, Second XI, and Third XI. The Roman Numerals are no coincidence. They match the Latin motto on the breast of the blazer, underneath the school crest: *Concordia Parvae Res Crescunt.*

"Which means what, exactly?" asks the headmaster Mr. Sinclair from behind his heavy oak desk, which might be the oldest thing I've seen in my whole life. There are five of us stood in front of it, all of us scholarship candidates. The magazines fanned across it, whose names I can read upside down, are all called things like *Quarterly* and *Review.* They have thick pages. They look like the kind you take, as opposed to the kind you read (*Auto Trader*). Moreover, the volumes in the bookcase are leather-bound, like expensive menus.

None of the other boys in the office know the answer. Mr. Sinclair blinks. He has a small mole on his lower-right eyelid that jumps when he does so. It looks like a fly resettling on a piece of meat. I feel my arm lighten by my side.

"No need to put your hand up." Mr. Sinclair laughs. And then, probably because he thinks he's seen me admiring the football pitches, "You're not appealing for offside."

"It means In Harmony Small Things Grow," I say.

"Indeed it does." He beams.

(At Grove End, our school motto is *"Pride In Achievement,"* but with no one's name outside the quotation marks, so it just seems sort of sarcastic.)

"And what do you suppose we mean by *harmony*?"

"Music?" offers a fat boy who's after a choral scholarship, his face laminated in a film of sweat so he looks like he's been vacuum-packed.

"No, that's good," says Mr. Sinclair. "Music's a part of it, certainly. And so is Sport. And Geography. And Politics and Theater. Well done. It's about having the correct *arrangement,* isn't it? Try and imagine your brain is an orchestra."

(I try, but it's difficult, because my brain is already a circuit board, a dog kennel, a water park, and a hostage negotiation.)

"It's made up of all these different *sections,* which are all entirely distinct and perfectly pleasant in isolation and all completely essential in their own right, but the whole thing only really comes to life when all of the sections are working together in perfect *harmony*. That's what gets the hairs on your neck standing to attention, isn't it? Is that what you meant to say?"

The fat boy secretes another sweat layer and nods too hard.

"So, as a school, or perhaps as a *conductor,* as our friend . . ."

"Philip," says the fat boy, this time 80% sure he's right (rising to 85% when Mr. Sinclair smiles at him).

"As our friend *Philip* might say, it's our job to cultivate The Whole You. And, of course, when I say 'job,' what I mean actually is raison d'être—"

"Reason for being!" I interrupt, banging the desk like I'm buzzing in on a quiz show.

"Quite," says Mr. Sinclair. "Quite so. Thank you . . ."

"You're welcome," I say, graciously.

"A footie fan *and* a Francophile," he purrs. "I suppose you know what a Francophile is?"

"Like Eva Braun."

"Okay," says Mr. Sinclair. "I didn't know that. Is that definitely right?"

"Yes," I reply. "She was sexually attracted to fascist dictators."

I like the way Mr. Sinclair laughs. The way it crackles reminds me of an open fire (especially since it makes Philip perspire even more). However, I have no idea why he's doing it.

"I hope to see you in September," he says when we're leaving. Although in English the second-person pronoun doesn't inflect for number (which is why the singular and plural forms look identical (i.e., *you* vs. *you*)), I'm pretty sure he's talking only to me.

Outside the study, Mum, who's taken time off work for the open day, asks how it went.

"Swimmingly," I tell her, which is subtly ambiguous, because I'm not allowed to swim. "I think he was impressed by my advanced lexicon," I elaborate. "Which means vocabulary."

"I'm sure he was," says Mum. "But what did *you* think?"

"I could see myself working under him," I say nonchalantly, reparting my hair with my fingertips because it's finally long enough again and I'm making up for lost time.

For lunch there is a choice between fish (plaice), pasta bar (carbonara, arrabiata, or pomodoro), and two types of meat (lamb or eggplant, which is American for chicken), which is a world apart from lunch at Grove End. (Once I forgot my lunchbox and I was stood behind Simon Nagel in the queue when he asked the lunch lady what sort of meat they were serving.

"Roast," she said.

"Roast what?" he said.

"Roast meat," she said. "You're holding up the line."

(In the end he had the VegeMince, which he claimed to find bones in. (The next time they were serving VegeMince, I made sure to get my hands on some, but when I dusted it down with the paintbrush I'd borrowed from Art, the only item of archeological interest I discovered was a tightly coiled gray hair.))) The food is just one of the reasons I've decided to come here. I got to try it the last time I visited, when I was applying for scholarship at 11+, but then I couldn't sit the entrance exams and I had to resign myself to another two years of packed lunches, so I can really empathize with those blind people you read about who regain their sight and then lose it again and wish they'd never bothered.

Mum has barely touched her Moroccan tagine. She looks old. (On average, people sleep for eight hours a night, which amounts to twenty-six years if you live to seventy-eight, which is the average life expectancy for someone living in the United Kingdom. This means that the typical British citizen is conscious for a grand total of fifty-two years. However, lately Mum has not been sleeping. This means she is aging at 133% the rate of the typical British citizen. If she continues to age at this rate, then she will have exhausted her allotted fifty-two years of consciousness by the time she's sixty-three years and three months old. (In contrast, I have been sleeping more and more recently. (At my current rate, I will live until I'm one hundred and eight.))

There are several telltale signs that Mum has not been sleeping lately, the two most obvious ones being the sharp drop-off in her sentence-completion rate (in other words, she is starting far more sentences than she is finishing), and that she has started wearing makeup to cover up the American Football–style stripes under her eyes. Moreover, ever since I dismantled my intruder alarm for Jaws 2's EEG, I have been noticing on waking faint imprints in my beanbag. These imprints have been appearing at a frequency of three a week for the past seven weeks, which has prompted me to carry out some experiments on the beanbag to determine its memory span. My findings suggest a direct correlation between the length of time someone sits in the beanbag and the length of time the beanbag remembers them. Judging from the fact that the beanbag is often still inhaling when I wake up, I can conclude that Mum sits in it for a long time.

I attribute Mum's insomnia to her concerns about The State of Her Marriage. It can be helpful to use the word *state* when describing a marriage because it makes you think of the people involved as particles. Right now Mum and Dad's marriage is a gas.

In addition to monitoring the beanbag, I have moreover been reviewing the position of Dad's car seats and his radio presets. So far this has not returned any useful data. (Dad's presets remain: AM1 Talk Sport, AM2 Five Live (909), AM3 Five Live (693), AM4 Classic Gold, AM5 Talk Sport. (He does not have any FM presets.)) However, two Wednesday nights ago Dad turned off the TV in the middle of a Chelsea match and challenged me to a game of chess. When I reminded him that he didn't play chess, he asked me to teach him.

"So," he said, once I had explained how all of the pieces moved (having decided to indulge him), "the king's kind of like a stay-at-home dad." Then he asked me how I would feel about him "scaling back" his "work responsibilities" so we could spend more time together "as a family."

———

(The fact that I have not yet uncovered any concrete evidence of Dad's infidelity is proof that I may have been wrong about The Act of Observation. Since his chess tutorial, he has canceled all his evening lessons except for Chloe's sister's on Thursday nights so he can spend more time trying to pretend he cares about us.)

Chloe agrees that all of this is suspicious. She is fast becoming the Watson to my Holmes, except a girl. This is why we have been spending so much time together. We have mostly been meeting up in the Harlequin Centre, taking it in turns to arrange secret rendezvous on MSN Messenger by typing the details in Wingdings and decoding them in unsaved Microsoft Word documents. Usually we meet in the Country Music aisle in Virgin Megastore or the Classic Literature section of Waterstones, because these are the places we are least likely to be disturbed by people we know, but on two occasions we have shared Oreo milkshakes in the food court. Chloe says that we know much more than we think we know, but not quite enough yet to act. She says the worst thing we could do at this stage is confront my dad about his shady dealings, because all this would do is let him know we're on to him, which would just mean a barrage of plausibly heartfelt reassurances and that we might never find out what's really going on. However, Chloe says, there are ways we can be certain. Having parents on the brink of divorce, she says, is like playing Doom 3 on

God Mode. Here though I had to stop her. I didn't understand the analogy. Mum doesn't believe in the trivialization of violence, which means I'm not allowed to play shoot-'em-ups.

"Oh, aren't you?" asked Chloe, rhetorically.

"No," I answered anyway.

And then she explained what she'd meant. When you're in God Mode in Doom 3, your life is automatically set to 100% and can't ever drop below that level because you are immune from all harm. This is the perfect analogy, says Chloe, because when you have parents on the brink of divorce, it is impossible for you to get into trouble. Then she told me to wait where I was (which was in the babywear department of Marks & Spencer). Ten minutes later, she returned with something under her hoodie, which turned out to be a copy of Grand Theft Auto: San Andreas. The instructions she gave were to install the game on my PC with my bedroom door open and play it on full volume, being sure to ignore the missions and concentrate instead on maximizing the death toll, until the song of the (police) sirens drew one or both of my parents to the scene. When he/she/they asked what I was doing, I was to reply that I was washing the scum from the streets. (For added effect Chloe suggested I limit my killing spree to a single race.) I was then to note the reaction and report back to Chloe at the next secret rendezvous.

The next weekend I reported back to Chloe the following tableau: my driving instructor father standing over my left shoulder like a bad conscience, breathlessly goading me into executing first a handbrake turn across a central reservation into two lanes of counterflow traffic to escape the attentions of the impromptu police cavalcade of which I was the head, and second, the blissfully unaware Hispanic prostitute who'd had the misfortune to innocently wander into the sight of my sniper rifle on her (probable) way home to relieve a friendly neighborhood babysitter. Not that I considered her family situation at the time, as I lazily lined up and snapped a bullet into her jugular, because by this stage in my hate-crime spree I was firmly in the thrall of the Desensitizing Effect of Artificial Brutality, which is tied with Skin Cancer in third place in Mum's All-Time Top Five Countdown of Biggest Parental Concerns 2004. When I mentioned this to Dad, who was busy applauding the distance the shot had put between the woman's head and her torso, he shrugged and said I was old enough now to make up my own mind. And speaking of which, wasn't it about time we took a look at my computer's online parental control settings . . .

Chloe nodded sagely while I relayed this information, and when I was through agreed it was ominous. Then, pretending to cross-reference the track listings of two Willie Nelson best-ofs, she outlined Phase II, which concerned diet and was designed to specifically target the matriarch, which is a better word for Mum. The purpose of Phase II (you could just tell by the way Chloe said it that that's how she was spelling it) was to test the matriarch's boundaries in order to establish how much, if anything, she knew about the imminent collapse of her marriage. The way to do this, Chloe had decided, was with a list she had compiled of the world's least nutritious foods.

———

(I am pretty sure by now that Chloe is my first girl friend, which is not the same as girlfriend. The gap is the same as the space between our faces when we're sharing Oreo milkshakes. It is less than a foot, but it is the longest foot on earth.)

Mum looked surprised in a good way when I asked if I could come with her to the supermarket. She let me get eight out of the fourteen items on the list (which I had memorized and then destroyed), which Chloe and I agree is inconclusive. Every night for the past week I have smuggled a selection of fresh fruit into my bedroom to eat in secret and requested one of Chloe's approved meals for dinner. On two out of five occasions my demands were met in full, on another two the meal was served in a healthier form (extra mushrooms on top of the stuffed-crust microwavable pepperoni pizza, the Rustlers quarter pounder presented minus the bun on a bed of rice with peas and carrots), and the grilled chocolate sandwich was refused outright. Moreover, on Tuesday evening, as per Chloe's instructions, I asked for a try of Dad's beer. Dad (as we expected) said okay, but Mum, who is never normally clumsy, accidentally knocked the can over before she could pass it to me. This is the detail that Chloe fixated on the most when I met her yesterday outside the newsagent with the *A* missing so the sign says NEWS GENT.

"Huh," she said, when I was finished briefing her, and then again when I asked why we were meeting there. "So she didn't actually say no?"

"What?"

"Your mum. If she didn't want you drinking, she could of said so, right? Said no, I mean."

I explained that there wasn't really time to say anything, what with the accident, because the kitchen table is unwaxed (and corrected her grammar).

"Freud says accidents are just unconsciously motivated designs," said Chloe.

"Who?" I asked.

"He's my dad's analyst. Dad's always on about him. Says there's no such thing as accidents."

"What about Chernobyl?" I asked, but Chloe didn't answer. Instead, she told me how Mum had most likely spilled the beer on purpose, and that the only reason she hadn't forbade me from trying some was so I didn't resent her, and because she wants to prove that she can be fun, too.

"Mum's not fun," I told her. "She calls bumper cars dodgems. And that's two reasons. And if you're saying it wasn't an accident and that she doesn't want me drinking alcohol, then that's good news, anyway, isn't it?"

However, before Chloe could reply we were interrupted by the homeless man who came out of the shop and handed Chloe a small yellow box and asked if he could keep the change and then blessed her when she said yes he could. The box said CAMEL SINCE 1913 on it and then, in a much less elaborate font, SMOKERS DIE YOUNGER.

"What the eff?" I asked Chloe, who didn't respond because she was busy gnawing at the box's corner like a squirrel with a nut. "If you need to smoke to impress people, then those people aren't your friends."

"They're not for me," she said eventually, spitting out a fleck of cellophane and tearing the wrapping off the packet so when she passed it to me it felt like being gifted an unpinned grenade. And then, by way of explanation, all she added was, "Phase III."

So here's what I told her: that this was where I drew the line, that each cigarette shortens your life expectancy by five minutes, that I now intended to live to a ripe old age thank you very much, that it was amazing what you could get done in three hundred seconds and anyway that in my experience when people said five minutes they usually meant anything up to half an hour, which means that every three cigarettes you smoke is potentially one must-see film you never get to see, and (in conclusion) that she could stick Phase III up her *arschloch*.

Chloe lets me say all of this with a grin on her face. Only once I've clarified that *arschloch* is German for a-hole does she explain further. She does this by emptying the cigarettes into a bin that's just for dog waste and crumpling the packet in her fist because actions speak louder than words. Phase III is all about taboos, says Chloe, which is why my parents have to discover the empty cigarette box among my possessions. This, she says, is the only way we'll find out for sure. If all their recent spoiling is just standard (post-)operating procedure and not the Coolest Parent Custody Pageant we suspect it to be, then (like I did) they'll draw the line at smoking (the Camel's pack will be the straw that breaks the camel's back (my joke, not Chloe's)). However, if Mum and Dad really are getting a divorce, then they'll each be so desperate to stay on my good side that neither will have it in them to administer the punishment I so clearly deserve. My sentence will lie there undelivered like a ringing phone it's someone else's turn to answer. The worst I'll probably get, says Chloe, is some vague theoretical lecture about the dangers of peer pressure and/or the evils of addiction, constructed from general terms and falsified personal anecdotes, and performed in such a nonaccusatory a-pro-po-nothing kind of manner that it may as well be an advert for Imodium Plus.

Before I went to bed last night I stuffed the cigarette packet in the back pocket of my good jeans. Then I put my good jeans in the dirty laundry basket.

Now I am playing the waiting game.

(There is no Phase IV.))

Instead of eating, Mum scrutinizes the Open Day itinerary which has the Tallow Chandlers' School crest in the top right-hand corner (it's a heavily militarized lamb silhouetted against a yellow sun like a partial ovine eclipse) and which I have already memorized. I know what she's thinking, so I decide to save us both some time.

"Debating society or the Audio Visual club?"

"Hmm?"

"The two o'clock clash. Do you want to go to the debating chamber or the media center for the Thirty-Six-Hour Short Film screening."

"Sorry, sweetheart. What?"

"They've got Thirty-Six Hours to make them," I explain. "They're not thirty-six hours long."

"I don't know," says Mum, laying down her knife and fork.

"Me neither," I admit. "I'd like to see the editing suite, but I also want to find out if drugs should be legalized."

"I don't know," Mum repeats. This time, though, I can see the equations. I can tell something is up, because her brow has underlined her hairline like it's a spelling mistake. "It's not the clash. It's the whole . . . Are you sure this place is right for you?"

"What's wrong with it?"

"Nothing. There's nothing *wrong* with it. Why, do *you* think something's wrong with it?"

"No."

"So you don't think it's a bit . . ." She looks around the room for the end of the sentence, as if it's written on flashcards. "White Bread No Crusts?"

"I don't even know what that means."

"I just mean . . ."

I give her a minute to collect her thoughts. When it's up, she takes my hand across the table, but I withdraw it because there's a time and a place (the place is In Private and the time is 1991–1999).

"Your father and I have been talking, and we don't want you blowing these exams out of proportion."

"I'm not."

"I know they probably seem very important at the present moment, but you've had a big year. We all have. And right now the thing to be concentrating on is enjoying yourself, and spending time doing the things that you want to be doing. And we just both feel that the scholarship might . . . It's too much pressure for you right now."

I think about the ice stretched across Letchmore Pond. "I mastered pressure in Year 6," I say, cracking an asterisk into the scalp of my Chocolate Crème Brûlée.

"We don't want you spreading yourself too thin."

"Actually, if you're worried about pressure, that's exactly what you want," I retort (felling pretty much a whole forest). This should win the argument. However, I know what we're really talking about. I lean across the table so no one else can hear. "You don't have to worry about the money."

"This has nothing to do with money."

"Well, good, because there won't be any involved. In a few weeks I'll be concentrating better because I can stop taking the anticonvuls—"

"You mustn't do that. Not until Mr. Fitzpatrick says it's okay."

"I know. That's what I meant. But it doesn't matter anyway, because the point is I've already decided to get the scholarship."

"You can't always decide these things."

"Why not?"

"Because there are forces beyond our control."

"I don't believe in Fate," I lie, looking quickly down at my palms, where the skin has grown back thin and pink. "It's a four-letter word. And I don't understand what it means anyway."

"It doesn't always matter what you believe," says Mum.

Chapter Sixteen

On the train home a pregnant woman offers me her seat. I tell her thanks but no thanks, but she insists and tells me that she's getting off at the next stop anyway. At the next stop she does indeed alight, which means get off, but I can see her get back on again in the next carriage and sit down again for a further fifteen minutes. Mum stands over me for the whole journey, hanging off the overhead rail like a shower curtain, which is really unhygienic, because there are companies that make signs to remind people to wash their hands that are kept in business only by people who forget to wash their hands. If I furrow my brow down over my eyes then she exists only from below the waist, like the woman in the *Tom and Jerry* cartoons. I do this for a few stops without looking up. Because it is rush hour, this means I get a whole parade of crotches in front of my face, which a few weeks ago probably wouldn't have set my mind racing.

Ever since Dad made such a big deal about disabling the parental controls on my Internet, I have been looking at porn pretty much every day. This is not for the purposes of masturbating (which Pete Sloss calls *master-bating* (as though it's something you have to perfect (which Pete swears it is))), because I am still waiting to have my first wet dream. (Pete is the reason I know about wet dreams. He claimed to have had one before we even started measuring our penises. The trick, he says, is to Sellotape a picture of a girl you like over your eyes before you fall asleep, so when your eyelids flutter (which is automatic for the people during REM sleep) she seeps into your subconscious and wanks you off.) Rather, my interest in pornography is purely educational, which is why I have been able to incorporate my daily viewings into my preexisting revision timetable without causing disruption. I have found pornography helpful for the following subjects:

1) Biology (obviously).
2) English (plenty of grammatical errors to spot, such as tautologies. For example, in the video title *Slutty Blonde Sucks and Fucks 4x Meat-Swords for Gangbang Facial* you do not need to say *Slutty*).
3) Maths (occasional stiffies (personal best so far 56.107 cubic centimeters)).

Moreover, pornography has taught me some miscellaneous lessons, which are arguably more relevant to my current situation. The most important of these lessons is about Human Relationships and The Power of Interpretation. I have (over)heard before (from Mum and Aunt Julie) many times about how pornography objectifies women, which means makes them into objects. However, I do not believe this to be the case. For example, consider these typical video titles:

1) *Blistering redhead begs for hot cock injection*
2) *Thirsty stripper slurps on tasty manaconda*
3) *Sizzling fuckslut rides flesh hydrant*

In all of these examples and many, many more the women are obviously not being made into objects. Rather, they are clearly the subjects (which you can easily see because they come before the verb), and it is in fact the men who are being objectified. This is also true from an artistic standpoint, because in the majority of scenes the only part of a man you can see is his penis. Sometimes this effect is achieved through camera angles and other times the man is literally hidden from view behind something physical (like a toilet wall or a cheese-and-tomato pizza), his penis poking through a hole in the middle of it like some exotic, floating vegetable. This is not to say that you don't sometimes get close-up shots of the women's genitals, too (usually it's a penis going into a vagina loads of times over, with that shallow echoey sound you get if you clap with cupped hands), but even then the camera will always eventually pull back to establish a wider context for the orifice, which you pretty much never get with the cocks. Moreover, in one scene that I saw in which a woman was giving a tug job (which is American for hand job), there was this disembodied male voice that kept saying, "Put me in your mouth." What the voice meant by this was "Perform inflatio on me," which (if you think about it) is basically the male performer admitting out loud that he's only a penis. (It was weird, almost like the man was proud of the fact that his entire existence had just tapered down to a single point.)

(I do not like this view of humanity. To me it says that we are simply crashing tides of genitals, just points and holes, two great armies of pluses and minuses coming together and amounting to nothing. However, this is not the lesson.)

The videos in the library on the site that I have been using (whose address I got from Pete Sloss in exchange for the promise of a photo of my mum) are sortable by several categories, such as Date Added, Duration, Top-Rated, and Most Popular. The difference between Most Popular and Top-Rated is that a video's popularity is determined by its total amount of views, while its critical standing is decided by aggregating its star ratings. Just like with normal films, the relationship between these two things is more complicated than direct proportionality: The Most Popular videos tend to be glossy and American, with name stars, familiar storylines, and high production values, while the Top-Rated are usually European and feel more real and upsetting. There are exceptions that prove these rules (I don't know how many exceptions it takes to *dis*prove a rule (or whether or not an exception that *did* disprove a rule would just be the exception that proved the rule that exceptions always prove rules)), the best example being a critically acclaimed series that has also found mainstream success called *Gloryhole Confessions*. *Gloryhole Confessions* (which has an average rating of 4.88 out of 5 (same as *Schindler's List* on IMDb)) follows the adventures of an unnamed Czech woman as she goes around a pretty European city that I think is Prague and alights with men in public toilets. The way this happens is that she enters a cubicle and sits down on the toilet and starts to masturbate herself off. This always occurs for between two and four minutes, at which point the woman pauses to survey her surroundings and notices something everyone else has already seen: an ominous circular ellipsis in the plywood wall about a meter from the floor and approximately fifteen centimeters in diameter. This is the "gloryhole," and no sooner has the woman noticed it than an erect penis sprouts through in such a way that suggests that the cubicle itself has grown the thing. (I have been watching *Gloryhole Confessions* on French revision nights because it helps remind me that inanimate objects can be masculine or feminine.) Then she performs inflatio on the penis, then takes off her pants and backs onto it until it sperms on her bum. However, this is not the weirdest thing about *Gloryhole Confessions*. The weirdest thing is how every time, just before she starts performing inflatio, the woman tells the penis (in subtitles) that she's never done anything like this before.

I have thought about this a lot. At first I assumed that the woman was a liar. However, that was before last week's Religious Studies class, when I found the clue in the videos' title.

Once you've noticed it, the similarities in dimensions between a toilet cubicle and a Catholic confessional are too obvious to ignore, and that's before you even start to consider the woman's posture during the act of inflatio, which is exactly like someone receiving communion (which, moreover, is the only other time you can put a whole person in your mouth). This means that the woman is not necessarily a liar, because in Catholicism once you've confessed your sins it's like they never happened in the first place.

This puts a completely different complexion on the matter. Back when I thought the woman was a liar I assumed that the penis in the wall belonged variously to different men in each installment of *Gloryhole Confessions,* because no one ever takes humbridge with her when she says she's never done this before (which they surely would if they knew it was bullspit (which they'd know for certain if the penis belonged to them on more than one occasion)). This would mean that the sex was random, impersonal, and anonymous, and nothing at all to do with emotions, which would have been really depressing and makes me feel hopeless and sad (which I think is why porn is sometimes called *blue* movies). However, if the woman isn't lying, but instead is preemptively confessing to the sin she's about to commit (and if the penis understands this (which it must do, because it represents the priest)), then there is no longer any reason to assume this is the case.

One of the things you learn how to do after watching pornography every day for a fortnight is to identify the male performers without being able to see their faces. Sometimes there's something obvious that gives the game away (a visual signature, like a tattoo or a scar), however, in the case of *Gloryhole Confessions,* there is very little to go on. Since I figured out the religious allusions in the series I have rewatched every episode of *Gloryhole Confessions* at least three times, pausing strategically and using my insect magnifying glass to study the wall penises for unusual markings. So far I have observed the following commonalities:

1) All of the penises are circumcised. (In itself this is not particularly surprising or helpful, because Prague has a large per capita Jewish population.)
2) When fully erect, all of the penises have a faint upward curvature of the shaft.
3) The skin of each penis is rubbed translucently thin in the heart-shaped valley beneath the bell end (as though through excessive masturbation or chronic chafing (which is a cause Pete Sloss is tireless in raising awareness of)).
4) Each penis is underscored by an evil-looking lattice of veins.
5) All of the penises are Caucasian.
6) All of the penises ejaculate in a series of quick then sustained then quick again bursts that look somehow kind of like an SOS sounds in Morse Code.
7) All of the penises are huge.

After cross-referencing with more than two hundred other high-resolution images I am 98% confident in saying that the reason for these striking commonalities is that all of the penises in *Gloryhole Confessions* belong to the same man. If I am correct in this conclusion, then *Gloryhole Confessions* is not the worst thing in the world (which I previously thought it might be) but instead the hopeful documentation of an enduring mahoganous relationship between two committed individuals who overcome significant obstacles (i.e., a wall) to be and stay together.

(This is the lesson: that sometimes something ugly is just something beautiful that I do not yet fully understand. Which is why whenever I think about *Gloryhole Confessions,* which I am doing right now, I get a warm rush of optimism.)

We are two and a half stops from home, and I am starting to anticipate the ambush that awaits me when we get there. Dad will open the door when we're still in the driveway. He'll have my good jeans in one hand, and in the other, held away from him between thumb and forefinger because what's inside it disgusts him so much, a see-through sandwich bag. It's Exhibit A, the cigarette packet, bagged and tagged, and taken down in damning evidence against me. At first, Mum won't understand. It can't be what it looks like. There must be an explanation, so she'll look to me to provide one. Her eyes are wide and pleading. She wants to believe me. I look at Dad. He's not saying anything. His face is a multiple choice with no right answers. I'll be grounded indefinitely for my own good. No more bad influences. Solitary confinement until I'm old enough to leave home. Or, better yet, they'll make me volunteer at a hospice full of throat-cancer patients. I'll spend my Saturdays playing Scrabble against old men with external voiceboxes, get cold sweats for the rest of my life any time I see someone using an electric razor. Or maybe they kick me out into the street. Disown me completely, like an adoption in reverse. I'll have to sell my organs in backstreet clinics or learn to play "Wonderwall" on the guitar. One day they'll pass me in a tube station stairwell. They'll be dressed in all their finery, up in town for dinner and a show. It's a special occasion. Their silver wedding anniversary. They won't recognize the toothless, ageless husk in the soiled sleeping bag as their onetime son, but on their way past they have the good grace to pause their conversation. Dad's hand disappears into a tuxedo pocket and emerges in a shower of dull, copper change, and then they walk on, their consciences clear, shivering for a second into each other, pulling the other tighter around them, and momentarily, unbeknownst even to themselves, mourning the memory of the child they've forgotten to remember.

At Burnt Oak, Mum asks me why I'm smiling.

I tell her it's something I remembered. Then I smile some more, because I am the boy who thought he had impunity but never did, because his parents never were splitting up in the first place.

However, when we get home, there is luggage on the porch.

Chapter Seventeen

In profile, the fine white down on the waitress's cheeks and nose makes her look like a cactus, which is appropriate because she gets prickly when Dad asks her if she *parlays onglay*. We are eating outside of a seafood restaurant in the Old Harbor. (In fact, we are eating outside of every seafood restaurant in the Old Harbor, it's just that the chairs, the table, and the waitress belong to one of them in particular.) According to Google, La Rochelle has a moderate tourist trade and is used to welcoming guests of all nationalities. However, at this time of year it is Not in Season, which means that, like a pineapple, it is much tougher to get into. This is not a problem for me, though, because I am a native.

Je m'appelle Marcel.

The sky is a clear, picture-book blue, and both the sun and I have got our hats on but the day is as cold as the dairy aisle. In French we have a phrase for days like today: *Le Fond De L'Air,* which literally means The Bottom of the Air. Above it, music from the market stalls drifts across the concourse and mingles with the strings twanging inside the café. Where we are seated is the exact point where two rivers of sound flow into an ocean of nonsense, which is precisely what Dad is making in his attempts to order a *carafe of low.* With his hands he carves an hourglass in the air and then with two fingers taps at his forearm like he's trying to bring up a vein.

"War . . . Tur?" he asks louder, even though Mum and I both speak French.

The waitress regards him with a mixture of amusement and unease, cocking her head to one side like he's a monkey in a zoo that's just done something uncomfortably human.

"*Du l'eau,*" says Mum quietly.

"War tur," repeats Dad, this time in a deep voice. But the joke, much like his request for The Carpe Diem, falls on a stony silence and fails to take root. In the end he orders with a stab of his finger from the Specials Board. Even though it is a gesture of defeat, the act of him ordering from the board at all forces me to Photoshop him and the waitress into a wild array of compromising positions. (It's easy to do. It is like every Romantic Comedy I have ever seen. At first they hate each other, but an hour and a half later they're together in the pushed-back passenger seat of Dad's car, kissing and space-docking (which is the one where you freeze a turd inside a condom and use it as a dildo).) The nausea rides up in me from my stomach to the penthouse. I swallow a burp and remember that I don't trust him.

Here in France, I try to remind myself, we have a far more progressive attitude toward adultery. We also have a word for that feeling you get when you're on a cliff and you think you might want to throw yourself off it: *L'Appel Du Vide,* which means The Call of the Empty. This suggests that the French know lots more about The Human Condition than the English, which is why when they say *Que Sera, Sera* it's not because they're going to Wembley. And if cheating *en Français* is an inevitable part of life (written into our DNA every bit as much as mahogany is written into the penguins'), then there is really no reason for me to think as little of my dad as I do right now. While he salts a slab of baguette and unfolds a map from A's six to zero I observe him through my new rose-tinted *lunettes.* With a great effort, I summon up all my vocab, run through as many *subjonctif* conjugations as I can think of, and pretend we really do live *en Français.* For a moment, it works. I see myself on the cliff edge, pouring respect into the *vide* between us, a thick, lavalike substance that will set solid as cement in the afternoon *soleil.* Next to me is Maman and on the cliff opposite is Papa, his arm draped gracefully over the slender shoulders of his hairy-legged mistress, whose name is almost certainly but not necessarily Elise and who Maman views with no more suspicion than she does the dry cleaner. (Sex is simply another thing in their life together that is just as easily outsourced.) Papa and Elise, I see now, have a cement mixer of their own. Theirs is full of trampled touchlines and shared interests, happy memories of Serge and I playing *au foot*. Across the soon-to-be-forgotten divide we wave to each other in a Gallic fashion. *Ensemble nous sommes une grande famille heureuse.*

But then Dad knocks over the vinegar and says Oopsie Daisy, which is not exactly meeting me halfway. If someone chokes, I will now have no option but to volunteer his services as a doctor.

("Vite! Est-il un médecin dans le restaurant?!"

"Oui! Mon pere, l'adultère!")

Otherwise, he could be lost to me forever.

"Le Rosh Hell?" Dad had echoed when I'd told him the place I would hypothetically go if I could go anywhere I wanted. "Above anyplace else in the entire world? Above *Disney*?"

"Yes," I had replied.

"What if it wasn't hypothetical?" he'd continued, after a few more chevrons had disappeared beneath us.

"What if hypothetically it wasn't hypothetical?"

"Right."

So, sat in the passenger seat of my father's dual-control mobile office on the way back from a hospital appointment that had it been an airplane we would've missed by the length of a film, I had tried to conjure up a hypothetical scenario in which I was being asked where I would go given the nonhypothetical situation that I could go anyplace in the world.

"La Rochelle," I had repeated.

"Why Le Rosh Hell?" Dad had asked.

"Pourquoi pas?" I had replied, enigmatically.

"Okay, then," Dad had said eventually. And then, after another mile, "Where even is that?"

La Rochelle is a small city on the west coast of France with a population of about 75,000 people (which makes it France's answer to Weston-super-Mare). After lunch I ask one of these people for directions to the library as revision for my French Oral, only to discover that there isn't one (unless you count the one in the university (which neither of us do)). Although I'm too proud to admit this to Dad, La Rochelle is not exactly how I imagined it. For example, so far the only swimming pool I have encountered is the one outside my hotel room window. Along with the boulangerie and the discotheque I was expecting the bibliotheque and piscine to be La Rochelle's central landmarks. If my textbooks are to be believed (which I'm starting to doubt they are), then these ought to be the North, South, East, and West on the townspeople's mental maps. (In French classes, you need only take the second left after one or continue all straight past another to arrive at any known destination.)

In the end, it doesn't matter so much what the town of La Rochelle does or doesn't have to offer, because as soon as Dad finds our location on his map (which is of the whole Charente-Maritime region) I get tired and a headache and have to go back to the hotel. In my room I try to do some Geography revision, but the Central Asian capitals get stuck on the tip of my tongue, and the East Asian ones further back still, so I put on my boxing helmet (because the room isn't seizure-proof) and shut my eyes.

I wake up to a kind of gulping sound, the sort of noise an embarrassed cartoon character would make while tugging its collar. The room is dark, the hotel is quiet (except for Dad snoring through the wall (which means he's been drinking)), and the clock reads 06:27, which has no special significance that I know of, apart from being at least fifteen hours after I shut my eyes. My headache is gone, but in its place is a surface of dust thick enough to leave footprints in. Moreover, my tongue is dry and furry, and when I try to swallow it clacks against my teeth like a typewriter, which is how I know that the second gulp isn't from me, either. It's not until the third one that I locate the source. They're coming from outside my window. I get to it in time to see a mysterious figure standing at the side of the swimming pool. He is encased from head to toe in a Samurai-black wetsuit and stooped under the weight of a heavy-looking oxygen tank, the flippers on his feet pointing ahead of him like misshapen shadows. I press my nose against the window and my breath fogs the glass and by the time I've wiped it clear the man has lowered himself down onto the concrete, his legs dangling into the water, his palms clamped together and his head bowed over the pool. He stays like this awhile in what looks from four stories up like prayer. And then he falls forward.

"Gulp," says the water, tugging at its collar a fourth time like it hopes no one's seen. (And no one has. Except for me.)

From where I'm looking, only one of the four divers is distinguishable from the others. Three of them are dressed identically in black, with their faces framed tightly in rubber, but a yellow vine runs up the spine of the fourth's wetsuit and blooms at the neck into a jungle of blond hair. I take this as a sign that he is in charge, a suspicion that is confirmed when the others congregate around him and he lectures them. Then he assumes the role of Baptist, plunging each of them through the water like he's converting Muslims. Only once they're all saved does he attach his own tank and join them underwater.

The bottom of the pool is checkered like a chess board, and for almost an hour, directed by the blond man (who stops them every other length to offer instructions), the divers comb it in straight lines rook-style. First they sweep horizontally, then vertically, and before they're done no square is left unexamined. However, when the sun begins to rise and the hotel starts to stir the unit emerges from the water empty-handed. Which can mean one of only two things:

1) Whatever it is they were looking for wasn't there to begin with.
2) It's still there now.

That day, we visit both the Maritime Museum and the Aquarium, and even though both are quite interesting (Mum buys me books from both), I find myself unengaged. According to the plaque in the lobby, the La Rochelle Aquarium contains 3,000,000 liters of sea water, which is why 800,000 tourists flock to it each year to explore The Mysteries of the Deep. However, none of these mysteries can fully distract me from the one outside my hotel room window.

"So what's the deal with you and the Gower girl?" asks Dad in the lift after dinner.

"We don't have a deal," I say, putting the clitoris bet to the back of my mind. "I just thought she'd want to look after Jaws 2 if we were away."

"She's very pretty," says Mum.

"I tell you what"—Dad winks—"you must've learned a trick or two from your old man after all . . ."

Before bed I set my alarm for 06:28 (two perfect numbers). Of all of the mysteries in my life right now, this seems like the one I'm best equipped to solve.

I'm awake ten minutes before my alarm like I always am so I can turn it off before it wakes up Mum or Dad, which would spell the end of my mission before it's even begun. The rain outside is hard enough to sound like a single note, which is also (it seems when I rip open the curtains) hard enough to discourage yesterday's divers. With my whole body beating like my heart is a one-man band, I pull the shower cap from under my pillow and stamp off my pajama bottoms. Beneath them, because I don't own swimming trunks, is a pair of black boxers with a yellow trim. Swimming is not something I'm an expert at. However, I do not anticipate this being a problem, as the main skill required of me during this enterprise is sinking, something I expect to come naturally.

The rain falls on the pool as a million different species, cats and dogs just two among them. Sitting on the side with my feet dangling and the downpour driving my head into a bow, I set the stopwatch on my Casio SGW100 to fourteen minutes and two seconds (which is exactly five minutes less than the world record (because I am Erring on the Side of Caution)) and make myself brave by saying my name twenty-two times. When it no longer sounds like my own, I fall forward.

If the water swallows, I don't hear because beneath it the whole world is on mute.

Chapter Eighteen

There are five stages to drowning. The first thing the boy in the year below who didn't know about Pressure would have experienced is Surprise, which occurs when the victim recognizes that he is in danger and becomes afraid. In all likelihood, at this point the boy would not actually have been far below the surface. What is most probable, in fact, is that his head was tilted back and his face and arms were above water. He would not have cried out, which could have saved him, because all of his energy would have gone into the desperate clasping for handfuls of air that would have eventually driven him under. This is when stage two would have begun. Stage two is Involuntary Breath Holding, which is the body trying to go into

Safe Mode. This is when the boy's epiglottis would have closed over his airway to prevent water from going down the wrong hole, which is what would have deprived him of oxygen. The lack of oxygen ushers in stage three, Unconsciousness or Respiratory Arrest, during which he would have sunk peacefully to the bottom of Letchmore Pond at a speed determined by the amount of air still trapped in his lungs. Once there the absence of oxygen from his brain would have triggered a violent seizure, which is called Hypoxic Convulsion and explains why when they found him the look cast across the swollen blue puppy fat of his face was one of blind terror. This is stage four.

Then he would have died, thus concluding The Five Stages of Drowning, which is when The Five Stages of Grieving would have begun. (When the boy's parents attended the memorial assembly as guests of the school, I would estimate that they were still at Denial, because the way they smiled up at Mr. Clifford when they shook his hand made it look like they were accepting a sports-day prize on their son's behalf.)

I am at stage two (Involuntary Breath Holding) when I feel myself lighten. I rise through the water like a bubble of oxygen but when I get to the surface I don't pop. Instead, I keep on floating, weightless and dry, up into the air and through the rain, until I'm where I was yesterday, looking down on a figure suspended below the water. In every way he looks like me, except chlorine has painted his eyes red. From four stories high, where my parents are sleeping, I watch myself in the third person. Miss Farthingdale was wrong, because there I am, a Photographic Memory waiting to be taken. Beneath the water, I look calm and at peace as though the fear has passed straight through me without me noticing it, which is how I know that my soul has left my body. In seconds I will fall unconscious and out of sight, but for now, with no one in the world awake to observe me, I am a subatomic particle in Copenhagen. I am in two places at once.

Across the courtyard from my room, a light comes on.

I return to myself in the flutter of involuntary leg spasms, which saves my life. My head punches through the water with a greedy gasp. Desperately, I flail my arms in the direction of land until my palm slaps against concrete, and only then do I recognize the sound of the rain drumming on my shower cap. It is the sound of the present. Which means I'm still here.

Slumped over the poolside, I spew a slug of spit down my chin and, waiting for the fire in my lungs to burn out, assess my options before realizing that I don't have any, because if you have only one option, then it isn't an option at all.

I need to know.

I reset my stopwatch for three minutes. Then I screw shut my eyes and breathe out until I feel myself empty.

This time I sink like a stone.

I open my eyes with my feet on a white square. Time feels stodgy, like in a dream (and my synaptic fluids nonconductive), but with the sun just moments from rising it is doubly of the essence, so as quickly as I can I decide on a bold Spanish Opening and stride ahead two squares as if to free the King's Bishop. However, as I lunge forward I lose balance. My left foot starts to drift away toward the surface, and turning to watch it go, I see that dawn has already broken. Overhead, the first beams of sunlight have broken through the clouds and flit across the uneven water like they're skim-reading Braille, which means soon the whole world will stir, which means this might be the only chance I get. In which case there is no time for strategy. I scan the board frantically, hopping illegally this way and that. I don't know what I'm looking for (only that I'll know when I find it), but for a slow second there's a part of me that believes all the answers I seek are hidden somewhere in this pool, from the mysteries of my parents' marriage to the capital of Mongolia. The question is only what form they will take. However, when my alarm blinks and my throat screams for air they've yet to take any, and still nothing especially makes sense. I am just about to admit defeat when the sun makes its move. Darting through a hole in the storm, it strikes the water and lands on the floor in front of me in a perfect Caro-Kann defense. And there, illuminated at the border of the occupied square, is my sunken treasure. I reach out to clasp it with the white, wrinkled fingers of a suddenly old man (as though the sight of it alone has granted me wisdom beyond my years), but no sooner has my hand closed around the doubloon than a force beyond my control straps an arm around my chest, causing me to breathe in a lungful of water.

The next thing I know I'm on the side of the pool. I recognize my assailant from the dripping shards of blond mane that anoint my head. I am laid flat on my back, the lion man on top of me, pumping furiously at my chest like he's trying to crush my ribs to dust. *"Qu'est-ce que tu fait?!"* he demands over and over, and then for punctuation pinches my nose, because on his patch the punishment for trespassing is death by suffocation. His bearded jaw yawns open like the pizza box at David Driscoll's house, and in it, for a second time, I see oblivion. But before he can plug shut my mouth, my torso erupts and a flume of watery sick darts down his open throat. Now it is his turn to retch, which gives me time to tighten my fist around the bounty. (If he wants it, he'll have to prize it from my cold, dead hand.)

"Fire!" I shout, at the top of my voice, which is what you're supposed to say if you're being attacked, because people don't run toward an assault. I fold up like a deck chair and trawl my mind for other survival tips, but the only one I can think of is about being buried in an avalanche and spitting so you know which way down is. "Fire!" I repeat, the rain lashing around us. "Fire! Fire! Fire!"

It works. By the time the lion man stops coughing, a confused receptionist has appeared by the poolside, which means now there are three of us, which officially makes a crowd. My bet is he won't be stupid enough to try anything in a crowd. And I'm right.

"*Fiyuh?*" he asks, scooping me into his arms, as though my well-being is his raison d'être. And then, to the receptionist: "*Allumez le feu!*"

In the lobby, the receptionist swaddles me in a blanket and sits me down in front of the electric fire. The flames burn blue like the lion man's eyes, which are trained on me like crosshairs from behind the desk, where he towels off his blond hair and tries to gauge what I know. As I return his gaze, it occurs to me that he looks exactly like Hitler should have looked. For a second, I consider a mocking salute. However, it will take more than gloating sarcasm to unlock my right hand.

I don't open it until I know I'm safe. Back on the fourth floor, in the bathroom with the door bolted behind me, standing shivering in front of the sink, I slowly uncurl my old-man fingers like I'm releasing a butterfly. Which is when I realize I've been holding my prize so tight that I've branded its shape into the heel of my palm. (The words are no less clear than if I'd pressed a key into a bar of soap.)

The next day at the airport when they ask me to empty my pockets, I tell them they're already empty.

"I knew it!" Dad says to Mum, when the metal detector beeps. "I knew he was a robot! And to think you told me you and C-3PO were just good friends."

The security guard takes one look at me and waves me on my way.

And on my way I go, secretly thumbing the object around my trouser pocket.

Chapter Nineteen

On the way back from the airport, once we've dropped Mum home because she's not feeling so well, Dad drives me to Chloe's to collect Jaws 2. As soon as her front door swings open, I understand what Dad meant when he said the conservatory wasn't the only thing that needed planning permission (if I knew what he was talking about (which I didn't)). Like the house whose entrance she bars, the breasts of the woman stood in front of me are the largest I have ever seen.

"Hello?" she says, her lips rounding out the O as if in homage to her best feature.

"You must be Maris," I say.

"Maris?" she replies.

(*Maris Piper,* I think, cleverly.)

"Are you collecting?" she continues. "Hold on, I'll get my purse. You poor thing."

In the driveway, Dad honks and waves.

"Oh," says Maris, "I'm so sorry. I didn't know she had a lesson today. Ella! *Ella!*" And before I can explain why I'm here, Chloe's sister, Ella, appears at the top of the staircase.

"Wait a second," she says into a mobile phone. "New new Mum needs me . . . Dunno, probably just misplaced her sense of self-worth again." And then, down the stairs to Maris: "Have you tried looking in your bra?"

"Actually, young lady," Maris says, smiling hard, "I think there's something you've forgotten."

"Have you tried looking in your bra, *slut?*" asks Ella.

"No. Try again." Maris laughs.

"Home-wrecker?"

"You've got a driving lesson."

"Err, no I haven't," says Ella, hoisting her middle finger and leaving.

"I'm so sorry," says Maris, turning back to me. "She's under a lot of stress, what with A-levels and . . . the Bird Flu epidemic. I'll be right back."

But before she can disappear up the stairs, I explain I'm here to see Chloe and apologize for calling her Maris.

Jessica (Maris's real name) shows me to Chloe's room, which is in the attic. There's no answer when we knock, and when Jessica opens the door we find Chloe sitting cross-legged on the bed, playing with a stress doll, her back turned to us and her head pinched between a set of headphones. The stereo stack that she's plugged in to is as big as a life support machine. It sits in the middle of the floor, next to Jaws 2 (who is asleep in his sphere), with its breezeblock-sized speakers at opposite ends of the room, laying facedown on the carpet like hostages in a bank robbery. Next to the sound system even the color-coded A0 revision timetable (which is pinned to the slanted ceiling (which makes me feel like we're in the turret of a castle)) seems irrelevant, and when Jessica pulls the plug I half expect Chloe to drop dead. Instead, a depth charge of noise turns the ground beneath our feet to quicksand (causing Jaws 2 to bolt awake and run into a wall), and Chloe spins round, whipping the headphone cord through the air.

"GET OUT!" she screams at Jessica, and flings away the stress doll.

"She's okay, really," says Chloe, about Jessica once she's gone. "But she won't last. Ella's decided. The speakers were her idea. Do you want a Dr Pepper?"

I nod, and Chloe opens her bedside cabinet, which is actually a mini-fridge. I must let my surprise show, because Chloe shrugs and says, "Divorce."

"Don't worry," she adds, handing me the can and sliding a laptop out from under her bed. "It's not all shit. And the bits that are you get used to. Do you want to watch *The Exorcist*?"

"Can't," I say. "My dad's in the car."

To confirm this, Chloe stands on her bed and pokes her

head through the window, then drops back down and draws the blind. Then she slides closer and tells me about a documentary she saw about a parrot who witnesses his owner's murder and testifies in court by repeating over and over the name of her ex-husband, who's the one that did it. The prosecutor, who's trying to charge another man with the murder (just because he's black), argues that the testimony should be discounted because the parrot can't be cross-examined, and in the end the witness is discredited and his statement stricken from the records because the court artist can't do feathers.

"And?" I ask, when it looks like she's finished.

"And the black man gets the chair."

"I meant why are you telling me? What's this got to do with anything?"

"That's what I've been trying to figure out," says Chloe. "I think this might be how Jaws 2 fits in. I think maybe he knew something about the affair and someone got to him."

"What do you mean?"

"What if he saw something he wasn't supposed to see? I've looked into it. There's this drug you can get, it's called Simvastatin. It's for fat people, to lower their cholesterol. You can get it over the counter. But guess what the side effect is. Guess!"

I ask for a clue.

"*You lose your memory!* Think about it. Didn't you say he was thinner?"

"Yeah, but—"

"Well, there you go," says Chloe, and stamps the enigmatic smile across her face like she's approving a package. But this time, I'm not standing for it.

"So," I say, in the language of a small island off the coast of Portugal called Sarcasm, "you're saying my dad wiped my hamster's memory with a weight-loss drug so he wouldn't let on what he knew about his secret affairs?"

"No," says Chloe. "Not necessarily. Could be your mum, too. I've decided. She knows all about it. Mine did. They probably just don't want you finding out till after the exams. That'd explain why she keeps looking at you funny. I was thinking about it—"

"Why?" I interrupt.

"Because she's feeling guilty," says Chloe. "Cos no one knows the long-term effects yet, so Jaws 2 might never remember who he is, like Richey from the Manics."

But that's not what I meant. (I've heard enough. (Inside, something's swung.))

"Why were you thinking about me?"

This stops Chloe in her tracks. Suddenly, she seems embarrassed. "Fuck off," she says, "I wasn't. I just—"

"You just what?" I ask, sensing an advantage. "You just couldn't stand the thought that not everyone's family's all effed up like yours is."

"What does that mean?" asks Chloe quietly.

"Fucked up!" I shout, feeling the words start to overtake me. "It means fucked all up! And it's how you'd swear, too, if your parents cared enough about you to pay attention!"

Chloe doesn't say anything to this, so to avoid an awkward silence I keep going. I tell her that just because her mum and dad didn't love her sufficiently doesn't give her the right to make up lies about mine, that she's just a jealous, home-wrecking slut, and that she is not my friend. And then, because she still hasn't said anything, I take a pound coin from my pocket and lay it on top of the stereo stack like a full stop.

"There," I say. "Now I don't owe you anything."

I notice the stress doll while I'm putting Jaws 2 back in his cage. It is naked, white, bald, and almost blank, its face in inverted commas made up of three equal-sized black divots spaced out like holes in a bowling ball to represent two eyes and a mouth, and I probably wouldn't think anything of it if not for the needle protruding from its right temple. When I pick it up to inspect it closer, I notice two things straightaway: first, that the whole head is dimpled like a golf ball, and second, that Chloe has scraped her initial into the rubber just above where its left ear should be. However, before I can speculate about the significance of this, Chloe is upon me.

"Don't touch that!" she screeches, flapping desperately at my arms and causing me to throttle the doll (which in turn makes her gasp (as though the figure has voodoo properties)). *"Give it back!"*

For a while we struggle, Chloe grabbing because she wants the doll and me withholding it for the same reason (because she wants the doll), until, after a moment or two, something about the strength of her determination frightens me and I relinquish my grip, letting it fall to the ground. Chloe rushes to its aid and scoops it off the carpet in both hands (the same way I taught her to pick up Jaws 2), and calls me a fucking dickhole. Gently, she cradles the doll like it's a wounded bird and starts to cry. Which is when it occurs to me that the capital C etched into the side of its head isn't her initial after all.

It's a surgery scar.

While Chloe wipes a sleeve across her sad white face like a bad mime artist, I have time to reexamine the dimples. This time their significance is obvious. (A feeling of dread unravels my intestines.) Every one of them is a needle wound.

"It's not what you think," says Chloe in a hurry, when she sees me staring down in horror at the black magic in her palm. "I can explain."

But before she can try I'm out the door.

That night in bed I reexamine the evidence against Mum and Dad in light of the new development that my coinvestigator is trying to destroy me. Then I think about my feelings, which is the bit that makes A Life in the Day so much harder than A Day in the Life. First come the obvious ones: Anger, Betrayal, and Confusion (easy as ABC). Anger at Chloe for trying to destroy me (and at myself for trusting her), Betrayal at Chloe for her betrayal (obviously), and Confusion at her motives. Next, though, is the weight pressing down on my solar plexus, which is harder to identify. At first, I assume this feeling is Relief, because without Chloe's testimony the case against my parents is suddenly flimsy, which means that I can drop the charges against them. However (if you think about it (which I just have)), Relief isn't a feeling. Rather, it is the release of waste emotions (like Shame or Anxiety or Fear), which is probably why urination is sometimes called *relieving yourself*. This means that Relief is the opposite of Despair: They are both acts of substitution, and therefore cannot have mass (which means that Relief can't be the thing pressing down on my solar plexus).

For a while I struggle to diagnose the emotion I am experiencing. It's the hardest I've had to think about something like this since the special sort of Pride I felt when I won a Nobel Peace Prize in one of Mum's dreams. However, pretty much the second I put my watch back an hour (because I'm back in England, where there's still no future), I realize that it's Guilt.

For a while, I think about the things I said to Chloe and start to wonder where they came from. (I think about what Mum said when I wished she was dead, that it wasn't me wishing it, and for a moment I relax, until I remember that I can't use that defense anymore, because whatever part of me it was that did the wishing then is now at the bottom of a bin bag.) However, the remorse that I feel over calling Chloe a home-wrecking slut is not the only reason for the pressure on my rib cage. The other reason I feel bad (the biggie) is that I do not feel better. In other words, I feel guilty for not being relieved. The reason this is so incriminating is it proves that all along I have secretly been hoping to find my parents guilty in order to justify the suspicions I have been harboring against them.

(I remember waiting for my test results, how afraid I was that the doctors would tell me there was nothing wrong with me, and how it felt instead when they told me what I had.)

———

For some time I toy with the idea of admitting Chloe's testimony into evidence despite her obvious conflict of interests, but whichever way I look at it, I can't ignore the fact that my findings are fatally compromised. After a while, though, as my body gets more tired, my mind gets heavier and starts to sink inevitably toward Jessica's breasts (which are large enough to exert their own gravitational pull), and when I fall asleep I dream that I'm a satellite in orbit around a giant, pink planetary sphere. The dream is silent like a really old film, which means that the orb doesn't have a name. To begin with, I find this unnerving and try hard to remember the names of the planets so I can identify the mass I'm revolving around. However, every mnemonic I remember just reminds me of another slightly weirder mnemonic, with each one in turn taking me a step further away from the answer until the whole thing loops back on itself and starts again from the beginning like a snake eating its own tail or someone performing inflatio on themselves (which Pete Sloss says you can do if you have your ribs removed). Each circuit of the mnemonics (from My Very Educated Mother Just Showed Us Nine Planets to My Very Economical Mother Just Saved Us Nine Pencils to My Very Elegant Mother Just Sewed Us Nine Purses to My Very Edible Mother Just Shat Us Nine Pizzas to My Very Elephant Mother Just Sawed Us Nine Porpoises to My Very Endless Mother Just Sank Us Nine Pygmies to My Very Enema Mother Just Sand Us Nine Problem to My Very Egg Mother Just Syphilis Us Nine Probably and back again) takes the exact same amount of time to complete, which I know for sure because they all coincide perfectly with one full revolution of the nameless planet,

and after a few round-trips I start to forget what it is I was trying to remember in the first place. Which is just as well, because it means that when it starts changing color I can just
enjoy the show.

As the sphere reinvents itself again and again in front of my
eyes I feel a great, wordless calm washing over me. All at once
I'm in orbit around a gadzillion different colors. Some of them
I recognize from places and faces and everyday objects, and
some of them are so unfamiliar that I'm convinced no one's
ever seen them before, but the one thing they all have in common is that none of them has a name, which for now at least
means that they have everything in common. Eventually, as I
continue to spin, even the letters in the mnemonics evaporate,
leaving behind just a residual melody that runs peacefully
around my mind until I feel an enormous quiet, this great infinity with all things, like I'm on the verge of understanding
something so basic it will change my understanding of everything. But before I can figure out what it is that I understand,
I become aware of something violent. The melody is speeding
up. Which can mean only one thing. That I'm orbiting closer
and closer to the surface of the sphere, which now I realize was
never a planet in the first place but actually a fiery star, which
makes me the planet and every round-trip I make a year. And
now the years are passing much too quickly as the melody
plays faster and faster until I'm a pebble rattling around a basin
toward a drain in ever smaller concentric circles and I realize
the star has changed color again, but this time to black, which
technically isn't a color at all because it absorbs every sort of
light, which means the star's imploding, so I try to shout for

help, which is when I realize that the hole has absorbed that, too, all my language and with it my power to think, which has only made it bigger and blacker and its gravitational pull stronger, and now I'm too heavy to escape the lure of the collapsing star, and in the seconds before I disappear completely into the expanding nothing all I'm left with is the silent, shapeless hope that Chloe will pop me with her giant, glinting needle.

Chapter Twenty

When I wake up I immediately conduct an inventory of all the words I know in no particular order, including proper nouns. However, I get distracted before I'm done because the covers are wet. At first I assume I've had another wind-down seizure but I don't have a headache and the dark patch on the sheets isn't me-shaped. Instead, it looks like one of the tests the school counselor gives you that doesn't have wrong answers. Moreover, in my belly button I find a pool of liquid. It reminds me of the translucent moat that surrounds the yolk in a fried egg before it's safe to eat.

(I remember the look on Pete's face when he told us all about his wet dream, how proud he was, like he'd come first in something. However, this doesn't feel like a victory. Instead, it reminds me of another thing Pete told me once, which was that if ever I really wanted to treat myself, all I needed to do was sit on my hand until it fell asleep. I had no idea what he was talking about and I remember furbatim what he said when I asked. (It seems appropriate now, in light of what feels more than anything else like my body's latest in a long line of mutinies. (Mutinies on board a ship that I'm not even sure I'm the captain of)):

"It makes it feel like it's someone else's.")

There are no more clean bedsheets in my cupboard which means once I've cleaned myself up I have to go downstairs to the utility room, which I haven't been into since Mum's photo habit got out of hand. I negotiate the landing in darkness because it's 04:12 and because I can. The carpet feels like sand between my toes, and when my foot touches down on the cold smoothness of the lino at the bottom of the staircase, I pretend I'm stepping onto Letchmore Pond. The whole way down the corridor I imagine that the ground could give way beneath me at any moment, and when the door rears up at the end of it I feel something in my stomach that's suspiciously close to Disappointment. The room beyond is the kitchen. There is no mistaking this, on account of the pool of color that bleeds under the utility room door.

The light is on in the darkroom. Which is weird.

———

I try the handle with my middle finger, pressing down as hard as I can at the most hygienic point, but nothing gives, so I inch away from the fulcrum and try again. Finally, after several unsuccessful attempts, I am forced all the way to the end of the lever (to a billion billion). However, when the handle does at last give way I realize the door is locked, which in this house we don't believe in. All of the keys in the house are kept in the key box, which is tacked to the kitchen wall next to the empty spice rack because one summer Dad was really into attaching stuff to other stuff. The word KEYS is carved into the front of the box (so as not to discriminate against blind burglars), which is shaped like a house in microcosm (so as not to discriminate against illiterate ones), and when I unhook the latch and the door swings open I have my pick of a dozen sets. Everything, in fact, except the one I'm looking for.

I find the key I'm looking for while I'm picking the lock on the utility room door with a paperclip I got from the clay frog on the windowsill. It's already in the door, which has been locked from the inside.

"Hello?" I ask the door politely, in the same voice I use to answer the landline.

No one says anything.

"Who's there?" I inquire louder, pressing my ear against the wood.

The answer is the same (i.e., silence). But this time the workings are different. This time it sounds like someone saying nothing.

"Hidden somewhere in that room," I say (courageously) to the intruder I'm now convinced is in the darkroom, "are two things. The first thing is a tiny piece of radioactive material, and the second is a Geiger Counter, which I've attached to a diabolical mechanism, a bit like the one in the board game Mousetrap." I pause to give him the chance to give himself up, which he doesn't take. "This is your first and final warning. Your chances of survival are increased twofold if you open the door so I can observe you." I pause again, this time for effect. "You have until I count to twelve, because, luckily for you, I don't believe in round numbers."

A dozen Mississippis later, the only sound inside the darkroom is the simple subtraction of someone holding their breath.

"Right," I hear myself announce. "I'm coming in."

I pick up the Get Well Soon card next to the clay frog. It's from Aunt Julie and Uncle Tony. I open it to the message (*Feeling ruff?*) and slide it under the utility room door to catch the key with, which is a trick I learned from a spy film that wasn't James Bond but thought it was. "It's got a dog on the front," I explain to the intruder. "With its leg in a cast. Cos I had an operation." I take the paperclip and set to work dislodging the key. "On my brain," I add, nervously. "I'm getting better now, but you still can't fight me, okay. Agreed?"

" . . . "

"If you agree, then don't say anything at all for six seconds," I command. Then I count twenty-four Niles. Then I jiggle the paperclip in the lock until I feel it loosen its grip on the key. With a nudge, I set it free and wait for it to rattle on the floor. But the noise never comes.

I can taste loose change in my saliva.

Gravity has stopped working.

Which would probably seem more remarkable if I didn't already know it was about to.

My whole body tingles like one big funny bone. I can feel myself shrinking inside it.

I don't know how long I'm away, except it feels like every second I've ever saved. When I come back around, I'm in bed, with Mum and Dad hovering over me, their brows furrowed like storm clouds. I try to ask what happened, but it comes out as a single word without vowels in it that isn't rhythm. There's still the taste of copper on my tongue, which is tender and swollen. I've bitten halfway through it.

"You had an event," says Mum, like she's somehow understood me. "What's the last thing you remember?"

I open my last saved version and scroll through from the start. In no particular order, I remember the following things: a sports-day race, the blood thumping in my ears the moment before the moment I realize I'm going to win, like the numbness that comes the second before you realize you've burned yourself, the taste of soap, Mum telling a joke backward because she's forgotten the start, walking past a lamppost at the exact moment that it lights up, the first time I see identical twins, sneaking downstairs during a dinner party and eating an olive that I think is a grape, the shock I feel before the realization that I like olives, a power cut, Dad putting the flashlight in his mouth so his cheeks glow red, my first swear word and the shape it makes of my mouth, a piece of graffiti on the side of a railway bridge that says GIVE PEAS A CHANCE, Mr. Brown accidentally saying erection results in History, a small boy with the same name as me sitting on his uncle's shoulders and peering into a casket . . . I skip to the end.

"I was in bed."

"Th-th-that's right," says Mum.

"What's today?" asks Dad.

"The day before tomorrow."

"And what day's that?"

"Monday."

He looks at his watch, then shows it to Mum. Over their shoulders, the sun is rising. "And what's the day after today?"

I consider my answer carefully.

"Today."

Chapter Twenty-One

The day after yesterday is Tuesday, which is the day of our first exam.

"If you don't know it now, you'll never know it," says Mr. Carson smugly to no one in particular outside the sports hall, while everyone fights over formulae (correct plural form) like ducks over bread crusts. I partake halfheartedly in the feeding frenzy. Pre-exam etiquette dictates that I pretend to be panicked and tell people I'm going to need it when they wish me good luck. However, secretly I am supremely confident (because Maths doesn't require what the school counselor calls Emotional Intelligence, hence the expression Safety in Numbers).

I finish the exam with fifty-four minutes to spare, which gives me time to check through my answers and work out my grade (minimum: 92%, maximum: 100%). After this, I still have half an hour to kill, not including the extra time that I'm allowed if I want it, so I look around. In the adjacent aisle Simon Nagel has the exam paper held up to the sports hall ceiling like a shopkeeper checking for forgeries. He tilts his head back underneath it and inspects the light dripping through it as though he hopes the real questions will reveal themselves (which they don't). Maths is his worst subject, because the questions are almost never about Nazis. He starts chewing on a pencil, which probably isn't kosher. In front of me Blowjob Frogley tucks a wisp of hair behind a totally unremarkable ear. Ever since she had the operation to pin them back, people have started to forget why they called her Blowjob in the first place. Now everyone assumes it's because she does them, which is why she gets invited to so many more parties than she used to. Six seats in front of Simon Nagel, David Driscoll coughs. It is crisp, clear, and mucus-free. He is only doing it because no one can prove he doesn't have to. Behind me, someone returns it with a cough of their own. To my right, someone blows their nose. In seconds, there's a chorus of cold symptoms bouncing off the brickwork. It is a pointless rebellion, but maybe that is the point. It almost sounds like birdsong.

I look around the whole sports hall and focus on each one of my classmates in turn. How we do in these exams, Mr. Clifford always tells us in Assembly, will determine our paths in life. Finally, I think I understand something. We are the form

that our Fates have taken. We are the forces beyond our control. (Destiny is just another word for living in the moment.)

In the seat between Beckie and me isn't Chloe Gower. Her
exam paper lays facedown on the desk, where it remains un-
touched until time is up and Mr. Carson collects it and shuffles
it together with the others like a Joker he needs for a trick.
This ritual repeats itself in Geography, Science, and French
(Written), but on Thursday, when Miss Farthingdale hands out
the History paper, she skips Chloe's place altogether.

Thursday afternoon I get off the bus home early at a stop
I've only ever seen before through a window. (Sometimes
when I look at things through glass it can feel like they're on
TV.) I ring Chloe's front doorbell four times before Jessica answers. She seems surprised to see me, but in a good way, and I
believe that she's sorry when she says she's sorry but Chloe's
not in.

"Where is she?" I ask.

By way of a response, Jessica ushers me into the house and
shuts the door behind me. Mounted on the back of the front
door is a cardboard sign. At the top of the sign in black felt-tip
is a heading: *WHERE ARE YOU?? BOARD VERSION 2.0.* With three
lines (two vertical, one horizontal) the board is divided into
four sections, which are labeled *IN, BACK SOON (i.e., before next
meal), BACK LATER (i.e., don't lock up!!!),* and *OUT (indefinitely).*
Attached to the *WHERE ARE YOU?? BOARD* are half a dozen
wooden clothes pegs, each one individually painted with the
name of the person they represent, in a manner (I assume) that

showcases an aspect of their personality. Chloe's peg is pink and glittery. It is in the far column, OUT *(indefinitely)*, alongside *WILF, SUSIE R.,* and (to my further surprise) *SUSIE B.,* which is also pink and glittery.

"She's at her mum's," explains Jessica. "But you're welcome in for cake and ice cream."

I am about to do with the offer what Madame Berger has trained me to do with all things irregular (and decline it) when I happen to notice the rest of the board. *DAD* is back soon (i.e., before next meal) and *ELLA* is back later (i.e., don't lock up!!!), but nobody is *IN*. This is because, I realize, Jessica doesn't have a peg. Which makes me feel sorry for her.

"Do you have any fruit?" I inquire.

Jessica serves me my banana on a plate with a knife, and for a second I think she is going to make banana butterflies like Mum used to before I asked her to stop because I was too old for them, but then she explains that the knife is to help me peel it because it's from the fridge. So I teach her the way monkeys peel bananas, which is simply to pinch the black bit between your thumb and forefinger and let the fruit reveal itself like a flower in bloom, which is much more efficient. This, I explain, is a good example of where evolution has hindered us. Most people have never seen a banana in its natural habitat. They think they come from supermarkets and that the stem is a handle put there purely for their convenience. (This is pretty much the biggest single problem with people as a species.)

"Wow," says Jessica, watching me eat from across the breakfast bar, a marble peninsula in the middle of the kitchen joined to the mainland by a cavernous chrome sink unit. "I think you just changed my life! I see I'm going to enjoy having you around."

"Say what, now?" I say.

"Well," she says and smiles, "it can't be long before you've got a peg of your own."

Suddenly, I feel a rush of heat in my cheeks. My stool wobbles. When I look down, the kitchen floor is lapping at my feet.

"It's okay." Jessica laughs. "You don't have to be embarrassed on my account. I was Chloe's age when I had my first proper boyfriend. Of course, he wasn't half as handsome as—"

"I have to lie down," I interrupt.

Jessica puts me in Wilf's room, which has black walls. Wilf is Chloe's brother that I didn't know about, and Susie R. is his fiancée. Thanks to the Monkey Method, I have just enough time to give Jessica my phone before I can't talk.

"Mum's under ice," I say.

"Under *ice*?" she repeats.

I hand Jessica my front door key, which is attached to my USB stick, which explains everything. "In Case of Emergency."

However, in my sleep Mum really is under ice.

(I am spread thin across the pond, my nose pressed against the surface. My breath fogs the glass, and when I wipe it clear, we are face-to-face. The look on hers is one of terror, and with

her hands she is gesticulating wildly like there's something behind me. I feel nothing, though, because through the ice she
looks like something on TV.)

I wake up with a headache and Jessica biting her nails.

"Mummy's on her way," she says, which normally I would
find annoying because she is not my sister. Now, though, I see
it for what it is (i.e., Empathy). "How are you feeling?"

I tell her, and she fetches my pills. Then she asks me whether
I knew that the body runs along meridians, which I didn't.
According to the Chinese, who have known about meridians
for fifteen hundred years, the body is governed through twenty
channels, each one responsible for supplying a vital organ with
Life Energy. This energy is called Qi, which I did know about,
but only, I admit, from the Scrabble dictionary. This is the
problem, says Jessica. Western medicine doesn't divide the
body along the same lines as Traditional Eastern Philosophy, so
it has no equivalency for the terms involved, which is why
Acupuncture is so often dismissed as Alternative Therap–

Here I stop her. "Acupuncture?"

"It's the easiest way to stimulate the flow of Qi along the
meridians. It's just another way to say making sure everything
gets where it's going."

"With needles?"

"That's what most people probably think of, yes." Jessica
sighs. "But really it's no different to damming a river."

At this point, Jessica keeps talking while I stop listening. I
am busy formulating a theory. When I zone back in, she is

talking about her training with a man she describes as one thousand and ten percent bonerfied.

"Does Chloe know about this?" I ask. Jessica smiles ruefully. "I've talked to her about it, if that's what you mean. But it's hard to know whether she's paying attention." She shakes her head. "Sometimes I think she'd rather I . . ." But she doesn't finish the thought. Instead, she tells me how often Chloe talks about me (often) and how high in her esteem she holds me (high). In conclusion, she says this:

"She really does like you, you know."

I think back to Chloe's bedroom, to the explanation I never let her give, the cratered skin of the rubber homunculus (which means little man).

"I know," I say.

The doorbell rings.

"She likes you, too."

Chapter Twenty-Two

If you think about it (which I have), Silence isn't the opposite of Conversation, because in a conversation you take turns, which makes two distinctions, which means that Silence and Conversation are too different to be opposites. If you think about it further (which I also have), there are two contrasting kinds of silence. $Silence_1$ is the good kind, because it is the opposite of Harmonizing, and $Silence_2$ is the bad kind, because it is the opposite of an Argument. (If you think about it even further (which I am only now starting to), it's weird that we have only one word for it.)

———

In the back of the minicab, me and Mum are completely silent$_2$. (Once, before Dad could turn off the TV, I heard a football commentator say about a penalty shoot-out that you could cut the atmosphere with a knife. This struck me as being especially meaningless, even by the standards of football commentary, because you can cut most things with a knife.) Right now you could cut the atmosphere with a spork. Mum is annoyed because I didn't tell her I was going to Chloe's, which caused her to worry about where I was. The fact that I am safe means that this Worry is now redundant, so her body has converted it to Anger, because that way it's easier to vent.

Turning to stare out the window, I consider the implications of my latest discovery. In theory, which is theoretically the same as in practice, Chloe's unswerving loyalty throws the spotlight of suspicion back on Mum and Dad. Next to me, as if to confirm this, Mum sneezes.

"*Gesundheit*," I deliberately do not say.

The music of tires on gravel distracts me from my deep thought by reminding me of what rain sounds like underwater and that we're home. Mum pays the driver with a single note and opens her door. But instead of getting out, she turns back toward me and fixes me in her gaze.

"I need for you to promise not to do that again," she says steadily, leaning heavily on *that*, like it's a concrete noun, which it isn't.

"Do what?" I ask, abstractly.

"Disappear," says Mum.

"Fine," I promise with fingers crossed.

"I need to hear you say it."

Instead, I say, "I need to know you trust me."

"Okay," she replies eventually. Then she shuts her door and gives the driver another note and asks for Woodside Leisure Park.

The minicab pulls up outside the Hollywood Bowl, where an ooze of older boys have gathered to spit, but to my relief Mum tells the driver to keep going until we're in the overflow car park around the back of the shop fronts. We get out by a wheelie bin, and I stoop down to untie and retie a shoelace to give Mum a head start because I am embarrassed to be seen with her. However, the second the minicab peels away from the empty curb, she strides off in the direction we've just come from and orders me to wait there.

For a while I count her absence in mountain ranges (Himalayas/Karakoram = 1 second, Atlas/Andes = 0.5, Alps = 0.25, Appalachians = 1.25) but then I get distracted thinking about the Karakoram range, which is the home of K2. Some people believe that K2 is the tallest mountain in the world, even taller than Mount Everest. However, this is true only if you measure from its base, which is thousands of feet underwater, which is exactly like measuring your penis from your bum hole forward. I think about what Mum said to Aunt Julie about life starting at the point of conception and try to imagine the circumstances of my beginnings. I zoom in to a biological level so as not to make myself nauseated and find myself in what looks like the Super Mario Land submarine level (Game Boy edition). The egg is the end of level boss, and every torpedo that her armor repels is another me that never existed, until eventually one pierces her shell and then I am. (Born into a bonus round.)

I am sitting down on the pavement with my knees hunched around my ears in a(n appropriately) fetal position, when twenty meters to my right a fire door explodes open. The noise is summer blockbusters and gratuitous violence, and the smell is oversalted popcorn and molten cheese. A face pokes out and a hand beckons.

They are both Mum's.

We take our seats in the front row just in time to see that the British Board of Film Classification has passed the following feature 18, only for persons of eighteen and over. Mum sinks into her seat and hands me a vat of pick-and-mix, which is the opposite of flossing. I look to her for an explanation, but her eyes are set on the blank screen, which looms infinitely above us like a starless night. Before I can calculate the marital/martial implications of what's going on, the titles punch through the dark with such force that I immediately forget myself. I plunge a hand into the sweets and smile because I know that the next two hours of my life will be perfect.

Which they are.

The film is about a troubled Russian mystic who is tricked at the end of World War Two by Adolf Hitler's top assassin into opening a portal to another dimension in order to recruit its most dangerous criminals for the fight against the encroaching Allied forces, and on the way out Mum and I agree that it's the best we've ever seen. Outside, it is still daytime, which surprises me, and the gaggle of boys have gone. On the ground where they were standing is a puddle of mucus that could just as easily be ectoplasm. My teeth feel furry like candyfloss, and I haven't got a care in the world, so when Mum offers me her hand on the way to the bus stop I don't think twice about taking it.

"I love you," she remarks quietly on the top deck of the bus.

I look around to check if anyone is in earshot, which they aren't. "And vice versa," I say.

When we get back home, I head straight to my room to practice hesitating in French in front of the mirror as last-minute revision for my Oral (French for *errrm* is *ooooh*). However, I have barely had time to adjust my jaw when I'm interrupted by a sound through the floorboards. In the kitchen, someone is playing the cutlery drawer, badly, in 5/4 time. It's Thursday night, which usually means takeaway, because Dad's out teaching Ella, but when I go downstairs to investigate I find two onions on the chopping board. From the living room, I can hear the printer hiccupping. It wheezes to a stop, and Mum enters clutching a piece of paper, which she slaps down on the counter in front of me. It is a recipe for Nigel Slater's Perfect Bolognese.

"Lord knows what I've been making." She laughs, pulling

on her jacket. Then she tells me that she won't be gone a minute and ruffles my hair.

Then she leaves.

Mum is true to her word. She is not gone a minute. Neither is she gone two minutes, three minutes, four minutes, or five minutes. After six minutes, I decide to start without her. The recipe calls for me to *dice* the onions, which sounds needlessly risky, so instead I opt to chop them. I am just about to make my first incision, the knife pointed away from me like an inverted moral compass, when I remember Chloe's mum's advice about how to stop yourself from crying, which I decide to take, even though it's ironic coming from someone with depression.

There is no room in the freezer. The top shelf is completely full of lasagnas and casseroles. Inside their frosted Tupperware, sealed away like classic action figures, these homemade ready-meals are busy not aging. Neighbors and friends of Mum and Dad's brought them round while I was in the hospital before they knew I was going to get better, and now that I am the cold has unionized them in a single block of ice. (They are striking against Time.) The other shelves are no more accommodating, so in order to make room for the onions I employ the knife and saucepan as a hammer and chisel (respectively (obviously)). However, this proves hazardous, and after a couple of near misses (which should really be called near hits), I retire upstairs to look for Mum's hairdryer. While I do this I wonder why people are always comparing onions to people. I consider all the ways in which they are similar:

1) They both have layers.
2) Most of these layers are pretty much identical, which means perhaps neither people nor onions are as mysterious as they can sometimes appear to be.
3) Some of them are French.

By the time I get back downstairs with the hairdryer in hand, the first bead of sweat has forced its way through the brow of the ice block. With the even application of warm air, it is soon followed by a deluge, which is a better word for flood. When the donations to the charity of me are free from their bonds, I can do what I want with them, which is what is meant by having liquid assets. First I stack them on the floor in towers depending on their size and shape, and then I do some Tetris with them to determine their optimum grouping, using my spatial awareness, which everyone says is excellent. Quickly, though, it becomes obvious that to make room for the onions I will have to reorganize the whole shelf, so I return to the freezer armed with my air gun. The space behind the ready-meals is partitioned off with a wall of inefficiently stacked hamburger packets, which date back as far as 2001 (before Dad developed diverticulosis). I tilt the hairdryer sideways, which is much cooler, and squeeze the trigger. After two or three minutes they immediately drop dead.

Behind the meat curtain there is loads of space, all of it

going to waste. The only thing in it is a white plastic bag, which I remove. The cold has contorted the bag into an irregular shape that gives no clues to its contents, so I open it. Inside is another irregular shape, which I pick up. The package inside the plastic bag is about the size of a fist and mummified beneath swathes of cling film. It seems to be leftovers of some kind (leftovers that never became washing up, on account of their suspension in time). Moreover, it intrigues me.

I unwrap it at the kitchen table, where we do Christmas.

Chapter Twenty-Three

By the time Mum returns I am barracuded in my room with the mattress pushed up against the door, feet first. She calls my name from the front door and again from the corridor, but once the kitchen door opens she doesn't make a sound. Not while she surveys the rubble of ready-meals strewn across the lino or while she identifies the broken fragments of her hair-dryer or sees the saucepan asleep on the back lawn on a bed of shattered glass. And especially not when she notices in the middle of the kitchen table a paw poking out from a cling-film chrysalis.

———

Now she is outside my door. I can hear the phlegmy stabs of breath. She knows better than to try the handle. She knocks. Six times, because it's a perfect number. Then time passes. Then she speaks.

She tells me she loves me.

She tells me she's sorry.

She tells me I am the most important person in her life.

That I am the best thing that ever happened to her.

I am her world.

If she could, she would die to protect me.

There are no rooms behind these doors.

Her conclusion is especially meaningless:

"Loving someone means being prepared to do anything to protect them. Even if the only thing you can protect them from is the truth."

She doesn't expect me to forgive her.

Chapter Twenty-Four

The next day my French Oral exam goes something like this:

Take 1
(Translation provided)

MADAME BERGER: *Good day, Marcel.*

ME: *Good day, Madame.*

MADAME BERGER: *Marcel, to begin with, can you tell me a little bit about your family? For example, do you have any brothers or sisters?*

ME: *In that which concerns my family, I have one big brother. As a pastime, he likes to play football with me each Saturday and set the table for an hour most evenings. He has fifteen years and what is more a sister who calls herself Agnes.*

MADAME BERGER: *Very good. Tell me a little more about Agnes. Describe her.*

ME: *According to me, she has white skin and black hair. As a pastime, she likes to listen to awful music. She is quite pretty, but also sad.*

MADAME BERGER: *Good. And your parents?*

ME: *I have one father. He calls himself Jean-Pierre. He wears glasses and has brown eyes. As a career, he is captain of a ship.*

MADAME BERGER: *Ah, yes? It is true?*

ME: *Yes, it is true, in my opinion. I have decided to live with him.*

MADAME BERGER: *Very interesting! And your mother? What does she do?*

ME: *. . .*

MADAME BERGER: *Would you like me to repeat the question?*

ME: *I would prefer not to discuss my mother.*

MADAME BERGER: *Pardon me?*

ME: *Ask me something else. Perhaps you would like directions somewhere?*

MADAME BERGER: *Please, Marcel, it is important that you answer that which I ask. Your mother. She is how?*

ME: *I have nothing to say on the subject of my mother. Please let it drop. To find the Found Property Office, simply continue all straight.*

MADAME BERGER: *Pardon?*

ME: *Do not turn left at the library, because it does not exist.*

MADAME BERGER: *Marcel, describe your mother, please.*

ME: *Stop the tape, please. I want to start again.*

MADAME BERGER: *I am sorry, but it is not possible. Do not worry! Everything goes well.*

ME: Stop the tape.

MADAME BERGER: *In French, okay?*

ME: *Please, Miss, put your clothes back on.*

MADAME BERGER: (stopping the tape) *Qu'est-ce que tu dit?!*

ME: I needed you to stop the tape. I'm sorry. I hope you understand.

MADAME BERGER: What ees ze mattuh wizz you?!

ME: Everything is cool beans and gravy. I just don't want to talk about my mum.

MADAME BERGER: Pourquoi pas?

ME: . . . Because she's dead.

MADAME BERGER: (gasping) Mon dieu! I yam zo zorry.

ME: Don't be. I'm not. It was her own fault.

MADAME BERGER: Ay deed not know.

ME: She drank herself to death. Like her dad.

(Madame Berger hugs me inappropriately. Her hair smells of smoke and cinnamon.)

MADAME BERGER: We can holwizz do zis anuzer time.

ME: No. I want to do it now.

MADAME BERGER: Rilly?

ME: Yes . . . As a dedication to her memory. She always had such a good one.

Take 2

MADAME BERGER: *Good day, Marcel.*

ME: *Good day, Madame.*

MADAME BERGER: *Tell me, Marcel, do you have animals at home?*

ME: . . .

MADAME BERGER: (stopping the tape and offering me a tissue, which I have not asked for and do not need) You has ol zee time in ze wold.

ME: (using the tissue but only to avoid causing offense) Maybe we could talk about weekends.

Take 3

MADAME BERGER: Remenzer, eet iz best somesing irregulere. Hockay?

(I nod)

MADAME BERGER: (pressing Record) *Good day, Marcel.*

ME: *Good day, Madame. How does it go?*

MADAME BERGER: *Errrm, it goes okay, thank you. And for you?*

ME: *Very well. Thank you for asking. I like what you are evidentially wearing.*

MADAME BERGER: *. . . Thank you.*

ME: *Of nothing.*

MADAME BERGER: *First of all, tell me, Marcel, what is it that you did last weekend?*

ME: *If I remember correctly, I played football with my brother, Serge, who has fifteen years, which is not to mention a sister who calls herself Agnes, who is pretty, but also quite sad. Afterward, I read two novels.*

MADAME BERGER: *Very good. Anything else, perhaps?*

ME: *Let me think . . . But of course! I drove my dad's car.*

MADAME BERGER: (stopping the tape) You droze your ded's car?

ME: (pressing Record) *I know. It was extremely irregular. It was in field.*

MADAME BERGER: *In a field?*

ME: *No, not in a field.*

MADAME BERGER: *Oh, good!*

ME: *In field. Because we were late for an appointment. Afterward, I passed the Hoover for two hours in my bedroom like a good son, is it not?*

MADAME BERGER: *. . . And what will you do next weekend, in the future?*

ME: *The future does not exist. In this country, there exists only this moment here, which calls itself now.*

MADAME BERGER: *. . .*

ME: *Now, if you would excuse me, please, I have a funeral to organize.*

Chapter Twenty-Five

Before David Driscoll's party, Dad helps me bury Jaws 2 in the back garden in a shoebox he insulates with cotton wool for "no reason that comes to mind" when I ask him. The service is intimate, which means that no one comes. The broken kitchen window is patched shut with a quilt of cereal boxes. Besides Dad and me, the only mourners present are Tony the Tiger, Snap, Crackle, and Pop, the Honeymonster, and the monkey from the Coco Pops box (whose name I don't know). Mum knows better than to show her face. She is giving wide birth to me. I am not a religious man, so instead of saying a prayer over the body, I read a formula that I got from the Internet:

"Triangle x triangle p is greater than or equal to h with a line through it over two."

I don't understand how exactly, but this has something to do with the Uncertainty Principle, which I find comforting, especially when I secure the lid on the box. However, when I toss the first handful of dirt down into the open grave, it plays a mini-drumroll on the roof of the coffin. Drums are hollow, which suggests that Jaws 2's soul has left his body for good.

While I am dressing for the party, Mum asks me whether I would like breakfast for dinner. She does this (sensibly) by sending Dad in her place, because I've made it known that I have nothing to say to her. He lurches into my bedroom with an overly jolly fence. It is all shoulders and knees, and it makes him look like the puppet that we both know he is. When I don't answer, he slumps down in the beanbag like his strings have been cut and tells me to give it here, meaning my tie. I watch him wrestle the snake of fabric around his thick, collarless neck and loop and tug and jimmy like a retired magician trying to remember a trick he hasn't performed in twenty years. When finally he's done he looks overly pleased with himself (and a bit like Fred Flintstone (and, moreover, ridiculous)). However, when he wriggles his head down under it and makes me bow in front of him to receive the medal, the knot slips and the whole thing falls through his fingers like sand. "Oh, well," he says with a shrug. "Maybe best we give them a sporting chance, anyway." He means the girls at the party. "After all," he adds, approving of my outfit with pursed lips, "they're not painted on." He means their eyes. "Is your friend Chloe going to be there?"

"Are you having an affair?" I ask in response.

"What?" asks Dad, even though my enunciation was perfect.

"Answer the question," I imperate. "Are you cheating on Mum?"

"Why would you think that?"

"I don't. Should I?"

Dad hauls himself out of the beanbag and puts his hands on my shoulders, makes an *h* of us. He looks deep into my eyes in which he presumably sees the reflection of his own in which he sees the reflection of mine and so on, which is called Infinite Regression. This goes on forever.

"I don't need to cheat," he says eventually. "I got Mum to marry me, didn't I?"

I nod. (Factually, this is uncontentious, if not obviously relevant.)

"So I've already won."

On the way to the party, I riffle through Dad's radio stations, partly to check for any changes and partly to try and get a rise out of him, which is getting harder to do every day. The presets have not changed. On AM1 and AM5 a serious-sounding man is chairing a phone-in debate about the England cricket team and whether or not it has a balanced batting lineup ("They ought to be balanced," says Dad. "Their tail's long enough"), while on AM2 and AM3 a slightly less serious-sounding man is reporting on the rising suicide rate amongst Scandinavian teens. On AM4 a third man is singing a song about jumping ("Might as well jump! Jump! Go ahead and jump! Jump!"). I toggle back and forth between AM4 and AM3 until the two things start to seem connected and Dad suggests we listen to something a bit more "you know."

Then he flicks over to FM. Something between a viola and a double bass saws through the space between us. The dial is preset to Classic FM. Dad doesn't like songs without words, because it's harder to tell if they're happy or sad. (I agree with him.)

"I didn't know you liked classical music," I say casually but not really, turning to look out my window.

"Neither did I," replies Dad.

It's been raining. Drops of water wriggle their way across the pane. They look like the sperm in the Biology video that changed everything.

"You're going to have to forgive your mother," says Dad, like he's reading the news.

I don't ask why.

"Because . . ." says Dad. "She's in your corner. You know that, don't you, kid?"

I turn away from the window and look across at my father. He takes his eyes off the road to look back, which I've heard him tell people never to do. He smiles. I smile back, marveling at how little he knows me to think I could be won round with a meaningless sporting cliché.

We drive past David Driscoll's door so Dad can drop me off at the end of the street outside a house with a broken washing machine and a chair with three legs in its front garden, except the washing machine isn't a machine anymore because it no longer changes the size or direction of an applied force, and the chair isn't a chair because you can't sit on it (now they are the same thing (i.e., rubbish)). This is Dad's idea. So as not to cramp my style. We agree that this is where he will pick me up from at twenty-three hundred hours, which means eleven o'clock.

I don't realize how nervous I am until I reach to undo my seatbelt and notice that my hand is out of focus because it's shaking so much. Dad must notice, too, because he immediately cuts the engine. For a moment, no one speaks. Then he says, "There, there."

When I open my mouth to reply, my teeth judder like loose xylophone keys. "Why do people say that?" I manage to ask over the clatter of my molars.

"I don't know," says Dad after a moment's consideration, but (thinking about it) I think I do. Then he reaches into his jacket pocket and takes out a shiny silver flask not much larger than a deck of cards.

When I ask him what it is he tells me it's his Irish percolator. "For making Irish coffee," he says, when I ask what it's for. Then he unscrews the cap and passes it over.

"What's Irish coffee?" I ask him.

"It's a coffee with no potatoes." Dad laughs. Then he steadies my hand and guides it to my mouth. "Try some. It's good for nerves."

The drink doesn't taste of much in my mouth, but when I swallow it firebombs my throat and carpets my gut in napalm.

It feels like a sicky burp in rewind, but Dad says it's meant to and that the first sip is always the worst. "There you go," he says, as I swig again, and then, when I'm off guard (trying not to vomit), he asks how things are going with Chloe. He laughs again when I don't answer. "Don't worry," he says, taking the flask and gulping back a mouthful. "This isn't what you think it is. Never mind about the birds and the beavers. I'm not going to embarrass us both by pretending you haven't done your research. Why do you think I got us broadband?" At this point my face must do something I haven't authorized, because Dad jokes that I'm free to leave at any time and central locks the doors. I know exactly what's coming next. It's the long-overdue Evils of Peer Pressure lecture (the one that Chloe predicted and is now about to become a bullet point in): that I shouldn't feel compelled to do anything I'm not ready to do just because other people are doing it, that most of the people who claim to be doing things already are almost certainly lying about it anyway, that I should never feel like there's anything I can't talk to him about, even/especially if it's something I don't want Mum knowing, that there'll be plenty of time for all sorts of experimenting when I'm older, and really when I think about it what's the big rush, that now's the time to enjoy being young and not having to worry about stupid shit like this (he'll almost definitely swear here so I know he has a vested interest in keeping this confidential, and that anything I might subsequently decide to tell him won't leave these four doors), that he could certainly tell me a story or two (followed maybe by a story or two), and finally that if I absolutely am sure that I'm ready for whatever it is I might be thinking about trying then both he and Mum would infinitely prefer I tried it under their roof, where at least they'd know I was safe, than out in the middle of a deserted car park or an abandoned factory somewhere . . . All of this delivered, of course, in the falsely neutral, strictly nonjudgmental *Are-you-having-trouble-with-diarrhea?* voice Chloe warned me about outside the NEWS GENT.

However, in actuality, Dad says none of this. "So . . ." he says instead. "Are you getting any?"

"Any what?" I ask, managing to sound more innocent than I really am simply by channeling my surprise at Dad's directness. (Unattributed pronouns in conversation between males only ever refer to one thing. (The classic e.g. is doing *it*.))

"It's okay," says Dad, handing me back the drink. "You don't need to play dumb with me." He grins toothily as I take the flask and wipe its mouth on my sleeve. (I think he also bails out of a wink by doubling up so it becomes a blink.) "I know you think I was born yesterday," he continues, "but, remember, I was young, too, once."

I leave this contradiction alone and take another swig of the mystery liquid. This time I do discern a flavor before the burn takes over. It tastes like melted licorice, the reassurance of which gives me the confidence to take charge of the situation.

I tell Dad I'm not an idiot, that I know for a fact half the time boys boast about fingering it's just Prawn Cocktail crisps from the tuck shop, and that even if it wasn't, it wouldn't matter anyway, because I never have nor would I ever in a quadrillion years submit to the evils of peer pressure.

"So, that's a no?" says Dad when I'm done.

"Yes," I confirm. "And don't worry, I'm not in any rush."

"Hmm," he remarks, and takes off his glasses. "What's the matter, is she frigid or something?"

There follows a different kind of lecture, one that really does sound confidential. While Dad talks, I concentrate on the Irish coffee mix so as to avoid making eye contact. Each sip goes down easier than the last until my mind starts to feel like my mouth after I've bitten my tongue (i.e., not big enough all of a sudden for all the thoughts it has to process). Dad's first time was when he was still in short trousers (if I know what he means (which I don't)). Looking back now, it was almost certainly a mistake but, as Dad puts it, "Making mistakes is the best bit about not being old enough to know better."

"What was her name?" I ask, with words that feel fuzzy round the edges, but Dad says that's not the point. The point is, he says, she was great practice for when he *was* old enough for it to mean something.

"Which," says Dad, "is what this time now's for. So when you are grown-up you can really hit the ground running. And"—here I can feel him stop looking at me, and from the corner of my eye watch as he attends himself to a smudge on his glasses lens—"if your friend Chloe isn't the sort of girl who's willing to make a silly mistake, then that's a lesson she'll probably never learn. And in which case maybe you shouldn't be wasting your time on her."

Instead, Dad says, I should be concentrating on the girls with the worst reputations, or, short of that, the ones with the lowest self-esteem. How do I spot the ones with low self-esteem? he asks himself, rhetorically. "That's the best part. You're teenagers. Everyone's got low self-esteem!"

When I reach for my seatbelt the second time, my hand's still out of focus, but this time it's not down to any oscillations. I can almost feel the loose connection somewhere between my retinae and my brain. On the plus side, though, I am no longer shaking, or rather I'm shaking with anger in the exact opposite direction that I'm shaking with nerves and the two things cancel each other out. I don't know what right Dad thinks he has to go poking around for details of my private life, but it's exactly this flagrant disregard for privacy that proves I was right to keep him under investigation for as long as I did.

He waits until I'm out of the car to deliver his closing argument. "Remember," he says, leaning across the empty seat to roll down the window (and by doing so erasing the raindrop tableau (and committing metaphorical mass spermicide)), "there's no need to tie yourself down to anything at this stage. No man in the history of History has ever lain on his death bed and wished he'd loved less."

Then he leaves and I am alone.

All of a sudden, I have never seen this street before in my life.

Then, just as suddenly, I've never seen any street.

Chapter Twenty-Six

I steady myself on the looming stalk of a cold metal flower. Above my head, it hums and blossoms into a full moon. Silver static falls across the white background of the glaring satellite and lands softly on my face. It feels light and calming and new. But then I hear a roar. In front of me, lit like a runway by a gallery of moons on sticks, is a pathway. From its near side a shiny bug-eyed monster bares a grille of teeth and flaps its eyebrows from side to side. When it sees me, its eyes light up.

(Slowly) it charges.

Without thinking (because I can't), I dart out across the course of the lumbering beast and strike it on the snout. It squeals with surprise and stops in its tracks, and I tear off down the passage without looking back. Behind me I hear a string of words I almost recognize. They sound like a leg of lamb falling repeatedly on someone's foot. Then, nothing. Then:

Vaf!

Vaf! Vaf! Vaf!

Which is a word I know.

I lean on a stalk and remember to breathe. As quickly as it left, my memory returns. The metal flower is a lamppost. Moreover, there is something tied to it. A sore, disheveled, chewed-up creature with patches of skin showing through thinning fur and a tail pebble-dashed with teeth marks. Around its scrawny neck, as though its head were a bulb, is attached a white plastic cone.

"Vaf!" it says (which is French for *Ruff!*), and tilts up its head to look through the falling precipitation. Slowly but surely the cone starts to fill. For what feels like a very long time I watch this graceless creature catching rain before I realize that I don't remember what it's called. All I have in my mind is the shape of the word. It looks like *god*.

Then someone says my name and asks if my mum dropped me off. Backlit in the doorway of the bungalow I'm standing in front of is a gangly silhouette with a glass in one hand and a stick of chalk in the other. He puts the chalk to his lips and sucks color into its tip. Then he doubles over, coughing. He looks like he's trying to suck himself off.

Pete Sloss shows me in, tells me to keep my shoes on, and offers me some of his drink, which looks like apple juice, which I don't like. Then he tells me to follow him. The carpet is beige and coarse, the cheap sort you get on kindergarten classroom walls. Set into it is a faded gray trail of children's muddy footprints that leads us all the way to the living room. There, sat in a coven on the floor around a black-labeled glass bottle, is the party. It is only six people. 66.66^{r}% look up and mumble hello. The other 33.33^{r}% is an older boy (probably fourteen) who looks like David but more so, and Chloe Gower. When she sees me she drops her chin and stares down into her own glass of apple juice, which is coddled in the intersection of her crossed legs, which she draws together like bellows when Pete slops down next to her. (As if on cue, he emits a plume of smoke.) I take a seat across from her, between Beckie Frogley and Gemma Overton, which completes the circuit and brings the older Driscoll to life.

"Everyone know the rules," he asks flatly, like it's an order, clamping a fat hand over the glass bottle. "Ones is tongues, twos is flat hands, threes is fingers. Boy gets boy you spin again, girl gets girl you don't."

"James?" asks David, quietly.

James lifts his hand off the bottle and uses it to thump David on his BCG scab.

"Arrgh!"

"I told you not to call me that. My name's ptk."

"Peter Kerr?" asks Susie Beckman, on behalf of everyone.

"ptk," says Driscoll Senior. It sounds like bubbles bursting in a pot of thick soup. "That's what I'm changing it to. When I'm eighteen. Try and shout it."

"What?"

"Go on, try."

Susie tries. More bubbles burst. "Oh, wow."

"See." He beams. "You can't. It's impossible. And if they can't shout at me, then good luck trying to stop me."

"Stop you from what?" asks Susie.

"Yeah, what?" says David. And then, once he's got his answer, "Arrgh! Stop doing that!"

"Who goes first?" asks Gemma Overton, who used to be respectable and likable before she realized people liked and respected her more when she wasn't.

"I do," says James, and spins the bottle. It lands on Chloe. Everyone laughs except me, Chloe, James, and Pete, who is too busy raking back apple juice. "Practice," says James, and spins again, this time harder. I watch Chloe as the bottle rotates. Her face is a salad dressing made with Relief and Humiliation. She shudders, and for a second they blend together to make something new and unrecognizable. However, the Humiliation is oil, so before long it rises to the surface. Just in time for the bottle to nominate her again. This time Pete laughs, too.

"Arrgh!" remarks David, because his brother has punched him a third time.

"Fuck off! It hit your knee," says James, which is a lie. "That's interference."

"It didn't!" squeals David, eyes starting to glaze.

"You know I know pressure points."

"I didn't touch it!"

"You did, kind of," mediates Susie, which means to be between two positions, which she literally is. "It sort of like brushed your knee," she adds, sort of like brushing James's knee.

"I didn't see," says Pete, unhelpfully, and burps.

"So shut up," says Gemma Overton.

"You can kiss me," says Beckie Frogley, to anyone who's listening.

Chloe says nothing.

"Maybe you should spin again," I say.

Chloe looks at me for the first time since I arrived.

"You are the worst person in the world," says her expression.

James spins the bottle again. However, there is something wrong with it because it stays perfectly still. No one else notices, though, because instead the room spins around it. It stops with Susie in the hot seat.

"That's cheating!" shouts David. "You cheated!"

"How?" asks Susie, plumping up her breasts and pointing them at James.

Then they kiss with tongues.

(It is only two people locking heads and probing a hole in the other's face. (But then again, you can do that with anything.))

Then it's Susie's go. This time I can't tell what's spinning (the bottle, the room, or my head), because either way, the entailment is the same. All I do know is when whatever it is (that's spinning) stops (spinning) the bottle is pointing to the gap between David and James. At first no one says anything except for some vowels. Then Pete Sloss suggests a "Three-

some!" which I think is his version of The Judgment of King
Solomon. However, both Driscolls stand their ground, so Susie
positions herself behind the bottle and lowers her head to the
carpet to look along its length for the purposes of extrapola-
tion, except that's not a word she would know. To do this, she
closes one eye, which technically I suppose might mess with
her depth perception and explain why she nudges the bottle
with her nose in the direction of the older Driscoll, who is
simultaneously shuffling around toward its decree.

David doesn't say anything (too heartbroken), and this time
they use hands.

"Get some room!" shouts Pete, which sounds like something he's only half heard.

Next it's David's go, but he's in the toilet, so it reverts to
Gemma, except Beckie complains that it should go boy girl
boy girl. Which means already it's round to me. This is one of
those times that I can easily identify my emotions.

I am scared.

My hand trembles as it floats out in front of me toward the
bottle, but as soon as I feel the glass on my fingertips a deep
sort of calmness descends. The feeling is rare but not without
president. I feel like I did when I found out that I had a brain
tumor, like a weight has been lifted. Only this time I know
what it is: It is the burden of Fate being removed from my
shoulders, the lightness that comes from no longer even pretending to be responsible. Now my Fate is over to Chance,
which is governed not by My Own Free Will (as written into
my DNA) but by the dual forces of Friction and Centripetal

Energy, who between them, without so much as consulting me, will determine the location of my first kiss.

Except they won't. Because the second I set the bottle spinning I taste copper.

And then my vision lifts and I see what happens next.

Chapter Twenty-Seven

Here's what happens next:

1) The bottle points to Beckie Frogley.
2) Beckie smiles.
3) I smile back.
4) I shuffle forward on my hands and knees into the middle of the broken circle. The carpet is scratchy, but I don't feel this. (I don't feel anything.)
5) Beckie joins me.
6) I lay my hands on her thighs, which tense through her jeans, and lean toward her.

7) We lock heads, and with clumsy tongues probe the holes in each other's faces.

8) My vision lifts again. I see further than I have ever seen before. My whole life is ahead of me. It is timetabled rigorously in various shades of highlighter. I see the following things:

a) Beckie and I passing notes in class. Her dotting the *i*'s with smiley faces. Me using exclamation marks to make clear when I'm being funny.

b) Abortive sexual exploration in the back row of cinemas showing political espionage thrillers that require complete concentration to understand the plot intricacies of.

c) Jagged, six-point hearts tattooed into the bark of ageless, nonconsenting oak trees. Initials and plus signs but no equals (like broken algebra). Adverbs spelled with numbers.

d) The arbitrary application and use of nicknames. (Beckie farts in front of me one time and I immediately christen her Gaseous Clay.)

e) The evolution in form/mutation of these nicknames. (Gaseous Clay → Mohammed Ali → Little Mo → Mo Mowlam → Ten Men Went to Mow → Tin Man → The Wizard of Oz → Ozzy Osbourne → The Bourne Identity → Harvey Dent → Dental Hygiene → Gene Pool → Paul Simon → Simon Schama → Simon Shawarma → Chicken Shawarma → Chicken Licken → Gangsta Trippin → Fat Boy Slim → The

Real Slim Shady → The Real McCoy → Walker Texas Ranger → Sharleen Spiteri.)

f) The eventual realization that we have forgotten the original reason behind the names with which we refer to each other.

g) Full sex.

h) A missing period (which (appropriately enough) is American for full stop).

i) A timely inheritance. Beckie gets a house. I get diverticulosis.

j) A fat girl in a white dress.

k) A bundle of joy, which consequentially unravels, because of Entropy, into:

(i)   a pile of professional compromise.

(ii) a heap of creeping resentment.

(iii) a mass of silent$_2$ martyrdom.

l) Casual sex (with each other).

m) A spontaneous pilgrimage to an ageless, tattooed oak. The discovery that this ageless oak has fallen foul to root rot and been chopped down.

n) A sudden obsession with Family Traditions, a phrase applied to any activity that occurs four times or more, through accident or design, in a given timeframe (e.g., fried breakfasts on Sundays, roast beef at Christmas, saying "bless you" in foreign languages).

o) Going on walks (as a family), which is not the same as walking.

p) Telling Beckie I love her <u>very much</u>, instead of just "I love you," as though love is not a binary thing (i.e., 1 or 0).

q) Calling Beckie "your mother" in the presence of our child.

r) Taking walks (alone).

s) Calling Beckie "Mum" in the presence of our child.

t) Casual sex (with other people).

u) Accidentally calling Beckie "Mum" while alone with her. Her not even noticing.

v) Serious sex with other people.

w) The whole family in the local branch of a mid-price chain restaurant, sat at our "usual table." Beckie and I smiling widely up at the teenage waitress as she takes our order and laughs professionally at a joke I've made a hundred times before.

9) I realize it's not even my life. It's my parents'. And I am doomed to remake it scene for scene with Blowjob Frogley as my leading lady. All because I gave her my first kiss at David Driscoll's thirteenth birthday party, because rather than at least trying to take responsibility for myself, I preferred to gamble my Fate on a horse (force) called Gravity.

Except I don't.

Because instead I kiss Chloe.

At first her mouth is small and stony. I can trace her teeth (like tiny tombstones) through her lips. But as I lap against her, I feel her starting to fall into me. Her fingers web my rib cage, and I stop hearing the audience's laughter, the words of shock that stretch their faces back over their skulls like tight, gangrenous ponytails. The whole thing is over in a matter of seconds, which is true of everything. We disengage. The distance between our faces is not enough that I can see her edges. In profile, we might just as plausibly be a wineglass.

"Fuck off," she says, quietly.

"Sorry," I say. "Déjà vu."

"Excuse me," says Beckie, and then scurries out of the room with something in her eye.

"Do you want to see my Samurai sword?" says James to Susie.

"Sure," says Susie to James.

"Do you want to see my Sarumai sword?" says Pete to Gemma.

"Be gone," says Gemma to Pete, and then goes herself.

"Wait," says Pete, following her. "It was a euphonium!"

And then we're alone together, just me and Chloe Gower at the center of the universe. Which in truth is a bit awkward.

"You were the biggest dick to me," says Chloe.

"What do you mean?" I ask.

"Jesus!"

"No, I know. I don't mean what did I do wrong. I mean, what you just said was ambiguous."

"It really wasn't."

I explain how it was. It all depends what Chloe meant by *were*. It could either mean that I *behaved* like the biggest dick and therefore still have some explaining to do or that I *used to be* the biggest dick, the implication being that now we've shared our first kiss—

"Shut up!" Chloe interrupts. "That's not my first kiss."

"It's not? I just assumed—"

"Why? Are you saying it was bad?"

"No. It was . . ." I try to think of a better word for nice, which you should never use in Composition. Then I hear myself start saying *perfect,* which is far too strong. "Perfunctory."

"What does that mean?"

"It's a better word for impersonal or workmanlike," I explain, and then immediately wish I hadn't. "Can we start again?"

"From where?"

"I didn't say all the stuff I meant. I mean, I didn't mean all the stuff I— Actually, either way. I don't know. I don't think I'm making myself clear. Jaws 2 is dead. You were pretty much right about everything. I'm sorry I said those things about you. You were only trying to help."

"How do you know that?"

"I know about the voodoo acupuncture."

Chloe turns Japanese, which means to blush (because your cheeks look like their flag, which is especially true in Chloe's case).

"I should have let you explain. Sometimes I'm not really in

control of what I'm feeling. It sort of overtakes me. You know when you put the wrong thing in the laundry and you want to get it out but you can't open the washing machine when it's on a cycle, so you just have to watch it through the window and wait for it to end, and you get all dizzy?"

Chloe nods sort of. Maybe. (I think.)

"It's sort of a bit like that. And even when it's finished you still have to wait for a bit, until it clicks, and by then it's too late anyway, because all the colors have run—"

"Was that your first kiss?"

Now it's my turn to blush. "No," I say in two separate syllables so it sounds like the world's first carpenter cum zookeeper. "I've kissed a multitude of girls."

"How many's a multitude?"

"Less than a plethora but more than my fair share."

"Between one and fifty?"

"Up to fifty," I say (technically not a lie).

"Closer to one or fifty?"

I tilt my eyes upward and try to study my lashes. I stay like this for as long as it would take to count to twenty-four. "One."

Chloe laughs. "You're the biggest dick," she says. However, this time it really does sound ambiguous. (Suddenly, *alone together* feels a lot less like an oxymoron.) Then she asks about Jaws 2, so I bring her up to speed and she says she's sorry for my loss. Then I ask where she's been all week.

"I had some stuff to sort," she says.

"But these exams will determine the path you take in life," I say in one-handed Scout's Honor–style quotations.

"I'm going away," says Chloe, and then takes her hand off my ribs, where I now realize it's been all along. This makes me aware of my breathing, which I notice requires concentration.

"What do you mean?"

"My dad got a job. I didn't want to go. But my mum can't really look after me anyway." She looks around the room, like she's tracking a fly. "And I've missed the exams now, so—" Her eyes land on the arm of the sofa, then a stack of old newspapers, then an ashtray, and (on the carpet between us) an old, orange grease stain. "There's an international school . . . And it's Hong Kong, so everyone speaks English. It's only for a couple of years, max."

Mississippis meander past. Their flow is glacial. There are only 31,556,926 of them in a year. "My name's not Max," I say, which, as we both know, isn't remotely funny.

I feel inverted.

"What does your dad do?" eventually asks someone, who, by a process of deduction, is me.

"He's in futures," says Chloe.

I feel a flicker of mirth like a punch in my gut and suck in a roomful of air. The spark ignites, and I burp up a chuckle.

"What?" asks Chloe. "What is it?" She wipes at her face like maybe there's something on it. "What?" But it's all just fuel for the fire, which is crackling in my throat.

I roar with laughter.

"What're you laughing at?" demands Chloe, with a crick in her voice. A flame leaps the divide and catches on her sleeve. "What I say?" she giggles. "What?!"

And then we're both ablaze.

By the time we've burned through all the oxygen in David Driscoll's house (wheezing for breath on our sides, as low to the ground as possible, eyes streaming), it's impossible to tell whose laughter is whose, which is when I realize that this is one of the moments that lasts, because it's not mine alone to forget, and I look forward to looking back one day and seeing myself in the middle of it.

"Y-ou w-ill m-iss me," I tell Chloe, as best I can in the space between gasps.

"What?" asks Chloe, serially.

"It-s Fr-e-nch," I say. "For I w-ill m-iss you."

Then someone must hit fast-forward, because the next thing I know time is whistling wordlessly through my hair like wind, like I'm orbiting too close to the surface of a collapsing star again.

Then I'm sitting on cold, hard, forgetful plastic.

Chapter Twenty-Eight

A tired nurse with an odd amount of eyebrows (either one or three) sits me down on the edge of a vinyl bed and squawks an instruction in a language I don't speak. She has a swollen, red face that looks like it's launched a thousand ships because someone was trying to save money on champagne. When I don't answer, she exits into the corridor and swishes tracing paper across the entrance to the alcove. I am in pain, which is not the same as having pain, because it's big enough to contain you. My legs hiss with carpet burns and my muscles ache like they've been marinated in acid, which they have, and every time I inhale a procession of fingers plays up and down my chest like a flutist practicing scales for Grade 3. I have to clamp my hands round the border of the bed to keep from falling off, because being in pain is like being in anything (i.e., when it moves, you move with it).

Then a doctor comes in, his face held parallel to the clipboard that protrudes on a perpendicular from his stomach. He murmurs something I don't hear that sounds like he has a cold and nods up to cross-reference me with his forms. Beneath the centimeter-thick lenses of his wire-rimmed glasses his eyes are shrunken and dry. They look how raisins must to grapes. Moreover, he has a bristly black goatee that makes his mouth look like a letterbox.

"βmu℘mhm ℘uτ m∞h, hmψ mmεum?" he asks, straining the words through his lip hair until they're completely uncucumbered by meaning (which is when something's unburdened because you've scraped all the extras off, like gherkins from a burger).

I ask him to come again, which comes out as "H∞h?"

"βmu℘phhm ℘um m∞h, hmh mmεum, ϖhhu . . . P∝m∂hϵ?" he repeats, turning his attention back to the clipboard and scribbling guardedly. "Γhφm puη ϖuh hhh∝m, λh'mu ξhum∂h? Hp lτu hεpϵh uhp bmmp?" Then he produces a penlight from his breast pocket and takes a step toward me. "Υpumh mu∝h, plumgη," he instructs, before clicking on the torch and jacking open my eye with thumb and forefinger. The shot of light tickles, which makes me sneeze on his lapel, which inspires a hasty retreat and a whole paragraph of notes. I wipe my nose on the sleeve of my shirt, which now I notice is inside out. The flutist's fingers are its buttons.

"⊗," says the doctor from a safe distance, still writing.

"PλamξP ∞pua, pa ℘ . . ." and so on until all of a sudden, like the old-style twisty radio in the kitchen, whose dial travels from station to station through a harsh white wilderness (like a Trans-Siberian Express train), he starts, out of nowhere, to make (a sort of) sense: ". . . not inconsistent with TLE, which, medical histories considered, in conjunction with what your girlfriend's already . . . All things being not unequal . . . I don't see as particular cause for . . . As for the removal of clothes and the hmmm *release* of . . . It's not something I wouldn't call not uncommon . . . In this instance, my suggestion, we chalk it up as a Road to Damascus-y type of . . . And try to look on the bright . . ." He glances up at me.

With his lenses between us, I feel like a TV program.

Then he smiles, stretching his lips humorlessly across his face and holding the pose for the count of ten, as though it's nothing more than part of his warm-down routine, which it turns out it is. "After all, if Paul the Apostle hadn't had a tonic clonic, we probably wouldn't celebrate Christmas."

With every step on the way back to the waiting room I hear the sound of the sea combing over an ugly pebble beach, which for a minute I think is what people must mean by a wave of nostalgia, until I look down and realize that the noise is actually a Nike swoosh, caused by the legs of my tracksuit rubbing together. Which is when I first realize I'm wearing somebody else's trousers.

In the waiting room, Chloe jumps to her feet and asks what they said.

A thick, syrupy confusion trickles through my mind, gluing my words together.

"ThatIhavetoremembertotakemypillsAndsomethingaboutanapostleHowiftheydhadKepprawhenJesuswasaboutthenBernardMatthewswouldbeoutofajob."

"Saint Paul!" She nods. "He had what you have. That's why he stopped persecuting the Christians, because he thought Jesus told him to, but really it was a grand mal and the blindness after, that was just post-ictal. You can see, can't you?"

I look at Chloe. And see her. (For the first time I notice she is perfectly symmetrical.) I nod.

"That's what you had, a complex partial seizure followed by a grand mal. It was over five minutes, so I made Gemma call an ambulance and I didn't let anyone put anything in your mouth. David's brother wanted to film it and put it online, but Susie told him he was a fucktard and David and Pete locked him in the garden. No one else thought it was funny."

"Whatsfunny?"

"Exactly," says Chloe. "That's what we all said. David was really good, actually. He knew the recovery position and about making the ground soft and everything. And he's the one that helped me and Ella get you in the car."

"What?"

"I know. He wanted to come with, but Ella hates having passengers, so he made me promise to call him the second I heard anything. I didn't know you were close."

Neither did I. But that's not what I meant.

"Oh," says Chloe. "I called her right after the ambulance cos Dad doesn't like me drinking spirits. I told her if she didn't leave right now I'd tell Dad she was the one cutting up Jessica's underwear, then she could explain why she let him sack the cleaner. She didn't even put the roof up."

I can feel the syrup clogging my synapses. There are two distinct flavors.

"Shedroveus?"

"Yeah, she dropped us off. I canceled the ambulance cos she got there first."

"Whendidshepasshertest?"

"Like a month ago. I think she must've flirted with the examiner, though, cos, no offense, she's pretty shit. Last week she was meant to take me to the Harlequin and there weren't two parking spots next to each other so we just went home. She still had your dad's number. I called him. He's on his way."

I look at the ground, where the legs of my trousers spill over the toes of my shoes like it's 2001 and I listen to Green Day, which it isn't and I don't. "Oh, yeah," says Chloe, as though she's just remembered something insignificant. "I spilled some drink on your jeans. I'm really sorry. We had to throw them out."

But she can't fool me. Because I am a pedigree liar.

Chapter Twenty-Nine

(According to *Roget's Thesaurus*, there are ten synonyms for the verb *to shimmy*, as in *he shimmied down the drainpipe to freedom*, listed here: *wriggle, clamber, scramble, lurch, wobble, careen, totter, falter, twitch, lollygag*. Of these ten, three (*falter, totter,* and *lollygag*) can be discounted for being too hesitant and, therefore, too risky, two (*careen* and *twitch*) for being involuntary, one (*lurch*) for being too sudden and, therefore, too risky, and one (*wobble*) for being too much like something a dessert would do at a blustery picnic. Of the remaining synonyms, *clamber* can be ruled out, as it implies too great a degree of difficulty, which could prove demoralizing at a planning stage, and *scramble* is insufficiently illustrative. Which leaves *wriggle*, for which *Roget* has the following suggestions: *wiggle, jiggle, flounder, flail, slither, crawl, slink, ooze,* and *shimmy.* Of these, *wriggle, wiggle,* and *jiggle* (too easily confused), *flounder* and *flail* (too undignified), *crawl* (too horizontal), *ooze* (too metaphorical), and *shimmy* (insufficiently instructive (hence *Roget* in the first place)) can all be ruled out. Which leaves me with two options for descending the drainpipe (*slink* and *slither*), both of which, oddly enough, make me sound less like the hero and more like a baddie.)

I spend the week following the latest betrayal of my trust alone in my bedroom, my time split evenly between revising for my final exam (English Composition, Friday p.m.), and plotting. In both of these activities I have found *Roget* to be a dexterous and amenable confederate, which are better words for able, willing, and accomplice respectively. To ensure the complete clandestinity (privacy) that my operation requires I have turned my Smithsonian Elements of Science Mini-Lab back into an intruder alarm and announced this fact to Mum and Dad in an email memorandum. Moreover, I have told Dad to tell Mum that I will be taking my meals at my desk until further notice. (Crucially, Dad doesn't know I'm on to him yet. Before he arrived at A&E, I had just time enough to brief Chloe about the situation. The story we agreed on was technically not a lie: I had had a seizure and she had called an ambulance. This would avoid any immediate confrontation about the phantom driving lessons, which would be more likely to provoke denial than provide satisfactory answers. It would also give Dad ample opportunity to further incriminate himself and me the chance to catch him red-handed.) This means that for five days straight I have only had three things for company: 1) my spiraling suspicions, 2) my increasingly irregular sleeping patterns, and 3) a now nameless hamster. (Moreover, Chloe and I have MSNed.)

It is Thursday night, and I have just finished a dinner of fish fingers and alphabetti spaghetti on white toast, through which Mum managed to communicate the message GOOD LUCK TO-MORROW X, which must have required her to open more than one tin, because of the number of O's in it. These are the first words we have exchanged since her dubious definition of devotion, and just like then, inside me now they mean nothing. While my digestive tract makes nonsense anagrams (DOCK TUX MORROW LOGO, OX MOGUL WORK DOCTOR, COD GUT LOX WORK-ROOM), I wonder whether she knows about the deception I am about to uncover—whether it's just another secret she's kept from me in the name of protection, or whether Dad shares her conviction that truth is a grenade and love is a helmet. I triple-knot the laces of my trainers and quadruple-check the time. It is 18:45, which on any other day of the week would signal the crack and sigh of Dad's first beer can (it sounds like someone saying poofta, which is late nineties for knob jockey) and Mum's subsequent darkroom hibernation. However, Thursday nights aren't for drinking beer.

I find Dad, as expected, in front of his beloved FD Trinitron wide-screen TV (flat CRT to reduce glare, three separate screen aspects, about seven stiffies and a semi-on). He is muttering at a quiz show and shouting a running tally of his score to no one in particular. When I arrive he is on fourteen, although I happen to know that he awards himself the point every time he gets the same wrong answer as one of the contestants, as a reward for sounding plausible. For several moments longer than I have budgeted for, I watch him watching the show from the doorway (me, not him). Perhaps it is the constant, noncommittal murmur of his voice as he cycles inaudibly through the conceivable responses to questions he can't answer, or perhaps it is his bald patch, which tonight is particularly monktastic, but for whatever reason it almost looks like he's praying. Then he gets one he's sure of. "Lake Titicaca," he announces proudly.

"Lake Titicaca," agrees the contestant, a bookish man with yellow skin and a creased spine.

"*Fif*teen!" shouts Dad.

"I'm sorry," laments the host. "I was looking for Lake *Maracaibo.*"

"Hi," I say.

"Hi!" He spins around and knocks over a bowl of peanut shells. "I thought they meant volume, not surface area. What are you doing out of your room? Is it Spring already?"

"Do you want to play chess?" I ask.

We set up the board on the coffee table that has never had coffee on it with Dad as whites and me, on the floor, as blacks. Just like I expect him to, Dad starts with an aggressive King's Pawn opening and a joke about a vacancy for royal sperm donors (a king spawn opening), and from there we disappear quickly into improbability. (The number of possible board configurations in chess after each player's first move is four hundred. After their second move this increases to 72,084, then 9-million-plus after their third and 288-billion-plus after their fourth. My all-time favorite fact is that after each player has made forty moves the number of possible patterns on a chess board is greater than the sum of every grain of sand from all of the beaches in the whole world. (My favorite thing about this fact is that a chess board is only sixty-four squares large. If you consider the size of the earth's surface, not to mention how many more than forty moves you have made, then you start to get some idea of how many different patterns you could have made of your life. (And yet here we are.))) I beat Dad in seven moves, two more than I planned on. Then I start to reset the board. Dad checks his watch and sucks air through his teeth. "I don't know if I can," he says, and then calls me "big man," which has never been my nickname.

"Please," I say, credibly. "I'll play left-handed."

Dad laughs. "Careful," he says. "I'll hold you to that. But it'll have to be another time, I'm afraid. Duty calls."

"Do you have to?" I ask. This time I'm so convincing I convince myself. It's the opposite of what the plan calls for, but, forthwith, more than anything I want him to say no. All of a sudden and with all my skin, which is the largest organ, I want the whole thing to be a harmless misunderstanding, no matter how unlikely or narratively unsatisfying. I make a deal in my head: I'll even forgive Mum, accept her explanation, that she was acting out of some mutated sense of parental loyalty, however misguided and weird, just so long as the three of us can go back to how we were (a unit, a solid, a family), if we could only ride the bumper cars on Brighton Pier together one (first and) last time.

Dad considers the question. Then he gets to his feet. "Son . . ." he says. "No score and thirteen years ago I swore a solemn oath"—he puts hand on heart—"to the road users of this great nation, to ensure their safe passage, free from the menace of P-plated teenagers who think undertaking's what funeral directors put on their CVs and ten and two means twelve." He takes a breath. I don't have a clue what he's talking about. But I'm ready to swallow whole whatever comes next. "And shall I tell you something?"

Anything.

He plants a foot on the coffee table. "Eleanor Gower, sister though she may be to that exceedingly charming young friend of yours, represents not only the biggest threat to the Great British motorist since someone Photoshopped a picture of a polar-bear cub bobbing up and down on an ice cube in the middle of the Artic Sea, but furthermore, the single greatest challenge to the solemnity of that promise." He leans over and laces his trainer. My heart rides all the way down to the basement. I didn't even know it could go that low. It must have been in the service elevator all this time. "Admittedly, there are probably safer ways to get my kicks. Base-jumping and heroin come to mind. But until that girl is fully proficient in the ancient art of road safety I would be remiss in my duty, were I not to attend myself to her education first and above all."

By the front door he shrugs on his jacket and pats it down for his car keys, which we won't find there, because I have hidden them to buy myself time. "If I'm not back in two hours," he says, "tell my son I love him."

"Will do," I say, and go back upstairs.

First I trip then reset the alarm. Then I secure my boxing helmet. Then I pocket my keys, my Maglite, and my Swiss Army Knife. Then I throw a pillow out the window. Then I slither down the drainpipe.

Rather than reverse into the drive, Dad has pulled in lazily, front first, which means I can crouch at the exhaust out of sight from the house. From this position, my job is simple. I fan out the dial of instruments and set to work with the Swiss Army saw, which exhaustive empirical trials have told me is the best tool for cutting through the particular type of shoelace with which the lip of the boot is sewn to the car's cocksix, which is Medicine for tailbone. As the saw's teeth gnaw away at the cord I see, as expected, a light come on in Mum and Dad's room, which is where the keys are hidden, reasonably enough (so as not to arouse suspicion) at the bottom of the dirty washing basket. This is the fifth most logical place to check, but Dad must not know this, because seconds later he cries out in triumph: "God'm!" My stomach lurches (X-CORD GLOOM WORKOUT, DOOM GROWL TOOK CRUX, COLD GOOK TUMOR ROW X). But then, just as the bedroom light goes out, my sawing arm jerks through fresh air. The boot twangs open. Now it's a matter of climbing in, threading through the replacement lace (which I've tanned in cold tea so it doesn't look too new), and stitching shut the wound from the inside before the front door opens and I hear footsteps on gravel. Which I manage with just a handful of rivers to spare.

Then there's some percussion.

Then some harmonizing: humming (Dad), coughing (the exhaust), humming (the engine), coughing (me).

And then we're on road.

Through the gormless crack in the darkness that provides my oxygen, I can track the first few turnings. First it's left onto Willow Walk, then right onto Lodge Hill Road and right again down Elm Park Lane, where I used to race milk floats, to Rutherford Road and across the high street to Eastheath Avenue where Simon Nagel lives (we slow down, and for a moment I picture Dad and Simon's mum doing it through a sheet (even though that's a myth and it's for Acidic Jews, not Alkaline ones, anyway)) and right once more onto Brockley Close. This continues for a while, familiar streets swinging into and then out of view as Dad picks his way across friendly terrain, until suddenly he spins a hard left onto a faster, noisier road and I have no choice but to give up my view and wedge myself lengthways between the walls with my toes flexed to keep from ricocheting off them.

(It is in this position, ensconced in what is starting to feel more and more like the belly of a whale, that I start to consider the wisdom of the phrase *Curiosity killed the cat,* which my whole life up until this moment I have harbored doubts about.

But maybe the Danes were right all along. And maybe if something is both alive and dead until the second you lift the lid to sneak a peek, then the absolute best thing you can do is leave that lid the eff alone.)

After ten something (seconds/minutes/hours), the pace slackens and we start again to weave as the street names get longer (the length of a street is always indirectly proportional to the length of its name) but no more recognizable. Now we are in somebody else's neighborhood, remarkable only for how similar it is to our own, except here I have to empathize hard to understand the special meaning behind pavements and pathways: Here's where someone else first rode without stabilizers, or mercy-killed a sparrow, or water-bombed a car. Soon I get into it, and after a while it's easy to imagine that in every house on every street is another me, which is when it occurs to me for the first time that it might not be just the one family I'm about to break up. However, it's too late for second thoughts, because the street names are getting longer and longer, and the gaps between turns shorter and shorter, and the next thing I know I hear what sounds like underwater rain.

Dad cuts the engine, and I stop breathing. My eyes are shut. I'm all ears as his door creaks open and his feet touch down on gravel. His seat sighs and then so does he and then he's off, his footsteps receding into the distance. I listen out for a knock or a buzzer, but I don't hear either. I count to ninety-seven. Then take a look. Through the slit I can make out a windowless double door without a handle, like the sort we have in the sports hall. It is cobalt blue with white letters stenciled onto it. They say:

THIS IS NOT A DOOR

The knot is the type that comes loose with one tug if you've tied it properly, which I have. I climb out of the boot and into the thin shadow of a squat, gray bunker of a building with a steep slate roof and a neat herbaceous trim. We are parked round back, where the only windows are squares in the ceiling, in a car park along with six other cars (four of them with Jesus fish on). From here I can see that the un-door refracts at its base into a gentle, concrete disability ramp. In fact, there is a dour wholesomeness to the entire architecture that almost *smells* of minibus appeals. It does not scream love nest. However, from the glow of the skylights it's clear there's someone inside.

I do a broken circuit of the building, stopping before I get to the entrance, where the light spill from the open doorway makes the risk of exposure too great, and doubling back on myself until I've traced a horseshoe around its rectangular base. Above the front door, patterned into the brick, is a stumpy *t* that looks more like the net of a cube than what it's supposed to (a crucifix). Nowhere are there windows at eye level, which is a problem I return to the car park to ponder. My original plan was simply to walk up to the front door of whoever's house I found myself outside and knock. I haven't prepared for this eventuality, that I'd be standing outside the address my dad has worked so hard to keep secret and still be in need of the decisive piece of evidence against him. It seems unlikely that anything too illicit could possibly take place inside a building this dull, but more unlikely still that the reason Dad's been lying to me for weeks is to cover up the fact he's plotting a Bring and Buy Sale.

Moreover, I decide, I haven't come all this way to leave open-minded.

Which means I need to see inside.

Just then an expensive car blinks and I hear footsteps wading toward me. I duck for cover and watch as a fat man with thin legs topples past and opens the passenger-side door. He leans over and his suit jacket rides up his back like the tide going out. When it comes back in, he's holding something. One of those fluffy green indoor footballs that wouldn't look out of place in a giant's tennis bag. He tucks it in the crook of an elbow, shuts the door, and waddles back toward the entrance, locking the car with a remote without looking back. However, just as I'm about to emerge from my hiding place, he stops dead in his tracks. For a full half-minute I hold my breath as he stands motionless at the edge of the car park, looking out into the empty road. There's no way he could have seen me. And sure enough, after thirty seconds he continues along his original vector and disappears behind the building. I suck in a lungful of foul-smelling air and realize I've been hiding behind a wheelie bin.

With the bags removed the bin is light enough to carry to the building's edge without making a racket, and with the bags gently lowered back in it is anchored sufficiently to support my weight. Using the disability handrail for a leg up, I am able (with great difficulty) to clamber onto its lid, from where my fingers just about curl round the margin of the skylight. Then (appropriately enough) it's a leap of faith to wedge my right foot into the guttering and pull myself up the roof until I can see inside.

Inside the hall are ten people sat in a perfect circle. Directly beneath me, so I can't see his face, is Dad. He is holding the giant's tennis ball, and his shoulders are heaving in a manner that would look like uncontrollable laughter if it weren't for the way the others are watching him. Their expressions have no regard for the laws of geometry: They clearly identify Dad as the corner of the circle. For some time, we all just watch. (He looks how I've always imagined The Loneliest Monk, who is a famous jazz musician.) Then the fat man, who is sitting next to him, reaches over a chubby hand and squeezes Dad's knee. He relieves him of the ball and says a few words of his own, but everyone still looks at Dad. Then he (the fat man) heaves himself up and bisects the circle to hand the globe to a man and a woman sitting opposite. They accept it together like a trophy they're being jointly awarded and smile up at the fat man. But there's something off about the smile. At the same time it looks proud and regretful. It's almost as though the ball really is a prize, only everyone knows it's got nothing to do with them, that they're just accepting it on somebody's behalf. It feels like a smile I've seen somewhere before, like déjà vu almost. Except I really have. I know this couple. They're the parents of the boy who drowned.

Then the gutter cracks.

With an orchestra of noise I scrape down the roof, bounce off the bin, and land hard on my ankle. The pain is sharp and loud, but I have it rather than the other way round, and if anything it focuses my mind. *Dad can't see me here.* I scramble to my foot as chair legs graze wood, and, as voices approach, hop down a verge and away onto the street. I don't look back or stop, not until the only sound is the thumping of my heart. Then I collapse on the pavement and try to think.

Is everything all right?

Chapter Thirty

"Here, lad!" says the voice, and then, with the stress in all the wrong places, so I know it must be repeating itself, and probably not for the first time, either: "Is everything all right?"

At the side of the road, backed onto the pavement in front of me with a hind wheel cocked in the air, is a dirty white van. The passenger window is wound down and the engine still running, but there's no driver in sight. Moreover, several beads of heavy liquid clinging to the tip of the quivering exhaust pipe do much to further the impression that the van is an independent being and has just finished marking his territory. And now he speaks again, this time to ask me what I'm on the *lang* from, which is a word I don't recognize.

"I don't know," I say in general reply, addressing the answer approximately to the wing mirrors as the vehicle's exhaust shakes loose a stubborn droplet, which, in the moment before the speaker heaves into view, bursts on the pavement under electric moonlight into a palette of colors. At first I don't recognize the man. He's as tall as a (short) tree. His face is gray and his hair, emerging first from behind the van, the fiery orange of a setting sun.

"Gis your paw," says the giant, sending down an enormous hand that takes forever to arrive. I reach up obediently toward it, half expecting from its size to feel foam beneath my fingers, and end up braceleted round a wrist, my fingers barely long enough to make a *C,* let alone an *O* or even a *G.* In turn the man takes hold of my arm (it's all his fingers can do not to lap themselves) and pulls me to my feet, which is when I remember the pain in my ankle. "Woah there, big fella," he says, taking my weight with the casual flex of a tricep as I collapse back down toward the pavement. We hold this pose for a moment longer than necessary, me suspended mid-fall, sitting squat on an invisible toilet, with the humongulus standing over me, enjoying his own strength, his pulse booming in the palm of my hand.

His eyes are two blue un-doors.

When I speak my voice is tiny and unauthorized. "I want to go home," it says.

The man considers this thoughtfully, like it's a joke he's heard before but never really thought about because he was too busy laughing the first time. Finally, he nods, as if in grave idea-logical agreement, which makes him seem even more like a homesick ginger Gulliver. "Ah sure. This is it like." He sighs and then yanks me back up with a scary ease. "So snap out yer buzz and get in the van."

I try to walk, but it hurts too much, like stepping into a bath that's so hot it feels cold. Even if I did know where I was, I realize, I couldn't make it back without accepting a lift from someone. And besides, there's something about this particular stranger, something distantly familiar, that makes me feel safer than I have any right to feel. Still, for reassurance I trace the shape of the Swiss Army Knife in my pocket and repeat over to myself the instructions for use: "Plunge and Twist, Plunge and Twist, Plunge and Twist."

The passenger-side door swings open like a question.

I answer in the affirmative by taking a hop toward the van. Which is when I notice the slogan stenciled across its side:

AN OF ICE WITHOUT PL NTS IS LIKE THE MAZON WIT OUT A RAINF REST. LOVE PLAN S WE DO.

The smell inside the cabin is of singed eyebrows and mis-used Bunsen burners, and the dashboard is flecked with the same dull, gray dandruff of scratch-card refuse that sometimes patterns David's school clothes. In the seat next to me, Mr. Driscoll steers with his knees. With his free hands he clamps a cigarette between cracked lips and sparks a match at the fourth attempt.

"So, like," he says, sucking in hard so his cheeks hollow and I can see the bones in his face. "What's the story?"

The question stumps me absolutely. In light of where I've just come from and what I've just seen (and only one day away from my Composition exam), I can't honestly say I know anymore. I think back over everything that's happened these past ten weeks and try to connect the dots, or, failing that, at least plot a line of best fit, because, as Miss Farthingdale always says, there's nothing worse than a narrator who doesn't know what kind of story he's in. However, right now I'm lost. I can't make sense of anything. Looking around, as if for some clue, I catch a glimpse in the rearview mirror. Behind us, in the back of the van, is a portable woodland. At a glance the foliage is thick and alive, and for a moment I'm transfixed by the secret skyline. It's only when I trace down the stems that I notice the plants are in captivity.

"I don't know."

Mr. Driscoll's laugh is grit and a phlegmy rattle. "*Jayzus,*" he says. "What *do* you know?" And with this he snakes a jab toward my chin. I jerk left, but he stops short and follows through in a slo-mo replay, as though reliving some faraway glory. "You a cruiser or a heavyweight like?" he asks, which is when I remember I'm still wearing my boxing helmet.

"Neither," I say, thankful for a question I know the answer to. I peel off the helmet and rake back my hair to show off my scar. But before I can explain further, Mr. Driscoll's eyes light up.

"Ah," he says, wagging the cigarette between courgette fingers, and asks if I know *his Davy.*

In the rearview mirror our gazes triangulate. (I think back

four years to a Saturday afternoon and then forward again a week or so to a Monday morning, the jaundiced skin of David's cheek, his eyebrow a swollen potato tuber, and the burst blood vessels that made ordnance survey maps of his left eyeball.) I can tell Mr. Driscoll is trying to place me by the way his forehead rolls down and pinches a ridge at the top of his nose. (My a-hole dilates because I am the boy who ruined his carpet, the one he found with his son dancing naked in the rain. (The one who never did catch chickenpox but got pneumonia instead.))

"Who?" I ask, steadily, glancing down at the row of knuckles that now prong the steering wheel like battlements, and in my pocket slip a fingernail into the furrow of the biggest blade.

However, before he can identify me, Mr. Driscoll looks away. "Never mind, lad," he says, leaking smoke from the corners of his mouth. "Davy's me young one. His best friend like." He takes a hand off the wheel again, reaches over and tussles the hair around my scar. "He's got a matching one of dem."

I get Mr. Driscoll to drop me off a street over from ours because I don't want Mum to know I've been gone. Before I get out I say thank you and then take another look at the private forest in the back of the van. I don't know why, but something about the sight of these plants, their feet encased solitarily in clay penitentiaries with limbs stretching skyward and their leaves touching, is like listening to classical music: I can't tell if it's happy or sad. When Mr. Driscoll asks what I'm crying for, which I didn't know I was, I blubber something about the high pollen count. However, the real reason is the sudden pang of what feels an awful lot like gratitude for everyone I know and all the hands I've ever held.

Shimmying up the drainpipe one-legged is not an option, even with all the synonyms in the world, so instead I go in the front door. I am halfway up the stairs when I realize that I can't get into my bedroom without setting off my alarm, which will arouse suspicion unless I pretend I'm leaving as opposed to entering, so I decide to empty my pockets and dump my helmet and then go to the kitchen for a glass of milk to help me think, which with Mum in the utility room will be like hiding in plain sight. However, Mum isn't in the utility room. She is asleep at the kitchen table, her cheek on her forearm, which is next to an empty glass and a bottle of wine that could split optimists from pessimists at fifty meters. Depending on which one you are, either Mum or the bottle is half drunk. Which is weird because, except for water and fruit juice, Mum is tea total.

I pour myself a glass of milk (in case she wakes up (which seems unlikely)) and sit down opposite her. Then I tilt my head until she's the right way up and really look at her. For some reason this reminds me of a riddle I heard once, that I haven't thought about in years: *A grandmother, a mother, and two daugh-*

ters go fishing. Between them, they catch three fish. Each of them goes home with one whole fish. How is this possible?

At the time I remember I didn't get the answer. It was the last day of term and there was a whole tray of Creme Eggs for the person who got it right first. (I don't remember who asked it or who got the Creme Eggs.) Now, though, it seems obvious: *The mother is a daughter, too.*

Then I notice the key in her hand. It is easy enough to release without waking her, so I do. I don't recognize it straightaway (because all keys look pretty much the same (which is ironic)), but when I unlatch the key box it's obvious which one it is because there's only one missing. I place the key quietly back on the hook, but then I change my mind because, I decide, I could really do with a new Photographic Memory.

First I turn off all the lights in the hallway and the kitchen, and then I navigate back to the darkroom door by the glow of my watch. Once I'm inside, I feel around the surfaces for a UV lamp, which, according to Google, is a must for every amateur photographer, and which I find on the cabinet above the washing machine. However, when I turn it on all the darkness leaks out of the room. This is because it isn't a UV lamp at all, just a regular one. Straightaway I turn it back off, but I know already it's too late. The damage is done. The negatives are destroyed.

Which means there's no further harm in taking a look around.

When I turn the light back on I'm not in a darkroom anymore, but not in an Uncertainty Principle way—rather, in the way that there is no photography equipment in the utility room. Apart from Mum's camera and a couple of used film canisters, the only difference I can spot is the logbook.

It is A4 and bound in black leather, with a red ribbon bookmark that splits at the end like a snake's tongue, which could be what beckons me in. The first page I open to has the day's date at the top (27 MAY 2004) written in black ink, which smudges under my touch, which means it's still wet. Then there's a subheading (DAY 7 W.T.) and a paragraph of writing:

Mum said once wished shed had stutter to ready for parenting. "If you cant start sentences with M cant put self first anyway." ~~Dont know if true. Who are you pretending for anyway?~~ D at group. Ha. Today lets talk grief v good grief!! & while were doing validation dont forget your parking tickets!!! Week now without talking. D says "take it day at a time." Exact same advice F gave. What everyone says. As though it means anything. Like theres alternative.

The entry ends there with a red wine ring stain, like a massive hollowed-out full stop. I turn back a page and read another two:

25 MAY 2004

Day 5 W.T.

On train to work woman handing out leaflets: "C H_ _C H. Whats missing?" Dont believe in God you told her. "Thats okay He forgives you." Could hear the capital. Wanted to scream at her: HE DOESN'T GET TO. Didnt. Ha. Isnt it funny? Guilt and Hope weigh the exact same. & isnt that just the kind of thing to make you believe in intelligent design.

24 MAY 2004

Day 4 Without Talking

~~I cant I cant do this. I can do this. I can do this. I can do this. I can do this. I can do this. I can do this. I can do this. I can do this. I can do this. I can do this. I can do this.~~ You must do this. Even if he never speaks to you again.

Then I flick to the start (6 MARCH 2004 Hope is not the thing with feathers. Hope is anchor. What keeps you from floating away. Despair is weightlessness. What now? "Take pictures."), and then forward again:

19 MAY 2004

F said last year: "Name of game now is Containment." Then game is fixed. Becos black absorbs light. Darkness spreads. Spot → Blotch. Room → House. You cant shut the door lock it away. Doesnt respect boundaries. I blame the parents. Ha. Only difference? There are no benign secrets. He was just there. Just other side of door. < foot away. "Lucky for you I dont believe in round numbers." Wanted to laugh throw open door hug kiss hold. Instead? Caught the key. And then. What did you feel? What was that? ~~Relief?~~ Stop it stop fucking crossing out. Admit it. <u>Relief.</u> Anything that preserves ~~your~~ your fantasy.

There's more.

But I stopped reading.

Part Four

And Then

TALLOW CHANDLERS' SCHOOL FOR BOYS
Gosling Lane • Oxhey Wood • Northwood • HA7 4HP

June 28, 2004

Mr. and Mrs. Graham
14 Pegmire Close
Bushey
Hertfordshire
WD23 8PA

Dear Mr. and Mrs. Graham,

    I hope this letter finds you well, but to save you from unnecessary anxiety I will dispense with further preamble. I am writing with mixed news. Following confirmation of your son's Common Entrance exam results I am delighted to formally offer him a September commencement with us. However, at this time we are not in a position to award an Academic Scholarship.

Although it is our feeling that on the whole Alex performed impressively in his exams—especially in Science, Maths, and French (spoken)—his failure to achieve a passing grade in English (composition) has led us to this decision. Entrance and scholarship are, of course, matters of our discretion, and while we recognize in Alex the clear potential to transcend the implications of such an aberrant grade, I feel it would be improper to bestow a scholarship in this instance.

It is my sincere hope that this decision will not affect your own I trust you will consider our offer regardless. On a personal note, young Alex made quite an impression on me when we met in May, and I would hate to think of us each missing out on the opportunity to learn more from the other!

Yours sincerely,
Mr. T. R. Sinclair
Headmaster

TALLOW CHANDLERS' SCHOOL FOR BOYS
Gosling Lane • Oxhey Wood • Northwood • HA7 4HP

July 4, 2004

Mrs. L. Graham

14 Pegmire Close

Bushey

Hertfordshire

WD23 8PA

Dear Mrs. Graham,

Thank you for your letter. I am afraid in this instance I am inclined to agree with you. In fact, for such a grade to have been awarded there must presumably have been *several* mistakes.

However, be assured that I share your consternation. As I alluded to in my first letter, Alex's English result does seem to represent something of an anomaly. It is, to say the least, unusual for a candidate to perform so ably in other essay-based subjects without recourse to the high literacy skills that the Composition module is designed to test. It is for this reason that I chose to overlook the result when offering Alex his place—an offer that I very much hope you are still considering.

In my experience, everyone has their off days. You should not let this result detract in any way from the pride you must surely be experiencing in light of the high bar that your son has already cleared. I am sure I need not remind you of the extremely competitive nature of our admissions process. To consider his acceptance anything other than an achievement in its own right would be to do a grave disservice to all involved.

Yours in anticipation,

T. R. Sinclair

Headmaster

TALLOW CHANDLERS' SCHOOL FOR BOYS
Gosling Lane • Oxhey Wood • Northwood • HA7 4HP

July 10, 2004

Mrs. L. Graham
14 Pegmire Close
Bushey
Hertfordshire
WD23 8PA

Dear Mrs. Graham,

Thank you for your swift reply. To address your points in order:

1) Yes, I was "trying to be funny." I recognize now that my attempts at levity were, in this instance, misjudged. I apologize deeply for any offense caused. Be assured that in no way did I intend to satirize the certainty of your claim.

2) If you remain adamant of the "impossib[ility]" of Alex's grade, then I suggest taking the matter up with the exam board. I am enclosing the appropriate forms. It is my understanding that any appeal must be lodged formally through the appropriate center—in this case, Alex's past school—and received within three weeks of the board's original decision.

And to make some points of my own:

3) While we encourage you to exercise your own discretion in this matter and by all means pursue an appeal

through the official channels, I must make clear that any subsequent change of result would be purely for your own personal satisfaction. At the time of writing we have awarded our full quota of scholarships for the upcoming academic year. Although we have so far been happy to hold a place for Alex—pending your decision—we would regrettably be unable to alter the terms of our offer, irrespective to the results of an appeal.

4) Without wishing to presume, we do recognize the occasionally prohibitive nature of our fees—which we believe are both appropriate to and essential for the standards of excellence on which we pride ourselves, as remarked on in this year's *The Good Schools Guide* and evidenced by our standings in the latest league tables (both enclosed)—which is why, in exceptional circumstances, we do offer a small number of means-tested bursaries. If you would like to be considered for one of these bursaries, then please contact the admissions office directly.

I hope this matter can soon be resolved to your satisfaction. I should be glad to receive written acceptance of Alex's place as soon as possible or not later than Friday, July 18, 2004.

Yours in expectation,

Mr. T. R. Sinclair

Headmaster

Grove End Middle School
Whippendale Road
Watford
Herts
WD17 1BB

July 14, 2004

Ms. L. Graham
14 Pegmire Close
Bushey
Hertfordshire
WD23 8PA

Dear Louise,

RE: Common Entrance Results Enquiry (OCEB)

A quick note post our phone chat to let you know we got your appeal forms okay and have now made an official Results Enquiry on Alex's behalf. I have discussed everything with Alex's English teacher, Miss Farthingdale, and we're both behind you 100% of the way on this one. Personally, my best guess is they got the papers mixed up. Between you and me these bastards couldn't organize a punch-up at a wedding.

We'll be in touch soon. And tell Alex not to let it get in the way of his summer holiday!

Best wishes,
Mr. Clifford

TALLOW CHANDLERS' SCHOOL FOR BOYS

Gosling Lane • Oxhey Wood • Northwood • HA7 4HP

July 28, 2004

Ms. L. Graham

14 Pegmire Close

Bushey

Hertfordshire

WD23 8PA

Dear Ms. Graham,

I have taken the liberty of interpreting your latest missive as a formal rejection of our offer.

As for your far-fetched accusations of misogyny and "condesension [sic]" I only hope these imagined slights are as real to you as the opportunity you have passed up on your son's behalf.

I trust you have his best interests at heart.

Yours,

Mr. T. R. Sinclair, BA, FRSA, FIMgt, MInstD

Headmaster .

P.S. If that's the kind of language you use around the house, then it's hardly surprising that your son failed his English exam.

Grove End Middle School
Whippendale Road
Watford
Herts
WD17 1BB

August 22, 2004

Ms. L. Graham
14 Pegmire Close
Bushey
Hertfordshire
WD23 8PA

Dear Louise,

RE: Common Entrance Results Enquiry (OCEB)

Sorry to be the bearer of bad news, but after the Results Enquiry OCEB has decided to uphold Alex's original English grade. Not to worry, though. All this means is they didn't physically lose the paper or give Alex someone else's grade by mistake—you'd be amazed how often that happens. Honestly, I just thank my lucky stars they chose marking over midwifery.

What this absolutely doesn't mean is that they weren't wrong to award the grade. Our next step is a Stage I Appeal. We have gone ahead and submitted this and a copy is attached for your records.

If you want to discuss this, or anything else, for that matter, feel free to give me a call at any time. Please know that our thoughts are with you.

Best wishes,
Mr. Clifford

Grove End Middle School
Whippendale Road
Watford
Herts
WD17 1BB

August 22, 2004

Mr. M. Duberry
Secretary of the Appeals Committee
OCEB
Cambridge Office
14 Mowbray Road
Cambridge
CB1 2EP

Dear Mr. Duberry,

Results Enquiry July 2004-07-14

Center:	16411 Grove End Middle School
Candidate:	5165 Alexander Graham
Syllabus No:	2869
Certification Code:	7684
Your ref:	EngCom

Thank you for your letter of August 18, 2004, which arrived at this center on August 20.

I herewith wish to inform you of our intention to proceed with a Stage I Appeal in the module referred to above as outlined in Part 9B of the OCEB Handbook for Centers.

The reason for this Appeal is stated below:

Those staff members who taught Alex comment that his record of work was consistently good. They spoke to the keen interest and intellectual curiosity that he brought to the classroom. His written work was described as imaginative, fiercely logical, strongly argued, lucid, and unwaveringly grammatical. His command of concepts was confident and advanced.

We were therefore surprised to learn that his grade in the module above was so low. In the professional opinion of those who taught him his work was certainly not of "U" grade standard.

It is our belief that in this instance internal procedures, as relating either to mark schemes, standardization or the arbitration of grade boundaries could not have been accurately followed.

I would be grateful for your acknowledgment of receipt of this letter.

Yours sincerely,
Tony Clifford
Headmaster

Grove End Middle School
Whippendale Road
Watford
Herts
WD17 1BB

September 6, 2004

Ms. L. Graham
14 Pegmire Close
Bushey
Hertfordshire
WD23 8PA

Dear Louise,

Sorry for the delay in contacting you. We had a bit of a setback: OCEB turned down the Stage I Appeal. But don't worry—this isn't the last they've heard on the matter. We've since told them we intend to pursue a Stage II Appeal. I have attached for your records copies of all correspondence.

The cost of the script return has been covered by the school. This is nonnegotiable. I will not accept a check from you. I've made it crystal clear to my secretary that if she cashes one she can start looking for a new job—so please don't even try it!

Yours,
Tony

OCEB*

RECOGNIZING EXCELLENCE

Head Office

1 King Street

Cambridge

CB2 1EG

Telephone: 1223 302302

Facsimile: 01223 302303

www.oceb.org.uk

Mr. T. Clifford

Headmaster

Grove End Middle School

Whippendale Road

Watford

WD17 1BB

August 24, 2004

Ref: EngCom/16411/5165

Dear Mr. Clifford,

CE Examinations June 2004: Specification 2869 EngCom
Appeal Against the Outcome of a Results Enquiry
Candidate: 5165

Thank you for your letter dated August 22, 2004, in which you detailed your wish to make an appeal in the above specification.

I have decided to reject this appeal on the following basis:

- There was no inappropriate application of the marking scheme as alleged by the Center

- There was no evidence of procedural failure nor any reason to doubt the accuracy of the grade(s) awarded

I would draw your attention to Part 9C of the OCEB Handbook for Centers, which describes the procedure for further appeals.

Finally, be assured that the matter has been reviewed in the first instance by a senior member of OCEB's staff who has had no previous involvement with the case.

Yours sincerely

Michael Duberry

Secretary: OCEB Appeals Committee

Enc: Appeals Against Results

Part 9 of the OCEB Handbook

Grove End Middle School
Whippendale Road
Watford
Herts
WD17 1BB

August 30, 2004

Mr. M. Duberry
Secretary of the Appeals Committee
OCEB
Cambridge Office
14 Mowbray Road
Cambridge
CB1 2EP

Dear Mr. Duberry,

Ref: EngCom/16411/5165

Thank you for your letter of August 24, 2004, enclosing the findings of your Stage I Report and another copy of Part 9 of the OCEB handbook, of which you can never have too many.

I note your conclusion that "there was no inappropriate application of the marking scheme."

I therefore intend to exercise my handbook-given right to take the matter to Stage II with respect to candidate 5165—or, as we all know him, Alex.

In the meantime, I make the following points arising from your letter:

a) Our appeal was not founded on the assumption that there was "inappropriate application of the marking scheme." This was never "alleged."

b) We appealed on wider grounds, namely, that "the internal procedures, as relating either to mark schemes, standardization or the arbitration of grade boundaries could not have been accurately followed."

c) In order to convince us that your internal procedures have been accurately followed, you must, surely, provide us with the following evidence:

   i. the written verdict of the original marker and the re-marker about the extent to which Alex's answer does, or does not, meet OCEB's assessment objectives.

  ii. a statement of how Alex's mark was, or was not, transformed into a weighted raw mark. Please show your working.

  iii. a copy of the script in question.

Finally, if you will permit a personal observation: Our specific concern for Alex and the accurate assessment of his work could well lead this center to consider more general issues regarding the board and its competence.

Awaiting your reply.

Yours sincerely,
Tony Clifford
Headmaster

OCEB*

RECOGNIZING EXCELLENCE

Head Office

1 King Street

Cambridge

CB2 1EG

Telephone: 1223 302302

Facsimile: 01223 302303

www.oceb.org.uk

Mr. T. Clifford

Headmaster

Grove End Middle School

Whippendale Road

Watford

WD17 1BB

September 3, 2004

Ref: EngCom/16411/5165

Dear Mr. Clifford

CE Examinations June 2004: Specification 2869 EngCom
Appeal Against the Outcome of a Stage I Report
Candidate: 5165

Thank you for your letter dated August 30, 2004, in which you detailed your wish to make a further appeal in the above specification.

As part of the review process, you are, of course, entitled to a copy of the candidate's script(s), as requested in section c(iii) of your letter. It is suggested that you use this evidence to inform your decision whether to pursue a Stage II Appeal. If you require access to script(s), please reply to this letter quoting reference EngCom/16411/5165 enclosing a check for the value of £8.50 made payable to OCEB. You will note that 14 days should be allowed for delivery of script(s).

It is recommended that you await arrival of the candidate's script(s) before formalizing any further appeal. Having myself read Alex's script, I would personally advise that this is a highly sensible recommendation.

Yours sincerely
Michael Duberry
Secretary: OCEB Appeals Committee

Part Five

The Dark Room

September 20, 2004

~~Day 116 W.T.~~

The letter arrived this morning. It's here right now, in front of me on the kitchen table in an A4 manila envelope. That's probably why I'm writing again after all this time, and in full sentences, too. Because I can't bear to open it yet. Ha. Or should I say Haha. I suppose it is funny, actually, or at the very least absurd, which I used to think was the same thing, at any rate, but I can't stop thinking about what might be inside. Obviously, it's either good news or bad news, but it's almost like once I've opened it it'll be one or the other, so until I do it's both. I know that probably sounds ridiculous—but even so, I need a few more minutes still.

So what can I tell you in the meantime? Well, last week was your first back at work. People are funny. "How *are* you?" they ask now, instead of just "How are you?"—and how proud they are to have done so! I can see it in their eyes. "Isn't it terrible, but at least I'm part of the solution." It's exhausting. Like watching someone recycle, or buy line-caught tuna. The worst part is how quietly everyone talks. It's as if they've all read the same bit of research: that grief improves your hearing. Aside from that, not much has changed. There's another new group of trainees. I can tell they don't know yet by the way they leave dictation: like they're not embarrassed to find it important. One of them signed off a recording with a message for me, asking me to deliver him a proof "Ace." At first I assumed it was a nickname he was keen to self-apply—he looks the type—but it later transpired it was short for "asap." I wish someone had told me when I was young and busy saving all that time that one day I'd have to spend it.

Some days every hour has a thousand minutes and every minute a thousand seconds. Another good reason to take things slow. Because once you open the letter that's it, you know. Good news or bad, it's over either way. There'll be nothing more you can do. It'll just be you and the rest of your life.

Last night I played his computer again. It was the first time since I went back to work. D was at group, but still I needed an excuse. "I'm just going to feed the hamster," I told myself. And then, once I was in his room I went straight for it. The first time I know why I turned it on. It's the same reason I have to make sure all the curtains are shut the second I walk through the door: because after dark guilt makes mirrors everywhere. But that never explained why I connected to the Internet and opened a Web browser. It must've been an hour last night. Sitting there in the dark and tracing the echoes of his Google

searches. Chasing him around the keyboard, suggesting pre-
fixes and watching as he whispered back whole words and
phrases. donkey oaty. double penetration. dow jones index. It
was almost like a duet. As though the two of us were sat beside each other on a piano stool, playing chopsticks. Ha. Like
you could play chopsticks. It must've been at least an hour
because by the time I was done D was back from group.

He asked me to come with again this morning. What exactly is it he said I would benefit from? A Vocabulary for
Grieving. That's it. "To help you put your feelings into words."
And then what? "And then into sentences, and eventually at
some point down the line into . . ." What, exactly? Perspec-
tive? No, he hadn't been about to say that. "Context." It's the
one thing we've argued about. The rest of the time we're perfectly delightful, which is no good to anyone, because what's
charm but yet another reflective surface? It must be a funny
thing to see the two of us, two charming people facing off, to
watch as small talk recedes into infinitesimal talk. It's ironic, I
suppose, considering everything that's happened, that these
days our conversations should be governed by the laws of
infinite regression.

This morning, though, was the exception. I could sense it
was coming. Here, in a nutshell, is his argument:

A wife who loses a husband is called a widow.
A husband who loses a wife is called a widower.
A child who loses his parents is called an orphan.
A mother who loses a child doesn't have a name.
This is because a) it's not supposed to happen.

And b) it's a taboo, which means THEY don't want you to talk about it.

But guess what? It DOES happen. It happens all the time. And there ARE people you can—nay, MUST—talk to. People who understand exactly what you're going through.

And here, in a nutshell, is mine:

This isn't something we're going THROUGH. It's something we're IN. And come to that how do you expect to put something into words when it's so big you can't see its edges?

There IS a name for a mother who loses a child. She is called a mother.

At which he sighed and told me something I can't stop thinking about. It's something someone else told him, a father whose son chased a football onto an icy pond:

"Take a look in the mirror. The person looking back, that's your best friend. Do you know how I know that? Because it has to be."

So, for the first time, I asked him. Do you think we did the right thing or the wrong thing?

He sighed again. "I think past a certain point it stops being an important distinction. I think punishing yourself isn't the same as mourning him. And I think in time you'll come to see that."

But that's just it, I told him. We're not on the same timetable. We didn't all start missing him before he was even gone.

"Yes we did," he said.

That's why I never came home tonight. At work it was someone's birthday, one of the trainees, I think, because the cake still had the right amount of candles in it, and there's a statute of limitation on that kind of thing. At the end of the day they must've noticed how long I was taking to gather my things because they asked me along for a drink. It's now 4:43 a.m. and I'm completely sober again. When I got home the letter was on the table and D was asleep on the sofa with the TV on. It was a world sports catalogue program, some ex-cricketer competing in the marlin fishing World Championships. On top of the screen was the picture of Alex from his first day of school, the one with his fly open, and in the bottom right-hand corner, as though she were standing on the water, a pretty young sign language interpreter. You never know what's going to set you off. "Are deaf people nocturnal?" he asked once. "Why would you think that?" I asked him. But he didn't answer. It was D who caught him in the end. He'd been sneaking downstairs in the middle of the night to watch TV.

On the dance floor I told "Ace" everything. What had happened, what I'd done, and, finally, how I would never forgive myself. It was too loud for me to hear the words I was saying, but the contortions of my mouth were enough to make it so. The whole time he danced at me. He couldn't hear a word I was saying. When I was through contorting myself, he asked what perfume I was wearing.

The time is now 5:38. Before long the sun will rise again, which these days is my biggest fear. Do you remember Chicken Licken? It took you a whole week of story times to make it even halfway through. He always was an inquisitive child. "But why DID the acorn fall on his head?" he kept asking every time you paused for breath—until eventually you abandoned the book and instead explained, as best you could, the properties of gravity. The next night, when you were tucking him in, he asked how come the sun didn't collapse under the force of its own gravitational pull.

One day, you told him, it will.

"And then what?"

And then nothing. That will be that.

"Because we'll be dead?"

You nodded.

"Even you and Daddy?"

Yes, you said. But that's all right, because you'll be dead, too, remember.

For a minute or two he chewed this over. Then nodded. "Okay," he said. "Night, night."

Grove End Middle School
Whippendale Road
Watford
Herts
WD17 1BB

September 19, 2004

Ms. L. Graham
14 Pegmire Close
Bushey
Hertfordshire
WD23 8PA

Dear Louise,

See attached. I'm sorry. There's nothing more we can do. I have withdrawn the appeal. Please forgive me for raising your hopes.

Yours,
Tony

OCEB*

RECOGNIZING EXCELLENCE

Head Office

1 King Street

Cambridge

CB2 1EG

Telephone: 1223 302302

Facsimile: 01223 302303

www.oceb.org.uk

Mr. T. Clifford

Headmaster

Grove End Middle School

Whippendale Road

Watford

WD17 1BB

September 17, 2004

Ref: EngCom/16411/5165

Dear Mr. Clifford

CE Examinations June 2004: Specification 2869 EngCom
Return of Script(s) for Formalization of
Stage II Appeal
Candidate: 5165

You will please find enclosed a reproduction of the candidate 5165's script(s) in specification 2869 EngCom.

I hope this goes some way to assuaging your fears regarding the board's competence.

Yours sincerely
Michael Duberry
Secretary: OCEB Appeals Committee

Enc: Script(s) for Candidate 5165 in
Specification 2869 EngCom

OCEB Examining Group
Specification 2689
ENGLISH COMPOSITION
June 2004
Time allowed: 60 mins

Instructions:

Ensure you have the correct question paper.

Write in black or blue ink.

15 marks will be awarded for accurate spelling, punctuation, and grammar.

QUESTION 1 of 1:

Describe in no less than 500 words your *Life in a Day.*

(100 marks)

Dear Mum,

Right now I'm really angry with you. However, I don't think I always will be. Therefore, I don't want you to worry.

I was here; I am there.

With love and thanks,
Alex

P.S. As official executioner of my will, I have two things for you to do:

1) My hamster is to go to Chloe Gower. Please give it to her. Moreover, tell her his name is Richey.

2) Go to my bedroom. In the tissue box on my bedside table you will find four secret compartments. One of these secret compartments has a picture of a monkey whose name is Coco on it. Inside this compartment is an object. It is something that I once guarded with my life. It is for you and Dad.

Epilogue

It's funny how the world looks out of a plane window. It's pretty much exactly like a paint-by-numbers puzzle. On the way out to La Rochelle it was foggy and moreover nighttime so I didn't get to see very much at all, but now, flying back into Luton on only my second ever airplane, I have plenty of time to look and think as the ground rises through the clouds. A minute ago the stewardesses came round and told everyone to get ready for landing, which meant stowing their tray tables and putting their chairs in an upright position (i.e., upright) and also making sure that the shutters on the windows were up. However, they didn't have to tell me the last bit. I don't understand how anyone could ever have their shutter down on a flight. Why would you read a magazine when you're thousands of feet in the air and there's a window to look out of?

I've never been very good at art, because I always draw

what I think I should see instead of what I actually do, so right now I'm trying extra hard to really look. However, the closer we get to the fields, the more I see a patchwork quilt. If you think about it (which I'm only really just starting to do), it's weird how neat everything is. All of the fields are color-coded and separated with straight lines into regular quadrilaterals (which is the plural of a square and a rectangle). The hedge-rows are dark and permanent-looking. For some reason they remind me of the time I started doing a crossword in pen be-fore I'd whispered in the answers first in pencil and I got all the way to the second-to-last clue before I realized I'd made a mistake. It's scary how someone obviously had the confidence to divide the world up like this, with such definite boundaries, especially because they won't know until the end whether they were right or wrong. I don't think I could ever be that certain about anything. It's like the Bolognese and the Ragú. Some-times one thing just becomes another.

I look over at my parents, who are asleep in adjacent seats, which is a better way of saying side by side. Mum's head is on Dad's shoulder.

There is only one thing in the world that I'm certain about. It's in my pocket, and when we get home I'll put it somewhere safer still.

It's a one-Franc coin, and it is mine.

Acknowledgments

Some essential thank-yous: my editor Jennifer Smith (for her guidance and expertise), my agent Gordon Wise (for his faith and wisdom), my friends and family (for their support and scutiny, in particular those who read and commented on early drafts: Tom Peters, Jonathan Hollis, Hannah Greene, and Darren Richman, who once sent me an email without which I probably wouldn't be writing this), my parents (who've really earned their dedication), Michael Mitchell (for his time and medical insight), and Imogen Haines (whose contribution cannot be measured between parentheses).

PHOTO: © IMOGEN HAINES

MATT GREENE was born in Watford, England, in 1985 and studied English Language at the University of Sussex, where he edited *The Badger* newspaper. He is the co-author of four plays, including the Edinburgh Fringe sell-out farce *The Straight Man*. This is his first book.